Look At Me

A Novel

by Tania Dilworth

Copyright © 2025 Tania Dilworth

ISBN: 979-8-9988490-0-8
Cover design by Tania Dilworth with AI Assistance

Published by Self-Published

One

The silence of the morning is a stark contrast to the violent chaos of the night before. I slowly open my eyes, my head pounding—the kind of pain that feels like a hangover, except I hadn't touched a drop of alcohol. Memories flash at the edges of my consciousness—heavy, menacing—but I push them away as I drag my unwilling body out of bed.

I glance at the other side of the bed. The sheets are tangled, the imprint of his body faint but unmistakable. He's gone. For now. Relief stirs, but it's buried under a heavier, colder weight — the knowing. He always comes back. And worse, some hollow, desperate part of me still wants him to.

With a deep, reluctant breath, I force myself downstairs. Pausing on the landing, my stomach churns as the memory of his hands tightening around my neck flashes across my mind. I can still feel the burn of his grip, the fear as my nails claw at his hands, desperate to break free. The sound of him stumbling backward into the wall echoes loudly in my ears. I shake my head, forcing the memory down like bile and continue down the stairs.

Coffee is the only thing keeping me moving.

The coffee maker gurgles softly, its rhythm steady against the stillness of the house. The rich aroma curls through the air, wrapping around me like a fragile lifeline. I grip the warm mug tightly, letting its heat seep into my fingers, grounding me for a moment before the storm inside me swirls again.

As I pass the hallway mirror, I catch a glimpse of my reflection. It's not pretty. I almost didn't recognize myself. My hair is a tangled mess of blonde, dark circles shadow my hazel brown eyes making them seem almost dim. I gently brush my fingers over the bruises beginning to bloom on my neck, my breath hitching before I turn away quickly.

Shame floods my chest—hot and suffocating—but I shove it down, determined to get through the day.

Coffee in hand, I head to my office to grab my journal.

The navy-and-gold journal feels heavy in my hands, the word "Believe" embossed on the cover catching the weak morning light. It is ironic, really—believing is the last thing I know how to do anymore. Tucking the journal under my arm, I make my way to the back porch.

The cool morning air nips at my skin, sharp and bracing, while I cling to the warmth of my coffee. The faint smell of damp earth mingles with the bitter tang of cigarette smoke, a combination that feels strangely fitting—both comforting and suffocating. Austin's weather seems to finally be shifting into fall.

My cigarettes are still on the black iron outdoor table. The chair screeches against the concrete patio as I pull it out, the noise jarring in the quiet morning. I sink into the seat, feeling the tension rise inside me.

I reach for the pack—I promised myself I'd quit—but today is not that day. The flick of the lighter seems louder than usual, a sharp spark that cuts through my thoughts. I light one, breathing in the guilt with the smoke. The familiar burn scrapes my throat, and I exhale slowly, watching the tendrils curl and disappear.

The relief was fleeting, but for now, it was enough.

Opening my journal to the next blank page, I write the date at the top of the page. *October 12, 2008*. A date that feels heavier than it should.

I scribble a few disjointed thoughts, but my emotions are tangled, a knot I can't untangle. The person I thought I loved is a monster. I need to change. I need to move on. But Bella…

My heart clenches at the thought of her. How could I leave her in this mess? We've grown so close; she is like a daughter to me. Lindsay and I have been co-parenting her for five years now—a partnership born of shared trauma that has blossomed into something like friendship. I didn't know if I was strong enough to walk away. The thought fills me with a mix of guilt and determination.

A memory wraps around me like a blanket. Last night, the aftermath of another fight. Me, sitting on the back porch, cigarette in hand, trembling under the weight of it all. I reached for my phone, finding myself dialing Lindsay.

"Hey," Lindsay's voice came through, warm but tinged with concern. "Everything okay? It's late."

I stared out at the horizon, searching for an answer I didn't have. "I've been better," I admitted quietly.

There was a pause, long enough for me to feel the weight of her worry. "Edgar? Talia, we need to talk about this. You can't keep living like this."

"I know," I said, my voice barely above a whisper.

"You deserve better," she continued. Her words were steady, but I could hear the urgency beneath them. "And so does Bella. You can't stay because of her. You'll always be in her life—no matter what. You know that, right?"

Her words hit me like a punch to the chest, and I struggled to keep my voice steady. "What if she feels like I'm abandoning her? I don't want her to think I'm giving up on her."

"She won't," Lindsay said firmly. "I won't let that happen. She loves you."

I closed my eyes, letting her words sink in. "I'm scared," I whispered. "What if I fail? What if... leaving doesn't make things better?"

"Failing isn't walking away," Lindsay said. "Failing is staying in a situation that's killing you. And you're stronger than you think, Talia. You just have to take the first step."

Tears blurred my vision. Lindsay—who had been through so much herself—had the exact words I needed to hear tonight.

"I don't know if I'm ready," I said.

"You don't have to be ready," she replied. "You just have to decide."

The wind picked up, rustling the leaves and the neighbors wind chime, ending the memory. But the comfort was still there. I blink, the yard comes back into focus, and I take another long drag of my cigarette. The fear is a living thing, a vine wrapping tightly around my body—but there is something else, however faint, beginning to awaken too.

I stare at my journal again. Lindsay's words echo in my mind, swirling with the emotions I've tried to suppress. A small spark of hope flickers in my chest. I take a deep breath and scribble furiously in my journal, the pen cutting across the page as if writing the words could carve them into reality. I write with purpose.

I am going to leave Edgar. I am going to get my life back.

My heart races as I stare at the sentence, stark and defiant against the page. It feels like standing in a room full of smoke—choking on the fumes—yet spotting a window cracked open.

The air is there. I just have to reach it.

Two

I stay in the safety of my house for the next week, avoiding my sisters' prying questions and my friends' worried looks. This wasn't difficult considering the distance I've put between us over the years with Edgar. I tell myself it is easier this way—less explaining, less pretending. Working from home makes this easier but the isolation only makes the memories louder.

I replay the scene over and over —the dim, smoky haze of the poker house, the stench of cheap whiskey and sweat thick in the air. I remember the way my stomach twisted when I spotted him, relaxed and grinning, a stripper draped across his lap like she belonged there. The way his hands rested on her hips, his head tilted back in careless, flirty laughter. The way my heart cracked wide open.

When I confronted him, he barely looked guilty—just irritated, like I had interrupted something. He scoffed, muttering excuses.

"She was just giving me a dance. She is a stripper. It meant nothing. You're overreacting."

His words felt like slaps, each one cutting deeper.

But it wasn't until we were back at home, and I tried to leave, that I felt the real impact.

That's when the rage hit.

It started the way it always has. His hand on my arm — too tight, too rough. I'm used to that now. I've told myself before it was nothing. Just anger. Just frustration.

But this time —This time, it's different.

His fingers sank deeper, bruising, locking me in place.

I gasped, startled not just by the pain, but by the look in his eyes — wild, glassy, dangerous.

I yanked back, shoving at him with everything I had, but he didn't move.

That's when I felt it — the shift.

His anger had always simmered under the surface, but now it boiled over, violent and unchecked.

His breath, heavy with alcohol, hit my face.

His body blocked the stairs — the only way out.

Panic spiked through me.

I shoved again, harder this time, frantic — but it was like pushing against a wall.

His hand shot out, grabbing me — and suddenly I was falling.

The ground slammed into my back, knocking the air from my lungs.

Before I could even process the pain, his hands were at my throat.

Crushing. Squeezing.

The world narrowed to the pressure around my neck and the roar of my own heartbeat in my ears.

I clawed at his hands, clawed at his face, desperate, disbelieving — but he only tightened his grip.

His face blurred above me — twisted, monstrous, unrecognizable.

This wasn't the man I loved.

This was someone else.

Darkness edged my vision. My body fought without thinking.

I kicked — wild, savage — my heel slamming into his ribs.

He staggered back, just enough.

I shoved him with everything left in me.

He crashed into the wall, the sound a sickening thud that seemed to echo through the house.

I stayed there, gasping, trembling, my throat burning, my heart thundering against my ribs.

The room tilted and swayed around me.

I stared at the ceiling, the white blur of it swimming above me.

Trying to understand what just happened.

How had the man who once adored me become the man who could just snap and break me without mercy?

This was the first time he physically hurt me like this—and I knew in that moment, with a sickening certainty, that it wouldn't be the last.

The worst part— Some hollow, broken part of me was wishing it wasn't real.

He blames the alcohol, the stress, and diabetes. He swears nothing happened with the stripper, calls me paranoid, says I was always so insanely jealous. His voice drips with indignation, but his eyes never quite meet mine. What's worse is he won't even acknowledge the fight at home, his hands around my throat, the terror that lingers in my bones—He exhales sharply, like this is hurting *him*, like *he's* the one suffering.

"I would never hurt you, Talia. If something happened, I—I wasn't in control. You know I'd never do that on purpose."

And for a second—just a second—I feel the guilt creep in, tightening around my heart. Because that's how it always is with Edgar. His pain eclipses mine. His suffering drowns out what he's done.

But this time I remember.

I remember the way his fingers tightened, the heat of his breath as he snarled through clenched teeth. The raw rage in his eyes. A terrifying, unrecognizable fury from the monster he turned into. And now, when he looks at me, I see it—the guilt he won't name, the shame he tries to bury, the desperate denial clinging to him like sweat.

He sees the marks on my skin.

And I see the lie in his eyes.

I try desperately to silence my thoughts by burying myself in work and curating playlists for CDs. This week's fitting fixation is Leona Lewis' *Bleeding Love*. There's something deeply therapeutic—almost cathartic—about music. It gives a voice to the emotions I'm too scared to say out loud.

As the song downloads, I hum along to the lyrics, while making my way through work emails. I glance absently at a photo on my desk. It's the three of us— Edgar, Bella, and me—smiling at the park near the house. A seemingly happy family, frozen in time, a stark contrast to where we are today.

Edgar's jet-black hair is meticulously styled with gel, spiked upward and away from his face, subtly elongating his round features. Though his skin is fair, his Hispanic heritage is evident in his deep brown eyes, which hold a certain intensity. Bella's smile radiates pure joy, her long golden-brown curls bouncing in the sunlight. She has a way of making everything feel lighter, even when my world is crashing down. I trace the edge of her face with my finger, my chest tightening. She deserves so much better than this —and so do I.

I think back to how it all started. It was my senior year of college at the University of Texas, and I was working at an Italian restaurant downtown. Edgar started working there too.

I barely noticed him at first, dismissing his flirtation as nothing more than playful banter. But he was persistent, slipping compliments into casual conversations, finding excuses to linger near me.

Like any skilled narcissist, he swept me off my feet with grand gestures, extravagant gifts funded by poker winnings, and words that felt like promises. I was captivated, drawn into the whirlwind of his charisma.

But the whirlwind became a trap. The man who had once showered me with love began pulling me into his endless dramas and financial debts. He was always the victim, and I was always his savior. That's how we started living together—he was behind on rent and being evicted, so I let him move in with me.

Slowly, his adoration turned to criticism—how I should keep the house, the clothes I wore, my friends, and my family. His charm unraveled, revealing cruelty beneath the surface. His anger flared. Just when I would give up, he would give me hope—a hint of love or change—to reel me back in. It wasn't real; it never was. But I wanted to believe it was so bad.

It wasn't Edgar who truly captured my heart, though. It was his daughter Bella. She was only two when we met, her sweet face and tiny voice stole my heart. I knew we'd have a special bond the moment she asked me for a pickle—my favorite, too. From then on, every other weekend with her became the highlight of my life. She's "my Bella," and I'm "her Talia."

My family sees Edgar for who he is—they loathe him. But Bella? She's won them over, just as she won me. It's been five years of this rollercoaster, and I'm not sure who I am anymore, much less what life is like outside of this toxic cycle.

Meanwhile, my older sisters are married and starting their families, their lives unfolding neatly like pages from a well-written script. The pressure to follow their lead looms over me, heavy and taunting, like a shadow I can't escape. I try to fit myself into the same mold, but the harder I try, the more I feel myself fading—suffocating—until there's nothing left. The fear of having to begin again and be further "behind" keeps me trapped.

The sound of the front door slamming jolts me from my thoughts. My heart races, and I instinctively tense. He's home.

"Hey, I'm home!" Edgar's voice booms from the hall.

"I'm in my office," I call back, keeping my tone even.

He strides into the doorway, leaning casually against the frame. His blue work suit and white striped button-up shirt hang loosely on his frame, sagging from the weight he's lost since his diabetes diagnosis. His black leather belt is the only thing keeping his pants in place —a stark contrast to the much stockier man in the photo.

"What's for dinner?" he asks casually, as though he hasn't shattered my life a hundred times over.

I swivel my chair away from my desk to face him, biting back the wave of irritation his question triggers. "Um, I don't know. We could grab something?"

"Fine. Let's go now. I want to hit the poker game later," he says, already heading toward the kitchen.

My palms are clammy as I grip the arm rests of my chair, trying to steady my breathing. The weight of the words I need to say press down on me, but I can't keep living like this. Not anymore. I take a deep breath, steadying myself. It's now or never. "Hey, we need to talk," I call out, my voice firmer than I expect.

He stops and turns, his expression annoyed and already darkening. "About what?"

"The lease on the house is up next month," I begin carefully.

"Yeah, so where are we moving?" he asks, his tone presumptuous but lighter. A smile growing on his face.

"I'm going to find an apartment," I say, pausing to meet his eyes. "For me."

His face twists, his smile vanishing in an instant. "What the hell are you talking about?" he snaps, stepping closer. His presence feels stifling, the air around him heavy with unspoken threats. My heart races, but I stand my ground, forcing the words out: "What happened the other night…" My voice falters, but I force myself to push forward. "I can't do this anymore, Edgar. I need my own space."

"Oh, that again?" he says, softening his tone as he steps closer. His voice shifts, laced with a practiced charm. "Come on, Talia. You know I'd never hurt you on purpose. I didn't even know what I was doing." He grips the arm of my chair, pinning my hands and pulling me in closer to him. The sudden movement startles me, and for a moment, I can't tell if he's about to kiss me or strike me. A slow, creeping grin on his face. "You're overthinking this," he murmurs, leaning in closer. "Let's not blow things out of proportion, okay?" He kisses my cheek.

I instinctively shrink back in the chair, pulling my hands free. His words would have worked on me even a few weeks ago but I hold my ground. "I can't stay," I say firmly.

"You're just going to abandon Bella and me?" His voice drips with guilt, each word a calculated jab. He stares at me, his face inches from mine.

"This isn't about Bella," I counter, my voice shaking but resolute. "I'll always be there for her. But I can't keep living like this."

"Fine!" he shouts, throwing his hands up and pushing my chair back. "Go find your stupid apartment! I don't need this shit. I'm out of here!"

Even as he storms out, slamming the door so hard the walls shake, a knot of unease twists in my stomach. Edgar wasn't the type to let things go, and I knew this wouldn't be the end of it.

I bring my knees up to my chest trying to calm myself down, my heart pounding. Relief and fear crash over me in equal measure. I did it. The first step.

The next day, I meet my parents for lunch at Z Tejas. I take extra care to straighten and style my hair, applying makeup to add a touch of color to compensate for my fading tan. I choose a light gray sweater with a modest collar, ensuring no trace of any lingering bruises are visible. Pulling on a pair of jeans, I note with a glint of satisfaction that, despite my recent weight loss, my curves—particularly my hips and full shape, courtesy of my dad's Hispanic heritage—remain intact.

My parents are in town for the weekend from Dallas, their visits always a blend of warmth and subtle concern. Sunlight streams through the restaurant's windows, casting a golden glow that feels both invigorating and disarming, perfectly complementing the cheerful mask I've decided to wear. When the server sets down a basket of Z Tejas' famous cornbread, I beam and dive into conversation with practiced ease. My voice is bright, my anecdotes lighthearted—updates about work, favorite new songs, and harmless stories from daily life—all carefully curated to reveal nothing out of place.

They don't ask about Edgar, and I don't offer any openings. I laugh easily, sip my Mexican Martini, and lean back in my chair, projecting an air of effortless contentment. Yet beneath the polished exterior, a familiar tension lingers, like a shadow they might sense if they looked just a little too closely.

Then, as if the universe has decided to offer me a glimmer of hope, I see her—Jenni. She's seated at the next table, laughing with a group of friends. Her blonde hair, sparkling blue eyes, petite frame, and infectious laugh are unmistakable.

Our eyes meet, and her expression softens. Years ago, we hadn't parted on the best of terms, but the tension that once lingered between us seems to have dissolved with time, replaced by something gentler, almost forgiving.

To be honest, Edgar was the reason we drifted apart. He'd been in one of his uncontrollable rages, smashing my new Burberry perfume against the sliding glass door, shattering one side completely. Jenni had come to my rescue, as she always did, but that time, she gave me an ultimatum: her or Edgar.

I chose Bella—and by extension, Edgar—and I hadn't heard from Jenni since.

"Talia?" she says, getting up and walking over.

"Jenni," I reply, surprised by how natural it feels to smile at her.

We fall into an easy conversation, and she tells me about her new job managing an apartment complex in Steiner Ranch. "If you're looking for a place, I can help you out," she offers with a grin.

My breath catches. "Really? That would be amazing."

"Come by on Monday," she says. "We'll find you something perfect."

We hug goodbye and I return to the table, the excitement swelling inside me at the idea of my own place, the start of something new.

"Well, it was nice to see Jenni again. You two used to be so close," my mom says, prying a bit.

I nod in agreement, not wanting to open up the conversation further. "Yeah, she's going to help me find a new apartment. Our lease is up," I add, cutting off the opportunity for a follow-up question.

We finish our lunch and exchange hugs before they head off to my sister Maya's house.

The house is empty when I return. I pause in the entryway, taking in the home that has held so much pain. Yet a sense of hope washes over me. Maybe as soon as next week, I'll have a new place of my own—a sanctuary I can fill with happier memories. The thought brings a bit of comfort.

Edgar doesn't return until late Sunday after a weekend bender at the poker house. His texts come in rapid bursts, as manic as his shifting moods. One moment it's: "I'm up $1,000! I'm taking you and Bella shopping next weekend." Then minutes later: "I'm down, but new people are coming in. I know I can get back to that $1,000." The desperation woven into his words makes me pity him. He truly believes this cycle will end differently each time.

He's been a gambler for as long as I've known him, but it seems to have worsened recently. His parents, hardworking Mexican Americans who built a good life for themselves and their sons, used to bail him out before I came along, praying he'd eventually find his footing like they had. But their constant rescuing only fueled the addiction. And now, I was the one bailing him out, caught in the same desperate cycle they had tried to break.

When he finally stumbles through the door, I pretend to be asleep. He climbs into bed without a word, flicks on the TV, and sinks into the sheets. The stale scent of alcohol clings to him, and I know he's been drinking again. My heart aches, but I stay still, barely breathing.

After a while, he shifts closer, his hand grazing my waist. I tense, dreading what comes next. His fingers trail gently down my side, his way of seeking comfort or closeness—but I can't give him that. Not tonight. Not like this. I freeze, my breath shallow, and hope he'll believe I'm asleep. After a moment, he sighs and turns away, the bed shifting beneath his weight.

I wait until his breathing evens out before I let my own tears fall. Silent, bitter sobs shake my chest, but I keep them muffled against my pillow. Eventually, exhaustion wins out, and I succumb to restless dreams.

Three

My alarm wakes me, and I roll out of bed, my limbs heavy with exhaustion. I nudge Edgar to let him know he'll be late if he doesn't get up. He groans and turns over, and for a moment, I just stare at him. The man who had once swept me off my feet now felt like a weight I couldn't shake.

He works part-time at a real estate firm. Despite my paying for his real estate license, he has yet to pass the test, so he helps with admin work here and there until he does. They've promised him a spot once he passes. I remain hopeful—maybe foolishly hopeful—that he'll succeed and finally get his own place.

He stops by my office on his way out, leaning down to kiss me goodbye like it's just another ordinary day. "Love you, babe. I'll see you tonight," he says, his tone light, casual—like he didn't just lose $2,000. Like I'm not about to go apartment hunting without him.

I force a smile, my cheeks stiff with the effort. "Yeah. Sure."

He doesn't seem to notice the edge in my voice. Or maybe he does and chooses to ignore it, the same way he ignores everything that matters.

As the door clicks shut behind him, I exhale, the sound shaky and frayed. Anger simmers just beneath my skin, hot and restless. But sadness tugs at me, too. I remember the man I fell for—the charm, the promises, the way he made me feel like I was the only thing that mattered.

How did we get here?

I press my fingers against my temples, trying to remember the last real conversation we had. The kind where he wasn't dismissing me or rewriting the truth to suit his own version of events.

"Did we even talk about the money?" I whisper to myself. Or did he just brush it off with a laugh and a kiss, like he always does?

I feel like I'm losing my grip on what's real and what's just another twisted version of his truth. And maybe that's the most terrifying part—realizing he's rewritten our reality so many times, I can't tell where the lies end and the truth begins.

Just then, my calendar reminder dings. Monday mornings are our usual team meetings at work. As a Sourcer for a boutique recruiting firm, I spend my days scrolling through profiles of top-tier professionals from best-in-class companies. My job is to identify top talent and pass their information along to our recruiters, who then pitch them job opportunities with our clients. My oldest sister, Maya, also works here and is the one who got me the job. Today, my goal is to find and submit ten names to the recruiters by two o'clock so I can meet Jenni afterward. I put myself into hyper-focus mode and dive into work.

By one o'clock, I finished preparing the email and hit send. Grabbing my keys, I head out the door.

The drive to Steiner Ranch is long but breathtaking, with rolling hills and glimpses of Lake Travis sparkling to the right. The weather is perfect today. I roll my window down taking in the fresh air before lighting a cigarette and turning up the music.

As I pull into the apartment complex, I'm struck by its grandeur. The Mediterranean-style architecture is stunning, with earthy stucco walls and a central building crowned by a gleaming copper dome. I pull up to an enormous gate and buzz for the office. The gates part and I pull in. Ornate balconies overflow with lush greenery, and a fountain bubbles softly in the courtyard. It's far more luxurious than I expected.

I walk through two giant wooden doors to the office. Jenni greets me with her signature smile and a big hug.

"Look at you!" she beams. "I know you are going to love this place."

"It's... already incredible," I say, still in awe. "Are you sure I can actually afford this?"

"Absolutely," she insists. "Trust me. You deserve this."

Her energy is contagious, and soon she's pulling me along for a tour of the property. The amenities are incredible: multiple sparkling pools tucked behind wrought-iron gates, a fully equipped weight room with floor-to-ceiling windows, and even a tanning bed. Each space feels designed with purpose—inviting and full of life. It's honestly perfect—better than I could have imagined.

"Okay," I say, shaking my head in disbelief. "Now you're just showing off."

Jenni laughs. "I told you this place was amazing. So... you ready to sign?"

By the end of the tour, I'm signing the lease for a beautiful tri-level, two-bedroom apartment. It feels like a fresh start—a tangible symbol of a new chapter in my life. The pen felt heavier than it should as I hovered over the lease. My hand trembled, but not from fear this time—from something sharper, something new. With a deep breath, I signed my name. The swirl of the pen on paper was both an end and a beginning, a quiet declaration of freedom.

"You okay?" Jenni asks softly. Her voice is gentler now, the teasing gone.

"Yeah," I say, swallowing the lump in my throat. "Yeah, I'm good."

Jenni slides the lease back across the table, her grin wide and infectious.

"See? I told you it would be perfect," she said, squeezing my hand. For a moment, I thought I saw something in her eyes—pride, maybe even relief. I smiled—a genuine, unforced smile that felt strange on my lips, but good.

"Hey, what are you doing Friday? Let's celebrate!" Jenni exclaims with her usual enthusiasm.

"I'm free!" I reply, matching her excitement. "Well, after I move everything in, of course," I add with a nervous laugh.

"Perfect! I will send you the details." she replies, giving me a hug as we walk out.

I walk over to the apartment and stand in the empty space, the keys cool in my hand. It was pristine, untouched, waiting for me to make it my own. As I ran my fingers over the smooth countertops, a sense of ownership bloomed in my chest. This space was mine. And so was my future.

I pull into the garage and see Edgar's car parked inside. My heart sinks. Part of me hoped he'd be out, giving me time to process everything before facing him. With a deep sigh, I gather my bag and make my way into the house.

"Where have you been?" Edgar's voice calls from the living room, low and sharp. He's sprawled across the couch, one arm resting on the back like he's been waiting for me. The TV flickers quietly in the background, forgotten.

"I... I found an apartment," I say, forcing as much confidence into my voice as I can muster. The words feel foreign, heavy on my tongue.

He turns his head, his eyes almost sad. "For you?"

"Yes." I swallow hard. "For me... and Bella when she wants to visit." The last part slips out softer, almost like an invitation. As if I'm still clinging to some thread of hope, some chance at peace between us.

Edgar's expression softens, just for a moment, and his lips tug into a small smile. "Bella will love that," he says quietly, almost wistful. The warmth in his voice stirs something painful inside me—a reminder of what we used to be.

I nod once, not trusting myself to say more. My feet feel heavy as I move toward the stairs. Halfway up, I pause, gripping the railing.

"Are you sure Talia?" Edgar calls from the couch. There's no venom in his voice, but it hangs there like something unsaid, like maybe he thought I'd change my mind.

"I am," I whisper, more to myself than to him.

I climb the rest of the stairs and slip into the bedroom. The weight of the day crashes down on me as I sit on the edge of the bed, clutching my keys as if they're the only thing holding me together. The silence of the room feels deafening, but this time it doesn't scare me.

This time, it feels like freedom.

Four

I've moved almost every year since leaving my parents' house, so I pretty much have this down to a science. The process has become familiar—methodical, even. I know exactly how to fold my clothes to maximize space in my suitcases, which boxes to label for easy unpacking, and the best way to stack furniture in the moving truck.

My routine is precise: I'll start by loading my car with all the daily essentials—the coffee maker, coffee cups, and, of course, coffee itself. I couldn't function without it. My computer and notebooks always follow, tucked securely in the front seat. Those are the first things I'll set up, ensuring I can still work even with boxes stacked around me. After that, I work my way through the rest, turning the chaos into something manageable.

There was a strange comfort in the rhythm of it—the familiar ache in my arms from lifting boxes, the satisfying snap of packing tape, the sense of order I created with each labeled container. It was exhausting, but packing had become a skill—a way to convince myself that no matter how chaotic my life felt, I could still control something.

Despite most of my belongings still being in boxes, I managed to organize my clothes and shoes in my new, luxurious closet by Friday. The space was a dream—custom shelves, soft lighting, and more room than I'd ever had before. I sat cross-legged on the plush carpet, running my fingers over the fabrics as I tried to decide what to wear.

Fashion has never been my strength. It was my sisters' thing—something they made look effortless, gliding through trends with ease, while I always felt like I was playing dress-up in clothes that never quite worked for me. But my body was different. Curvier. No matter how much I tried to mirror their styles, the fit was always off, the proportions unflattering.

It had been a while since I truly went out with friends and got dressed up. I know Jenni will show up looking gorgeous, so I reach for a little black dress—simple but striking. It hugs my curves in all the right places instead of fighting against them. I pair it with leopard-print pumps for a touch of flair. To finish the look, I choose a bold, classic red lipstick that makes my blonde hair seem even brighter against the dark fabric of the dress.

As I studied my reflection in the mirror, something shifted. Maybe I would never have my sisters' effortless style, but tonight, I didn't need it.

Tonight, I felt like me—and for once, that was enough.

As expected, Jenni was dressed to kill. She was striking in a black lace cami paired with some perfectly fitted jeans and black pointed heels. Her straightened hair fell in sleek perfection.

Her new love interest and restaurant manager, Jeff, secured us a prime table on the patio at Fion, a cozy French bistro tucked away just down the street from the apartment. Strings of fairy lights crisscrossed above us on the patio, twinkling against the dark velvet sky. The air was crisp but pleasant, and the scent of warm baguettes wafted from the restaurant's open doors.

Thomas, Jenni's friend from our apartment complex, joined us for dinner. His bleach-blond hair was styled to perfection, and his impeccable fashion sense—a lightweight, cream-colored sweater paired with tailored navy chinos and polished leather loafers—exuded a classic Banana Republic vibe with a touch of New York chic. From the moment he sat down, his animated expressions and razor-sharp wit had us in stitches, effortlessly drawing everyone into his enchanting charm.

I felt a sliver of freedom. There was something about being there—the weight of Edgar's volatile moods seemed worlds away. For the first time in what felt like forever, I allowed myself to exhale, savoring the quiet rebellion of being exactly where I wanted to be.

As our server approached, I looked up—and froze. He was tall—easily six feet—with a short, clean-edged haircut and an easy, confident smile that was utterly irresistible. His deep, chocolate-brown eyes locked onto mine, and for a second, it was like the air shifted—thickened. That gaze was intense and smoldering, threaded with something that seemed to reach across the space between us.

The fitted black button-up shirt he wore, sleeves rolled to the elbows, showcased strong forearms and a lean, athletic frame. The rich, deep hue of his skin seemed to catch the dim light, smooth and magnetic. But it wasn't just his appearance—it was the energy he carried. Raw strength softened by warmth. Charisma mixed with a kind of quiet intensity that made my heart race.

"Hi, my name's Damian, and I'll be taking care of you tonight," he says, his voice smooth and low. The sound of it slides over me, dark and warm like whiskey.

I realize I'm staring. Heat rushes to my cheeks, but I can't bring myself to look away. Jenni smirks, wasting no time ordering a bottle of prosecco.

"Sounds good. Jeff has some appetizers coming out for you all as well," Damian adds, his eyes lingering on mine just a fraction too long before he walks away. The scent of his cologne—a mix of something woodsy and sharp—lingers in his wake, teasing my senses.

I turn to Jenni and Thomas the moment he is out of earshot. "Holy shit, he's hot," I whisper, trying to play it off as a joke, but my voice comes out breathless.

They burst out laughing, nodding in agreement. But even as we sip our prosecco, my gaze keeps drifting toward Damian. It was like trying to resist gravity.

"You look amazing," Jenni says, her smile wide, genuine. "It's so good to see you like this, Talia. You deserve to feel happy again."

Her words hit harder than I expected. I swallow, nodding as I raise my glass. "To new beginnings." My voice is firmer than I feel.

Throughout the night, Damian seemed to appear whenever I thought about him—refilling glasses, clearing plates, or simply passing by. Each time, his gaze would find mine. Quick, almost imperceptible, but enough to set my pulse racing. I couldn't help but wonder if he felt the same spark I did.

By the end of the night, a mix of prosecco and courage leads me to ask Damian a few pointed questions, including the big one: "So…do you have a girlfriend?"

"Yes," he says, his expression unreadable. Of course. Figures. Not that I have any room to judge, still tangled in the mess that is Edgar.

But something flickers across Damian's face—a hesitation, like he was weighing what to say next.

"What's her name? Do you have a picture?" I ask, trying to sound casual, like we are old friends.

He laughs softly but answers. "Nicole." He says the name like it tastes bland. Then, with a shrug, he pulls out his phone and shows me a photo.

"Oh," I say, tilting my head. "Not what I expected."

He raises an eyebrow, a hint of amusement breaking through his guarded expression. "Oh yeah? What did you expect?"

My mouth opens, but the words tangle. The truth? I expected her to look more...put together. Glamorous, confident—someone who matched the magnetic energy Damian gave off. Not this average-looking brunette with a smile that seemed more strained than happy.

I hesitate, suddenly aware that I am about to describe, well...myself. "I don't know. Blonde, maybe?" I trail off, feeling ridiculous. Quickly, I add, "Your dog is adorable!" I point to the tiny, black and tan Min Pin in the photo.

"That's Tucker, my little buddy," he says, his smile warming. "What about you? You have a dog?"

"I used to have a Min Pin too," I admit, my voice softening. "But my ex took him. Now I have a Yorkie, Harvey"

Damian's brow furrows slightly. "Oh, so no boyfriend?"

"Um, well... kind of, it's complicated," I stammer, my cheeks burning.

He nods in a way that makes me feel he understands exactly what I mean. His gaze holds mine, steady and searching, as if he was trying to peel back the layers. The spark between us is undeniable, even if it is fleeting. Or so I thought.

As the last customers trickle out, Jeff saunters over to our table, throwing his arm around Jenni with easy familiarity. "Join us, Damian," he calls over, his tone effortlessly commanding.

By this point, I had a solid buzz going, the prosecco warming my veins and dulling my usual inhibitions. When Damian slid into the seat next to me, his presence pulled me in like gravity. It was absurd how aware of him I was—the heat radiating from his body, the subtle brush of his arm against mine.

"It's getting cold out here," I say, my voice a little too high, too eager. Without thinking, I place my freezing hands on his forearm, my fingers curling instinctively around the firm muscle. "Wow, you're hot."

The words slip out before I can stop them, and my stomach drops. But Damian's reaction wasn't what I expected. His laugh was rich and effortless, like I'd just gifted him a secret he'd been waiting for me to confess.

"Yeah? Thanks." His grin was the kind that sent heat racing through my skin.

The words replayed in my head, even as I
laughed. I knew they'd haunt me the next day, but in
that moment, they felt unfiltered and honest.

Touching him felt electric, like breaking a rule I
didn't know I'd set for myself, and yet it was
impossible to ignore how right it felt—how right *he*
felt.

Up close, he was even more striking. The sharp
lines of his jaw, the way his eyes lingered on mine like
he was cataloging every reaction. I felt exposed in the
best possible way.

"So, California, huh?" I said, desperate to sound
casual. "You don't strike me as a Texan."

He shook his head. "Born and raised on the West
Coast. Nicole and I came out here to try something
new. You know... change of scenery."

"But?" I pressed, catching the way his gaze
flickered away.

"But..." he hesitated, his fingers tracing the edge
of his glass. "Texas hasn't exactly been what I
expected."

"That bad, huh?"

He laughed, but it was thin, strained. "More
like... I'm not sure what I'm doing here anymore."

The way he said it made me think it wasn't just
Texas he was talking about. His words carried a
weight that didn't match his easy smile. And suddenly,
I felt bold. Or maybe just reckless.

"Maybe you're looking for the wrong things," I
said, my voice dropping lower.

He lifted his eyes to mine, and the heat between us seemed to thicken, pressing in from all sides. "Maybe. What about you? Are you from Texas?"

"I moved here when I was twelve, so yeah. Guess that makes me a local." I try to keep my tone light, but something slips through—regret, maybe. "I wanted to go away for college, travel... but it hasn't exactly worked out that way."

The admission surprises me, my own words sounding heavier than I intended. Like I've been stuck here, stagnant.

"But Austin's cool. You should give it a real chance." I add quickly, like it's some sort of apology for my own inertia.

"We'll see." Damian's eyes shift with something I can't quite read. "Maybe you're right. Maybe I just haven't been looking in the right places."

The conversation shifted to simpler topics— music, food, random complaints about the weird Texas weather. But even when the subject was mundane, I felt the undercurrent between us, sharp and undeniable.

Jenni and Jeff decided to keep the party going, inviting everyone back to Jeff's place. The kind of casual invitation that meant drinking and joking and a night that stretched on far too late.

I asked Damian if he was going. Part of me hoped he'd say yes. Another part of me hoped he wouldn't.

"Maybe," he said with a small smile. But he never showed up.

As I lay in bed that night, Damian lingered in my thoughts like a song I couldn't stop replaying. Something stirred inside me—soft and hesitant, yet impossible to ignore. It wasn't just attraction; it was the faint whisper of possibility, a glimpse of a world beyond the walls I'd spent so long building around myself.

The thought felt wrong somehow—like I didn't deserve it. My confidence was threadbare, worn down to nothing. Who would want me, broken and unsure as I was?

But still... there was something. Something awakening, fragile yet insistent, reminding me I was still here. Still capable of feeling. Still worthy of something more.

The last weeks of October blurred together—a haze of cardboard boxes, restless nights, and a dull, unanswered longing to see Damian again. On top of that was Edgar's unwelcome return, weaving everything into a tangled mess I couldn't seem to unravel. Each day felt like trudging through mud, a cycle of uncertainty that left me drained and raw.

But there was one thing I managed to control—my new space. The moment I unlocked my front door, I made it mine. I attacked the unpacking with purpose, tearing through boxes until each room felt organized and whole. I arranged my bookshelves just how I liked them, hung framed photos on the walls, and filled the kitchen with fresh flowers and candles that gave the air a warm, comforting scent. This home, with its clean lines and cozy corners, felt like a breath of fresh air, a space that belonged only to me. For the first time in a long time, I felt settled, like I could exhale.

Jenni had gotten Damian's number from Jeff, and we tried reaching out—inviting him to a few gatherings, sending casual messages that I hoped felt warm but not too desperate. But he either didn't respond at all or replied with polite yet distant excuses. Each unanswered message felt like a tiny cut, sharp enough to sting but not deep enough to draw blood.

Was he avoiding me on purpose? Or was I just hoping for too much? Thoughts of him made my stomach twist with something dangerously close to desire. I hated how much I noticed him. Hated how much I wanted to see him again.

In the middle of all that uncertainty, Edgar managed to slip back into my life like a slow-moving shadow. Lindsey and I had agreed that Bella should still come to my house every other weekend, especially since Edgar had yet to find a place to live and was couch-surfing. That arrangement, of course, opened the door for Edgar to drift in and out whenever Bella was visiting.

Those weekends were bittersweet. Bella's laughter filled my home with warmth, and our moments together felt precious—like I was still holding on to something good. But Edgar's presence turned those visits into something strained. He'd make empty promises to Bella about taking her shopping or to the park only to oversleep or leave to play poker. Monday would roll around, and somehow, Edgar would still be there— his presence polluting the space I'd worked so hard to build, offering vague promises about "helping with bills" and "getting things sorted." Promises that never materialized. He left shoes by the door, his keys scattered on the table, and dishes piled in the sink. My home no longer felt like mine; it felt invaded.

The worst part wasn't his presence—it was the way it felt so familiar. As if I'd slipped back into an old life I thought I'd left behind. Like waking up from a dream only to realize I was still trapped in the same nightmare.

"You deserve better."

Lindsey's words echoed in my head, clear and sharp. But what did *better* even look like? I barely knew anymore. The lines between hope and disappointment, between comfort and regret, had blurred so much that I wasn't sure where one ended and the other began.

The one bright spot in it all was Jenni. Somehow, we had fallen right back into our old rhythm. She felt like a lifeline—a constant reminder that, at least in one part of my life, I still had a choice. With her, I didn't feel like I was drowning. With her, I could breathe. She made me realize how much I missed my friendships.

Five

November brings Jenni's birthday—and with it, an unexpected encounter. I had plans to pick up the birthday girl at her apartment at 6 p.m. so we could head downtown together. I hit the gym to shake off the restlessness that's been clinging to me all week.

Sweaty and full of endorphins, I walk in through the back patio door to the apartment. To my surprise and immediate annoyance, Edgar is standing in the kitchen with his head buried in the fridge. My stomach sinks.

"Oh, hey!" I said, forcing my voice to sound casual, but my anxiety had already started to rise.

"There's no food in this house," he mutters, his tone flat and accusing, like it's my personal failure.

His audacity never fails to surprise me. I bite back a sigh. Same old Edgar. Complaining about things he's perfectly capable of fixing himself.

"Yeah, well, I have Jenni's birthday dinner tonight, so I wasn't going to go to the store until tomorrow," I shot back, sharper than I intended. I didn't want him to drain my good mood.

"Birthday dinner? Where are y'all going?" he asks, his eyes narrowing like I've just sprung something on him.

My shoulders tense, but I keep my voice even. "Kai Sushi." Should have lied. Picked somewhere uninteresting, something he'd brush off with disinterest.

"Oh, perfect! I've been wanting to try it. I'll come with you," he says, like it's the most natural thing in the world.

Of course. Why wouldn't he? Edgar's always been like this—casually inserting himself into plans he wasn't invited to, like he's doing me a favor. And maybe, at one point, I would've believed that.

Now, it just feels exhausting.

"Sure," I say, keeping my tone neutral. It's not worth the argument. Not tonight.

As I climb the stairs to shower and get ready, I take a deep breath trying to calm myself. I wasn't going to let him ruin the night.

I shoot Jenni a quick text to let her know the change in plans.

The private room at Kai Sushi, tucked away in an upscale downtown spot, was an oasis of soft lighting and modern elegance. The sleek wooden floors gleamed under the dim red glow of overhead lanterns, and the delicate scent of fresh fish and wasabi mingled in the air, tantalizing my senses.

Jenni, of course, was dressed to perfection. Her emerald-green dress clung to her slender frame like it was made just for her, the fabric flowing effortlessly to just above her knee. Her hair was perfectly straightened, gleaming with a polished sheen that caught the light in every movement, and the high heels she wore added an extra layer of sophistication. With every step she took, her presence commanded attention.

Laughter and conversation flowed easily, but I was too distracted to enjoy it. Out of the corner of my eye, I see him—Damian.

He was here.

My stomach twists. *Yay.* No, *not* yay. *Shit.* Edgar is here.

Damian made his way around the table, his easy smile disarming everyone in his path. Celebrations seem to come naturally to him, and for some reason, that only made him more captivating.

When he stops beside me, his smile widens. "Hey, Talia." His voice is smooth and low, but there is a note of familiarity in it that hadn't been there before.

"Hey, Damian." My voice came out faint, barely a whisper. The fact that he remembered my name sent a thrill through me I wasn't ready to admit.

To my horror, he slides into the seat next to me. His arm brushes mine as he adjusts his chair. A tiny, innocent touch, but it felt deliberate. My skin prickled with awareness, a heat that spread through me too quickly. My heart skips, then thuds painfully against my ribs. I shift slightly away, but there's nowhere to go.

Edgar's eyes darken. His shoulders square, and he leans in closer, his voice sharp. "Who's this guy?" he demands, the edge in his tone slicing through the easy laughter around us.

I stiffen. Don't make this a thing. Please don't make this a thing. I force a smile, the muscles in my face straining. "Just a friend," I say quickly, the words tumbling out too fast. My voice sounds thin, brittle.

Damian's grin doesn't falter. "Yeah, just a friend." The way he says it, light and almost playful, felt like a challenge. His eyes lingered on mine, a flicker of something unspoken passing between us.

Warmth blooms in my chest — unwanted but undeniable. It coils low in my stomach, a feeling I can't remember craving until now.

Edgar's arm slides around the back of my chair, his fingers brushing my shoulder. The touch was firm, almost possessive. His hand settles there, firm, his fingertips digging in just enough to leave a message. My breath catches. The pressure isn't painful, but it's enough to leave me frozen. It was just Edgar being Edgar—staking his claim, letting me know I was his, whether I wanted to be or not.

Damian's presence beside me was impossible to ignore. He was so close—warm, solid—and for some reason, that terrified me almost as much as Edgar's grip. Damian felt like both a lifeline and a threat—something I wanted and something I couldn't afford to need.

Jenni caught my eye from across the table. Her smile was practically smug, like she'd orchestrated this whole thing. You're welcome, her expression said.

But all I could think was, *I'm not sure what you've just started.*

Later, the party spills onto the rooftop of Molotov, one of the most popular bars in the city. The skyline glows in the distance, neon lights reflecting off glass buildings, the music thrumming beneath my skin.

My little sister, Karina, is already there, perched at a high-top table with her best friend, Ana, cocktails in hand. She's freshly sun-kissed from her whirlwind backpacking trip through Europe, her deep brown long hair was lighter, her energy effervescent.

The second she sees me, her eyes light up, and she jumps from her seat, pulling me into a tight hug.

"Finally!" she squeals. "I was starting to think you forgot about me!"

I laugh, squeezing her back. "Never. I'm just so happy you're home."

Over her shoulder, I catch the exact moment her smile fades.

Karina doesn't even try to mask her distaste when Edgar appears. She fakes a tight, polite smile but makes zero effort to step closer. No hug. Not even a forced greeting.

I see the irritation cross Edgar's face, but he brushes it off with an overconfident smirk, like he doesn't care.

I care.

The moment stretches just a little too long, the weight of unspoken truths thick in the air.

I clear my throat, breaking the tension. "I need a drink," I mutter, slipping away before Edgar can latch onto me.

I weave through the crowd toward the bar, the night buzzing with the energy of laughter and clinking glasses.

Damian found me at the bar, leaning close as I ordered my drink, his presence a dark, tantalizing shadow. His confidence seemed fueled by liquid courage, and when he spoke, his voice dropped to a whisper that only I could hear, a teasing, almost seductive edge to it.

"You look cute tonight." His eyes traveling down my curve-hugging blue dress, lingering at the dip of my cleavage before returning to my gaze. The proximity between us was exhilarating, making my skin hum with awareness.

I blinked, caught off guard. "What are you doing?" I ask, suspicion lacing my voice as I narrow my eyes.

"What?" He shrugs, his smile easy and unbothered. "I can't compliment you?"

"Not when my boyfriend is here. And not after you've been avoiding me for weeks."

He hands me my drink, his fingers brushing mine in a way that feels deliberate, sending a jolt of heat through me.

"You're trouble, you know that?" I whisper, my lips curving despite myself. How could I feel this pull with Edgar just across the room? But I couldn't stop the pull, the magnetic force drawing me toward him.

He leaned in just slightly, his voice teasing. "So are you."

The tension between us was palpable, charged with something I couldn't quite define. It was electric, a crackling undercurrent neither of us could ignore. Damn, he was sexy. His confidence, the way he carried himself, was impossible to look away from. Our eyes kept locking across the room, a silent conversation unfolding with every glance before being shattered like fragile glass when Edgar's arm slid possessively around me, pulling me back to a reality. It was dangerous—reckless even—But the thrill of Damian's attention was hard to resist.

As the night wore on, Jenni—being Jenni—became completely wasted. The group began figuring out rides, and I focused on getting her safely into a cab. I slid in behind her. My phone buzzed, and I glanced at the screen, my stomach lurching at the message:

Edgar: *We'll meet you back at Jenni's apartment. I got a ride with Damian.*

My stomach dropped. *Why is he with Damian?* They barely acknowledged each other at dinner, Edgar's gaze turning cool and calculating anytime Damian was near.

My mind raced. Was Edgar just trying to size him up? Or was he testing me—trying to gauge my reaction by pairing off with the one person I couldn't seem to stop noticing? The entire journey to Jenni's felt like an eternity.

Once there, we settled on the patio, all smoking cigarettes. My eyes kept darting toward the door, scanning the parking lot, dreading and anticipating their arrival. Edgar finally walked through the door—alone.

"Where's Damian?" I asked, fighting to keep my voice even.

"He went home." Edgar's grin widened, satisfaction gleaming in his eyes. "Nice guy."

"Why'd you ride with him?"

He shrugged. "He offered. Seemed like he wanted to talk. Guess he's just friendly." His smile sharpened, eyes never leaving mine. "Too friendly, maybe."

My pulse quickened. Was he trying to catch me in something?

"What did you guys even talk about?"

"Nothing much. Work. The city. You." His voice was casual, but there was something underneath it, an edge meant to put me on notice. "His phone went off at one point. Girlfriend checking up on him, I guess."

The words landed like stones in my stomach. *Girlfriend.* Of course. And now Edgar wanted me to know. To remind me who I was supposed to be loyal to.

I forced a shrug. "Oh yeah, his girlfriend, Nicole."

Edgar's smile twitched, like he hadn't expected me to sound so indifferent. "Yeah, seemed like a decent guy. Loyal, too." He said it like it was a challenge, his eyes locked on mine. "Lucky girl, I guess."

He flicked his cigarette ash, leaning back with the air of someone who'd just won a quiet, private battle. "People who know what they have… they don't go looking for something else."

My jaw tightened, heat prickling beneath my skin. The message was clear: Damian was off-limits. And so was I.

Six

I couldn't focus on work that week. My thoughts kept drifting back to Damian—his playful smirk, the way his voice lowered when he spoke to me, like he was letting me in on some secret only we could share.

It wasn't just attraction. It was the way he made me feel *alive* again, like something Edgar had buried in me was clawing its way to the surface. Damian's flirtation wasn't heavy or demanding—it was light, effortless, the kind of attention that made my pulse race and my cheeks flush before I could stop them.

With Edgar, everything felt like a negotiation—his control, his jealousy, his constant need to remind me that I *belonged* to him. It was exhausting. I'd grown so used to monitoring my words, measuring every reaction, that I'd forgotten what it felt like to simply exist without being scrutinized.

But Damian? He was easy. Fun. A breath of fresh air I didn't even know I'd been starving for.

And yet, the confusion gnawed at me. For weeks, Damian had been avoiding me. No messages. No accidental run-ins at the restaurant. Nothing but silence. I'd told myself to forget him, that whatever fleeting connection I'd felt was nothing more than a mistake.

But then he showed up at Jenni's party, smiling at me like he'd never kept his distance, his flirtation easy and unguarded. Like he hadn't spent weeks pretending I didn't exist.

Why now?

The question spun around in my mind like a broken record, its edges frayed and sharp. Was it me he'd been avoiding? Or something else? The sudden attention was thrilling, yes, but it also left me feeling unsteady, like I was standing on the edge of something I couldn't quite see.

And worse, I couldn't stop myself from obsessing over every detail. The way his gaze lingered, the teasing comments, the warmth in his smile that felt too genuine to be an act. It was like he'd seen something in me I hadn't realized was still there. Something worth wanting.

But if that was true, then why the distance?

Was I just some passing thrill for him? A distraction from his own problems? I didn't even know what those problems were, but I could feel them lurking beneath the surface. The easy charm, the casual flirtation—it was real, but it was also a mask.

Or maybe I'm just imagining everything. The thought twisted my stomach, part shame, part frustration.

Edgar had me second-guessing everything for so long that I wasn't even sure I could trust my own instincts.

But every time I thought of Damian, there was that spark—that reckless, exhilarating pull toward something I couldn't define. Something I wasn't sure I deserved but desperately wanted.

And that terrified me. Because what if it wasn't real? What if I'd only imagined the spark between us? What if I was just fooling myself, clinging to a fantasy because the reality of my life felt so suffocating?

I stared at my computer screen, the words blurring together. I'd been re-reading the same email for ten minutes without absorbing a single line.

Ding. An instant message pops up on my screen, saving me from the black hole of overanalyzing I have clearly fallen into.

"Where are we with the Honeywell Marketing leaders?" my recruiter, Stacy, messages, her tone sharp even through text.

I cringe. Shit! I've been so distracted I haven't sent anything yet.

"Almost done. I have eight names I can send you now," I reply quickly, hoping to buy myself some time to find the last two.

She agrees, and I dive back into work mode, fingers flying across the keyboard as I chase my target. Ten minutes later, I have the final two names and hit send, exhaling in satisfaction.

This wasn't my dream job—not even close. It was a far cry from the life I once envisioned—working in the State Department, traveling the world, making a real impact. But I couldn't deny that I was good at this. Really good. I had a knack for tracking down even the most elusive candidates, digging up hard-to-find people in half the time it took others.

Still, it was just a job. A means to an end.

With a final click, I log off, ready to leave work behind and disappear into the evening.

Dinner is hardly glamorous—a simple cheesy broccoli dish I whip together in minutes. Just as I'm plating it, the back patio door swings open. I startle, my heart jumping, but immediately relax when I see who it is.

"It's me, and I brought prosecco!" Jenni announces, kicking off her heels as she breezes inside.

My apartment is right across from the main office at the complex, so her dropping by at the end of the day is a regular—and very welcome—occurrence.

I grab two large wine glasses, and we head out to the patio to recap the day.

"Wait… is Edgar here?" she asks, glancing around like he might slither out from the shadows at any moment.

"Nope. He's either at work or hanging out at the poker house with strippers. Who knows? It's a fun little guessing game I try not to play," I say sarcastically—though, let's be honest, I'm mostly not kidding.

"Oh great! Ok so how fun was my party?" she asks, her grin suggesting she already knows the answer.

I laugh, shaking my head. "It was awesome—except for the awkward Damian-and-Edgar scenario. I mean, he hasn't wanted to hang out any other time, and of course, the one night Edgar decides to tag along, Damian shows up."

"I know. I'm sorry!" Jenni admits, her voice laced with guilt. "I was going to tell you, but I wasn't sure if he'd actually show up, and I didn't want to get your hopes up."

She shrugs, lighting her cigarette with a flick of her lighter before passing it to me. I light mine, and we clink our glasses together, tapping them lightly on the table in our unspoken ritual. It's something we've done countless times—almost like a spell cast to ward off the heaviness of our lives.

I fill her in on the captivating moments Damian and I shared—the stolen glances, the lingering tension at the table, the way his voice dipped just enough to make my pulse stutter.

She smirks, leaning back against the chair. "You just need to get rid of Edgar once and for all and go for Damian already."

I let out a dry laugh, swirling the prosecco in my glass. "If only it were that easy." I sigh, watching the bubbles rise and pop. "He's so confusing—avoids me for weeks, then flirts with me at your party."

Jenni tilts her head, considering. "It's complicated for both of you. But you're never going to figure it out unless you see him again."

I hesitate, biting my lip. "Maybe you're right."

Jenni claps her hands together, eyes lighting up. "Alright, that's it!" she declares. "I'm inviting everyone over to my place on Saturday. Drinks, snacks, the whole deal. Well… except Edgar, obviously."

I chuckle, but there's a heaviness underneath the humor. "Fun. Okay." A small pulse of excitement flows through me, quickly drowned by doubt. "Hopefully, Damian will actually show up this time."

The truth I don't say out loud is that part of me is terrified he will. Because every time he looks at me like that—like he's already figured out everything I'm trying to keep hidden—I feel myself slipping.

And letting go would mean finally tearing myself away from Edgar's hold.

Even worse, it would mean facing whatever part of me still believes that's impossible.

Thursday rolls around, and Karina texts me about meeting her and her friend Molly at Speakeasy downtown.

I smile at my phone, a flicker of excitement stirring—something I haven't felt in a long time. Having Karina back feels like stepping into sunlight after months of gray. She's always been the vibrant one, her energy contagious and her humor quick.

Growing up, Karina could turn the dullest
moments into something unforgettable—a
spontaneous dance party in the kitchen, a pizza-movie
marathon that stretched until sunrise. We share the
same offbeat humor, the kind that turns a passing
comment into a joke that lasts for years.

With her, I can be my truest self—fun, unfiltered,
free.

I haven't seen Holly since high school, so
catching up sounds like a breath of fresh air—a
reminder that I existed before everything got so
heavy.

Jenni and Thomas, of course, are always game to
try a new bar. Somehow, they've made it their mission
to explore every trendy spot in the city.

As I set my phone down, I feel something stir—
hope, maybe. Like I'm finding my way back to the
person I used to be.

On the drive downtown, Jenni glances over. "You
should text Damian and see if he's working tonight,"
she suggests casually. "I heard he's at Perry's
Steakhouse now. It's close by."

"Why not?" I shrug, pulling out my phone to text
him.

*Hey, Jenni said you're working downtown now. We're
headed to Speakeasy if you want to come meet us.*

By the time we walk in, Karina and Holly are
already lounging in a cozy seating area surrounded by
plush couches and armchairs. The warm, moody
lighting adds to the relaxed vibe.

My phone buzzes.

Damian: *Yeah, I'm just down the street. My friend and I just got off work; we'll meet you there.*

I lean over to show Jenni, and her face lights up. "Hell yeah," she exclaims, loud enough to earn curious looks from my sister.

"What's that about?" Karina asks, raising an eyebrow.

"Oh, our friend Damian is coming by," I say, trying to sound nonchalant.

She shrugs, though her knowing smile suggests she's intrigued.

A few minutes later, Damian and his friend Rodney walk in. Both are still in their work uniforms—crisp white shirts and black slacks. Damian's eyes find mine almost immediately, a grin spreading across his face.

The grin that makes my pulse stumble.

"Hey, you made it!" Jenni says, hopping up to greet Damian with a hug. He makes his way over to me.

"Hey, good to see you," he murmurs, his voice low and smooth, like he knows exactly what he's doing. His arm slips around my waist, casual but confident, fingers pressing just firmly enough to send a jolt of heat through me.

The air between us feels charged, like everyone else in the room can sense something unspoken.

Introductions follow, everyone laughing and exchanging pleasantries. But Damian's gaze keeps drifting to me, his attention impossible to ignore.

Damian sinks into the armchair directly across from me. As the conversation flows, Damian leans forward, his elbows resting on his knees, shrinking the space between us.

"So, how's it been, working downtown?" I ask before taking a sip of my cocktail.

His smile turns teasing. "Busy," he says, his gaze never wavering. "Between the late nights and long shifts, it's hard to get much time for anything else." He pauses, his smile deepening. "Unless there's a good reason to stick around after hours."

I feel my face heat, but I smile back. "Oh yeah? Like…?"

"Like you," he says.

I start to say something else, but his unwavering focus unravels my thoughts, leaving me flustered. His eyes—intense and undeniably gorgeous—make it hard to think straight. His attention feels heavier than casual interest—intentional, irresistible, impossible to ignore. The chatter from the rest of the group fades into a dull hum, the air thick with something electric.

Jenni smirks from the couch, nudging Thomas, who's pretending not to notice. Karina, ever the opportunist, leans back and throws a cheeky question into the mix breaking the tension. "So, how do you two know each other again?" She asks her finger pointing to the two of us.

Damian shifts slightly, his gaze flicking to Karina, but his body remains angled toward me. I decide to take the lead. "Oh, we met through Jenni at Fion," I say, keeping my tone light.

"Ah," Karina says, drawing out the syllable. "And you just came out tonight to see Talia?"

Damian chuckles softly. "Yeah, we work at Perry's down the street, so we figured we'd stop by."

"Convenient," she replies with a smirk, clearly enjoying herself. "That's right I saw you at Jenni's party at Molotov."

The group laughs, but the tension between Damian and I is palpable. Every glance, every word feels charged. I wish I knew what he was thinking.

Rodney and Damian head to the bar for another round. Clearly amused, he leans over to Damian and murmurs something that earns a subtle smirk in response. Jenni catches my eye, giving me a conspiratorial wink. He's definitely into you," Jenni whispered, nudging me with a grin. Across from us, Karina raised an eyebrow, her expression somewhere between amusement and curiosity. "You should tell me about him later," she said, her tone teasing but knowing.

When it's finally time to leave, we all walk out together. The cool night air wraps around us as Jenni turns to Damian. "Hey, by the way, I'm having people over Saturday night. You should come."

Damian doesn't hesitate. "I'm working lunch, but yeah, I can make it," he says, his eyes meeting mine as he speaks.

I smile, my heart racing, though I try to keep my excitement under control. He has a way of saying yes and then not showing, but for tonight, the possibility feels intoxicating.

Jenni and I climb into her car, exchanging a knowing look that says everything. Karina's already in the backseat, phone pressed to her ear, her voice light and animated. The sound of it surprises me—full of something I haven't heard from her in a while: genuine excitement. I knew she had to be talking to the new Australian she met on her trip.

"Is that Oliver?" I ask in a teasing voice, twisting in my seat to glance at her.

Karina's eyes flick up from her phone, and she rolls them dramatically. "Yessss," she groans, but there's no hiding her smile.

"Ohhh," Jenni chimes in, dragging out the word like a song. "It's *Oliver*."

"Let me talk to him," I say, motioning for the phone.

Karina hesitates, but then sighs and passes it over with a playful warning: "Don't embarrass me."

"Hello? Oliver?" I ask, lowering my voice slightly for effect.

"Hi, yes, this is Oliver," he replies in the cutest Australian accent. His voice is warm and easy, like someone who doesn't take life too seriously.

"I hear you want to come visit Karina," I say, adopting a mock-serious tone.

"Yes, that is the plan," he answers, a slight smile evident in his voice.

"Amazing," I reply. "Can't wait to meet you." I pause, imagining him as a koala—the mental image makes me giggle. "I don't know why," I add with a laugh, "but I'm picturing you as a koala right now. Tiny, fluffy, just... hanging out in a tree."

Jenni snorts with laughter, and Karina grabs the phone back, shaking her head. "Ignore them," she tells him, her voice still bubbling with happiness.

We all laugh as Karina says her goodbyes and hangs up. The warmth in the car is infectious, filling the air like sunlight.

"I think he's a keeper," Jenni teases.

Karina's smile softens. "Yeah... me too."

Jenni cranks up *Kings of Leon's "Sex on Fire,"* as soon as she hangs up and within seconds, we're all screaming the lyrics at the top of our lungs, the windows down, the night air whipping through the car. I feel alive again, the weight of everything else momentarily forgotten as the music thunders through the car, fueling my energy.

Seven

Saturday afternoon is spent running errands, stocking up on drinks and snacks for the gathering. As we wander the aisles, Edgar texts, asking where I am. I casually reply that I'm with Jenni, spending the day hanging out. I conveniently leave out the part about the party.

His next text comes almost immediately: *All you do is hang out with Jenni now.*

The jealousy drips from his words, heavy and possessive.

I try to keep my tone light, hoping to avoid a confrontation. *We're having fun and doing girl stuff you hate doing,* I type back, attempting to convince him this isn't a big deal.

His response is quick, dismissive: *Fine, whatever. Have fun, I guess.*

I probably should feel more guilty but I don't. I feel excited.

By the time we're back at Jenni's, the place is buzzing with preparations. Thomas, of course, is the first to arrive. "I'm here, the party can start now!" he announces as he walks through the door.

"We are in my room, almost ready!" Jenni hollers back as she finishes putting her lipstick on. I throw on my sweater and walk out to greet Thomas who is already walking toward us with drinks in hand.

"Cheers lovelies!" Thomas says as we raise our glasses.

"To an epic night ahead!" Jenni responds before taking a sip.

As the house fills with people, the evening starts to take shape. I'm out on the patio, chatting with Thomas and a few other friends, when Damian finally walks in.

He steps onto the patio like he owns it—self-assured, his gaze sweeping over the crowd before landing on me.

He's wearing a fitted black shirt that clings to his broad shoulders, a sleek grey jacket tailored to perfection. His presence is effortless, commanding. But it's the way he looks at me—intent, unguarded—that makes my nerves kick in.

I can't stop myself from fidgeting with my belt on my black leather pants as he makes his way through the group.

Within minutes—almost as if fate itself intervened—Damian and I are alone on the balcony.

He drops into one of the newly vacant chairs, leaning back with an effortless confidence, one arm draped over the backrest. The pose is casual, but there's a simmering intensity in his gaze that sends shivers along my spine. I'm leaning against the railing, facing him, a cigarette between my fingers. The cool, crisp air mingles with the faint hum of city life, but it all feels distant, muted.

Out here, the balcony feels like its own little world—quiet, secluded, suspended above the sparkling lights of the city.

"So, what's the deal with Edgar?" he asks, his voice steady but probing.

I shrug, avoiding his eyes. "He's an ass, honestly." The words tumble out before I can stop them. "Last month, I caught him at a poker house with a stripper on his lap. He swears nothing happened, but…"

Damian cuts me off, his expression hardening. "Something definitely happened," he says, scoffing with a knowing tone.

I stare at him, startled and defensive. "How do you know?"

"I just know," he says with unshakable confidence. "I've known guys like him, trust me."

His certainty unsettles me. Part of me wants to push back, to argue that he doesn't know Edgar like I do. But I can't. Because I know he's right. And admitting that means facing a truth I've been burying for years—Edgar is never going to change.

I hesitate, my fingers tightening around the railing. I leave out the part where Edgar came home drunk that night—the shouting, the fight, his hands tightening around my throat as I scrambled to get away on the stairs. The memory slices through me like a cold blade—sharp, immediate, unforgiving. I push it down. I always push it down.

"It's complicated," I say, my voice sounding strained and brittle. "He has a daughter, Bella. And she means a lot to me. It makes it hard to fully walk away and cut him out when she loves him so much." I pause, my gaze dropping to the ground. "Her mom and I are great friends. I know Bella will always be in my life, no matter what. But... it's hard. There's this constant pull to stay for her."

Damian's expression shifts, something softening in his gaze. "I get that," he says, his voice quieter now. "It sounds like you care about her a lot," he adds.

He doesn't push. Doesn't judge. Just lets the words settle.

I force a smile, desperate to change the subject before I unravel completely. "What about your girlfriend?"

"We're breaking up," he says simply, leaning back in his chair. "I'm moving back to California in two weeks."

I freeze. "Why?"

He looks away for a moment, his jaw clenching like he's trying to decide how much to reveal. "It's just time," he says with a shrug and a half-laugh. "It's not working out, and I don't like Texas. Moving here was supposed to be a fresh start. Some kind of last-ditch effort to make things work. But... we don't fit.

Never really have. She wanted Texas, and I thought I could make it work because she wanted it so badly."

He pauses, his fingers tracing the edge of his glass, his eyes distant. "But it's more than that. I realized I'm looking for something else." His gaze shifts to me, and there's something raw in his expression.

The words hang in the air, heavy and unspoken. I feel my pulse quicken, a strange mixture of fear and hope twisting inside me.

I nod slowly, but something in his tone feels heavier than his words — like there's more he's not saying.

"You sound pretty sure," I say carefully.

"I am," he replies, but there's a slight hesitation — a flicker of doubt that's easy to miss if you're not listening closely.

His eyes shift back to me. "But... I don't know," he adds, his voice softer now. "Sometimes you leave a place and realize you're walking away from something you didn't expect to care about."

He says it like it's nothing — casual, like he's just filling space in the conversation — but the way his gaze lingers tells me it's not. He's not talking about Texas.

I feel a knot form in my stomach. My mind scrambles for a response, but I don't know what to say. I *want* to ask what he means — to see if he's really saying what I think he is — but I can't. I'm too afraid to ask for something I'm not sure I deserve.

"Yeah," I say finally, my voice too thin.

His smile is faint, almost sad. "Yeah," he echoes, but the word feels final — like a door quietly closing.

My phone buzzes loudly, breaking the moment. We both look down. It's Edgar.

Where the hell are you? I need your car to go play poker!

I roll my eyes, but dread coils in my stomach. Another fight feels inevitable. I text him back quickly:

On my way now.

The words feel like chains — cold and heavy, wrapping tighter with every buzz of my phone. Even when he isn't here, he controls me — makes me question every move I make.

"I'd better head home too. I'll walk you out," Damian says, his voice low, carrying a hint of reluctance.

We stop by my car, a silver Volvo sedan that makes me seem older than I am, like I have it all figured out. I lean against the hood, the cold metal pressing into the back of my legs. The night sky stretches above us, a canvas of sharp, shimmering stars. The air feels colder now, biting at my skin. I shiver.

Damian steps closer, his warmth radiating toward me. The heat of him brushes my skin, sending a jolt of electricity through me. My face is just inches from his chest, his steady breath brushing my hair. My pulse stutters, hammering against my ribs. I stare down at our shoes — my feet planted firmly on the pavement, like some fragile anchor to reality.

63

"Look at me," he says softly, his voice low and steady — a quiet but demanding request.

I shake my head, my breath shaky as I refuse to meet his gaze. "If I do... I'll want to kiss you."

His voice drops even lower, the words a quiet challenge. His hand slides gently to my chin, his fingers warm against my skin, coaxing me to look up.

"And that's a bad thing?"

I swallow hard, my chest tightening. "I don't know," I whisper. My breath catches, my body frozen in place. I can't look up — I'm afraid of what might happen if I do. Afraid of how much I *want* it.

His hands move to my arms, his fingers tracing slow, soothing lines across my skin. The tension starts to unravel — like his touch is melting away the weight I've been carrying. We stand like that for what feels like an eternity — the world outside fading, time stretching and bending around us. I don't want this moment to end. I don't want to step away from this closeness — the heat of him like gravity pulling me in.

My phone buzzes again. I don't take it out of my pocket. We both know who it is.

"Goodnight, Talia," Damian finally says, his voice low and lingering.

As he turns and walks away, the air feels colder, emptier. The weight of my indecision presses down on me — heavy, suffocating, filled with regret.

But beneath it all, something stirs — a quiet hope, a raw desire — something I haven't felt in a long time.

When I get home, Edgar is pacing in the living room, his face a mask of irritation.

"You didn't tell me your girl stuff was going to be all night too," he says, his tone deceptively calm.

My stomach churns, dread creeping up my spine. I brace myself for the argument that's surely coming, but instead, he just slams the door behind him as he storms out. The sound of my car pulling away feels like a relief — like I can breathe again.

I sit on the edge of my bed, the room quiet and still.

What am I doing? Why didn't I kiss him? My thoughts race as I try to untangle the mess I've created. I really like Damian — more than I want to admit — but now he's leaving in two weeks, and I'm still here. Still trapped in the same patterns, the same cycles.

Eight

The next morning, I wake up and roll over, still thinking about the night before. Damian's body so close to mine, his gentle touch, the quiet pull of his presence. The way I wanted to turn to him, to kiss him, still lingers like a warmth beneath my skin. I sigh and pull the covers off, forcing myself to shake off the thoughts threatening to consume me.

Coffee—I need coffee.

I head downstairs, the quiet of the apartment making me pause. Edgar never came home—or maybe he's still out. Who knows? He has my car, but I don't need to go anywhere today, so I let it go, grateful for the peace in my own home.

On my way back upstairs, I grab my journal and a pen before stepping out onto the patio. The morning air is colder than I expected, sharp and biting against my face. I tug my cozy sweater tighter around me, grateful for its warmth, and pull the sleeves over my fingers sliding my thumbs through the worn-down holes I have created. My sweatpants are soft and comforting, a perfect match for the chill in the air.

I light a cigarette, my eyes narrowing as I watch the end burn red.

I open my journal and write: *December 14th, 2008.*

What am I doing? I stare at the words, frustrated. *I was getting my life back—piecing things together, finally breathing again—and then the universe throws me a curveball. A very handsome curveball. But still. Edgar is still here... and yet not. Physically present, emotionally absent. I feel like I'm stuck in between—one foot in the past, one foot reaching for something new.*

I press my pen harder against the page. *I just need to keep moving forward, choosing myself, and what makes me happy.* The words feel important, like a message sent from somewhere outside of me.

Choose you, Talia.

I close the journal and pick up my phone. It's almost noon. My eyes drift to my last message with Damian. My fingers hover over the keyboard before I type carefully:

Me: *Hey.*

Damian: *Hey. Thinking about you.*

I smile despite myself.

Me: *Oh yeah? For real?*

Damian: *No, for play-play.*

I laugh softly, biting my lip.

Me: *Lol, okay. And what exactly are you thinking about?*

Damian: *You…last night.*

The heat rises in my cheeks as I read the words.

Me: *Same.*

The tension is there—unspoken yet unmistakable—but for now, this is enough.

I smile again and set my phone down, staring out at the skyline.

This. I choose this, I tell myself, feeling lighter than I have in weeks.

Thursday night Jenni, Thomas, and I are having dinner at our favorite little Mexican taqueria. The air is filled with the enticing aroma of sizzling fajitas and freshly made tortillas. Between bites of tacos and bursts of laughter, Jenni leans in.

"Hey, we're going to Kiss Fly downtown tonight. You have to come," she pleads, her eyes sparkling with mischief.

I hesitate, glancing at my phone. "Ugh, I told Edgar I'd be home after dinner. Plus, we're getting Bella tomorrow," I say, torn between duty and the tempting escape.

Jenni rolls her eyes dramatically. "So cancel. Who cares? It's Edgar. He's an ass and will probably just go play poker or something anyway."

Thomas nods in agreement, his tone conspiratorial. "She's not wrong, you know. Come on, live a little."

The idea nags at me, a flicker of rebellion sparking to life. *I could go. I should go.*

"It does sound fun…" I say, the words slipping out slowly, like I'm testing them. "And maybe I could, I don't know, invite Damian."

Jenni's face lights up. "Yes!"

"Absolutely," Thomas chimes in, practically buzzing with excitement.

My pulse quickens as I pull out my phone and type the message:

Want to meet us at Kiss Fly tonight?

The reply comes almost instantly.

Sure. See you there.

My heart stumbles, a warm rush flooding through me. I need to get home, grab a change of clothes, and get out before I lose my nerve.

Jenni drops me off at my house, and we agree I'll meet her at her place to carpool downtown.

When I walk through the door, Edgar's on the couch, his face lit by the glow of the TV. His beer bottle sits half-empty on the coffee table.

"I'm going out tonight," I say, heading straight to the bedroom.

"What?" His voice sharpens. "No, you're not."

I pause in the doorway. "Yes, I am."

He's off the couch in seconds, his voice rising. "You said you'd be home tonight."

My fingers tremble as I grab my make-up bag from the bathroom counter, ignoring the tension squeezing my chest. "Jenni invited me out, and I'm going."

"All you do is hang out with Jenni these days," he snaps, stepping into the doorway like a barricade. "What about getting Bella in the morning?"

"We will get Bella in the morning," I fire back. "Go play poker, go do whatever it is you always do."

His eyes darken, and his hand curls into a fist at his side. "You're not going."

The room feels smaller, the air heavier. My breathing falters. I brush past him to the closet, grabbing the black top I know fits just right.

"Where are you even going?" Edgar demands, voice low now — colder.

"Out," I say, yanking a pair of jeans from the dresser. "Why are you making this a big deal? You go out all the time."

He steps closer, close enough that I can feel the heat of his body behind me. "You think you can just do whatever you want now?"

Fear spikes through me — sharp and immediate. I spin around, my heart pounding. "I'm leaving," I say, voice shaky but firm.

I shove past him again, grabbing my purse and my keys.

"You're not serious," he mutters behind me. "Get back here."

I'm already halfway down the hall.

"*Talia!*"

I don't stop. I throw open the front door and practically sprint to my car, my heart hammering so hard it feels like it's trying to break free from my ribs.

I slam the door shut, jamming the key into the ignition with trembling fingers.

Just go. Just go.

The wheels screech as I back out, my side mirror clipping the edge of the garage with a sickening crunch. Glass shatters, scattering across the pavement. For a split second, I freeze — but then I shove the car into drive and floor it down the street.

I don't care. I don't care about the mirror. I don't care about the yelling or the fight waiting for me tomorrow.

All I care about is getting away.

The air rushes in through my open window, cool against my flushed face. The tension in my chest eases, and suddenly I'm laughing — breathless, shaky laughter that spills out of me like a release.

And in that moment, all I can think about is Damian—his smile, his voice, the way his fingers felt on my arm that night by my car under the stars.

I want to see him. I want to kiss him. I want to choose something just for myself.

I press harder on the gas, racing toward Jenni's. Toward *him*. Toward whatever comes next.

Kiss Fly is a moody, pulse-pounding bar in downtown Austin that draws you in with its dark, intriguing energy. Inside, red neon lights flicker against black walls, illuminating a packed dance floor where bodies move in rhythm to the heavy bass thumping from the DJ booth. The air is thick with sweat, liquor, and the faint scent of something sweet from the cocktail bar tucked in the corner. It's loud, chaotic, and impossible to ignore.

Step outside, and the energy softens. The outdoor patio is strung with warm Edison bulbs, casting a glow over scattered tables and wooden benches. The music still hums, but quieter — enough for conversation to drift easily through the air. An outdoor bar is almost empty compared to inside.

When Damian arrives, I get a text: *They won't let me in because I am wearing Jordans.* I grab Jenni immediately, knowing her knack for knowing everyone. Of course, she finds the manager, works her magic, and just like that, Damian is in.

We head to the outdoor bar to grab drinks, and he turns to me, a hint of curiosity and mischief in his voice. "I'm surprised you asked me to come."

"Why do you say that?" I ask, tilting my head feigning confusion as I lean against the bar top.

"Well, last time, you wouldn't even look at me when I wanted to kiss you," he says, his tone teasing but sincere.

I blink, caught off guard. "You wanted to kiss me?" It's more a statement than a question, but I can't help the disbelief in my voice.

"Yeah," he admits with a small shrug, his smile laced with that familiar charm. "I was going to try."

"Maybe you should try again," I say, my voice soft but deliberate.

He looks at me, his eyes sparkling with something dangerously enticing, and that signature grin of his grows wider. "Oh really?" he murmurs, leaning in. His hand comes to rest against the bar, trapping me between him and the cool metal counter.

I look up, meeting his gaze without hesitation this time. "Yes," I whisper, my pulse quickening, my heart racing. Before I can say another word, his lips find mine, soft but insistent, and for a moment, everything else fades away. The weight of Edgar, the fear, the guilt—it all dissolved under the heat of his touch pulling me closer. This wasn't just a kiss. It was a spark catching fire, a reminder that I'm still alive, still capable of wanting something for myself.

The warmth of his kiss spreads through me, igniting every inch of my body. Somewhere behind us, I hear Jenni and Thomas cheering and clapping, but their voices are distant, barely registering in the haze of this perfect moment.

Damian pulls back slightly, his breath warm against my lips. His dark eyes search mine, a small, knowing smile playing on his mouth. "I've been wanting to do that for weeks," he murmurs.

"Then why'd you wait so long?" I tease, my fingers still tangled in the fabric of his shirt.

He chuckles, tucking a strand of hair behind my ear. "Because I needed you to look at me to know, to be sure." His thumb grazes my cheek, his touch sending warmth through me.

We spend the rest of the night entwined in each other, lost in a whirlwind of conversation, searing kisses, and forgetting the world beyond the electric pull between us. Every time his lips find mine, it feels like he's unraveling me, piece by piece.

Between kisses, I murmur against his skin, "This feels so right…but you are moving back to California."

His lips still against my shoulder, his exhale warm and heavy. After a pause, he lifts his head, his gaze locking onto mine with something undeniably raw.

"I know," he says, voice thick with something I can't quite name. Then, softer, "But I'm here now. Tonight."

The words hit me like a slow ache, settling deep in my chest. One night. That's all we have. But right now, it feels like enough.

I swallow, my heart pounding. "Come over," I whisper, barely recognizing my own voice.

Damian exhales sharply, his grip on my waist tightening. For a second, I think he'll say no, but then he nods. "Yeah… yeah, okay."

I quickly check my phone, scrolling through a string of angry text messages from Edgar. It takes a moment to piece together, but I finally decipher that he's gone — off to play poker like I hoped. Relief floods me, my heart racing as I rush home. I tidy up in a blur, my mind spinning, the memory of the kiss playing on repeat.

I wait, checking my phone every few seconds. The minutes feel like hours. Finally, a message lights up my screen. I stared at his text, the words blurring on the screen. *I decided to go home.* My chest tightened, the excitement from earlier draining away like air from a punctured balloon. For a fleeting moment, I'd let myself believe in the possibility of something more—something real. But maybe I was wrong.

The next day, I force myself through work, relieved no one is really in the office for the holidays. The kiss had been reckless, but it had also awakened something I thought Edgar had destroyed—a part of me that wanted more, needed more. But now, the guilt wrapped around me like a vice. All I could think about was Damian's hands on my waist. The way he looked at me—like I was someone worth wanting, someone worth more than what I'd settled for.

I squeeze my eyes shut, willing the memories away. I wanted him to come over. I wanted more. But what would that have changed? He was leaving. And no matter how much I craved the way he made me feel, I couldn't let myself get lost in something that had no future.

I exhale sharply, shaking off the weight of last night. I have to focus.

Today, I get to pick up Bella, and we're going Christmas shopping together. With just a few days until Christmas, I'm ridiculously behind.

She is what matters. She always has.

Our first stop is Target, our favorite place. As expected, Bella's eyes light up, and she starts asking for everything she sees. I remind her that Christmas is around the corner, but of course, I cave a little. That sweet smile of hers could melt the hardest heart.

"And I want a Hannah Montana microphone! And new princess dresses! And also, maybe like... fairy wings." She giggles, her cheeks flushed with excitement.

"I'll see what I can do about that." I laugh, ruffling her hair.

Bella's eyes sparkle as she clings to my hand, her gaze roaming the toy aisle. "Daddy says he's getting me the best Christmas ever. With all the things I want."

My smile falters slightly. I swallow the bitterness, trying to keep my voice light. "Daddy likes to make big promises."

Bella nods, her innocent faith unshaken. "But you and Mommy always get me the best stuff." She looks up at me, her eyes filled with a pure, unfiltered adoration.

My heart squeezes. Bella's trust is too precious, too innocent. A tiny part of me wants to shield her from the truth about her father, but I know that day will come eventually.

"Hey," I say, squatting down to her level. "No matter what, you're going to have an amazing Christmas. Okay?"

She nods enthusiastically, her arms flinging around my neck. "I love you, Talia."

"I love you too, Bella."

We meet Edgar for dinner, where he puts on his usual best dad performance for Bella. He's all smiles and boisterous laughter, bending down to scoop her into his arms as if he's a hero returning from war.

"There's my little princess!" Edgar crows, spinning Bella around until she squeals with delight.

I can't help but notice how the act drops the moment his attention shifts away from her. The smile on his face becomes strained, a performance cracking at the edges.

"So, what do you want for Christmas, kiddo?" Edgar asks, his voice full of enthusiasm.

Bella's eyes light up. "A Hannah Montana microphone! And new princess dresses!"

Edgar chuckles, but the sound is hollow. "We'll see, sweetheart. Daddy's got some big things planned."

I resist the urge to roll my eyes. The grand promises are his specialty. Tangible follow-through? Not so much.

After dinner, as we settle into the car, Edgar leans over and drops the inevitable bomb. "I'm going to play poker tonight," he says casually.

I suppress the urge to roll my eyes. "You know, to make some Christmas money and pay you back for all the gifts," he adds, a blatant lie. I know he has no intention of paying me back. If he wins, the money will vanish just as quickly—probably into another poker game.

"You're leaving, Daddy?" Bella asks, her voice small and sad.

"No, baby. Daddy has to work, but I'll be home when you wake up, and we can get breakfast together."

The lie rolls off his tongue so easily it's almost poetic.

Bella looks unsure but nods. I jump in to lighten her mood.

"How about we watch *Hannah Montana* in my bed and eat popcorn?" I suggest.

Her face brightens, and she smiles. She loves that plan—it means she doesn't have to sleep alone in her bed.

The next morning, I wake to a cute but stinky foot in my face. Bella is sprawled upside down, taking up most of the bed. I chuckle softly and gently move her foot away.

"Hey, little mama," I whisper, brushing her hair back from her face. "Let's go get some breakfast before we meet Mommy."

"Breakfast?" she mumbles groggily, blinking up at me. "Can we get pancakes?"

"Of course," I say with a smile.

Downstairs, Edgar is still passed out on the couch, snoring lightly—a reminder of when he stumbled in only a few hours earlier. I shake my head, grateful for the peace Bella and I shared upstairs.

After breakfast, I meet Lindsey at our halfway point. She's heading to Houston with Bella, where Bella will spend Christmas Eve and part of Christmas Day with Lindsey's family. Then, we'll pick her up in Houston so she can spend time with Edgar's family.

Lindsey steps out of the car, her eyes lighting up as Bella twirls around the parking lot, singing her *Hannah Montana* song with abandon. "She's been going on about that microphone Edgar promised her," Lindsey whispers. "He didn't actually buy it, did he?"

I shake my head. "No. I picked it up last week so she wouldn't be disappointed. I knew he'd forget or blow the money."

Lindsey's mouth tightens. "It's not fair, Talia. He gets to make all the big promises, and we're stuck holding things together."

"That's what worries me," I say, hating the idea of Bella being disappointed.

Lindsey's gaze sharpens. "You don't have to stay with him for Bella's sake. We'll figure it out. We always do."

Her words land like a stone in my chest—heavy, undeniable, and impossible to ignore.

Bella darts over, beaming. "Bye, Talia! I love you!"

"I love *you*, Bella." I force a smile, but Lindsey's words keep echoing in my mind.

I watch Bella climb into Lindsey's car, her tiny hand waving through the window. My heart squeezes—a mix of relief that she's happy and safe, and an ache that she's leaving. The house feels quieter without her already.

The thought of traveling with Edgar weighs heavily on me. My mind drifts back to *that kiss*—Damian's hands on my waist, the way I felt alive and happy for the first time in so long.

That night Edgar gets drunk at dinner and admits he lost yet another substantial amount of money at poker the night before. As Edgar slurred his way through blaming me for making him go, another excuse, I felt a twinge of something I didn't want to name—pity, maybe. Or regret for the person I thought he was when we first met. But those feelings were fleeting, drowned out by the exhaustion of years spent cleaning up his messes and the anger burning in my chest. I didn't love him anymore—I wasn't sure I ever really had. He stumbles into the kitchen looking for more tequila.

"I can't do this anymore," I whisper, barely audible over the clanking of the bottle hitting the countertop.

"What are you talking about? Stop it. Come here," he says, his breath heavy with booze as he staggers toward me trying to pull me into a kiss.

"Stop! Get off me!" I yell, pushing him away and surprising us both.

"I kissed someone else," I blurt out, my voice trembling but resolute. "And it made me realize something, Edgar. I don't love you anymore. I can't do this. We're done."

His face twists with rage, his jaw tightening as his hands clenched into fists at his sides. "What did you just say to me?" he growls, closing the distance between us.

"You did what?" he hisses. "Who would want you?" he spat, his voice low and venomous. He stepped closer, and I could smell the tequila on his breath, sharp and acrid. My heart pounded, but I held my ground, refusing to shrink under his glare.

"It doesn't matter," I say, steeling myself. "I just know it's time. It's been time. We're done."

"You're a whore! How could you do this to me?" he shouts, his hypocrisy almost laughable.

Smack! He swings, but he's so drunk he barely grazes my cheek before stumbling backward and falling onto the floor. I freeze, my heart pounding. To my relief, he doesn't get up but instead passes out there on the living room floor. Even as Edgar's words stung, my mind drifted back to Damian—the warmth of his hands on my waist, the way his eyes lit up when he looked at me. That kiss wasn't just a kiss. It was a reminder that I didn't have to settle for this, that there was something better out there for me. That I deserved more.

The next morning, I'm on the balcony, smoking a cigarette, my nerves still raw. I've filled Jenni and

Thomas in—they're ready to help me if I need to get Edgar out.

The balcony door creaks open. Edgar steps out, fully dressed. "You almost ready to go?" he asks, his tone casual like nothing happened.

"Go?" I echo, confused.

"To Houston," he replies, annoyed.

"But... last night?"

"You're not even coming to Christmas with my family? It's the least you could do after kissing someone else," he snaps, his voice dripping with thinly veiled manipulation. "What, are you trying to make me look bad in front of my parents?"

His words sting with guilt, but they also fill me with a simmering frustration. My mind races, bouncing from thoughts of Bella and the Christmas I promised her, to the kiss that changed everything, to the fact that Damian is leaving and didn't even bother to come over that night.

With a heavy sigh, I push my feelings aside and start getting ready, the weight of it all settling over me like an unwelcome shadow.

Houston is a blur of forced smiles and awkward silences. My thoughts keep drifting back to Damian and the kiss. I go through the motions, but all I can think about is taking my life back.

When we finally get home, I head straight to the shower, eager to wash away the holiday tension. The hot water cascades over me, but it does little to quiet the storm raging in my mind.

Stepping out, I wrap myself in a towel, only to freeze in the doorway. Edgar is sitting on the edge of the bed, holding my phone, his knuckles white as he grips it.

"What are you doing?" I snap, my voice sharp, cutting through the thick silence.

He looks up, his eyes blazing. "I found your little boyfriend. Is it really that dude from sushi?" he sneers, his words laced with venom.

I take a steadying breath, my heart pounding. "It doesn't matter, Edgar," I say, my voice firm but unwavering. "You and I are done. You need to move out. Today."

For a moment, I brace myself for an explosion, for him to turn and lash out, but it never came. He slowly stands, his jaw tightening as he looks down at me and he begins throwing his things into a bag. The tension in the room is heavy as he moves wordlessly.

At the door, he pauses, turning to me, his eyes burning with hatred as he bitterly smirks. "I'll leave," he says, his tone low and biting, "but you'll be begging me to come back in no time."

The door slams behind him, and the sound echoes through the apartment. Relief crashes over me like a wave, leaving me breathless and trembling. Exhausted, I crawl into bed and sleep until my phone buzzes with a text from Jenni: *Hey T, we're going to a new bar for New Year's Eve. Let's go shopping for dresses this weekend!*

I muster a response: *sure* before falling back to sleep.

Jenni pulls up to my apartment, her music already blasting as I slide into the passenger seat. She looks effortlessly chic, her oversized sunglasses perched on her head and a knowing smirk on her face. As we browse the aisles of our favorite boutique in South Austin, I fill her in on the Edgar drama.

"Well, finally! Thank God!" she exclaims, tossing a blouse over her arm. Her relief is palpable, her tone bright with genuine excitement. "This might actually be the end of Edgar."

I laugh dryly, shaking my head. "Hopefully."

Jenni tilts her head, eyeing me. "What about Damian? Have you two talked?"

I sigh, fiddling with a rack of dresses. "No, we haven't. Besides, he moved back to California. What would we even say? What would we do—date long distance?" My voice is laced with skepticism, as though the idea is too far-fetched to even consider.

Jenni stops, turning to face me with a raised eyebrow. "Talia, come on. You should text him. See where it goes." She steps closer, her voice softening but full of conviction. "You two had something real. There was fire between you, I saw it. You practically lit the bar on fire with that kiss. You can't just let that go."

Her words settle over me like a challenge, daring me to confront the feelings I've been pushing aside. We leave the store with two new dresses and are ready to ring in the new year.

That night at the bar, I still couldn't stop thinking about Damian. A few drinks in, I decide Jenni is right and start scrolling through my phone to send him a message and my stomach twists. The words jumped off the screen: *The kiss was a mistake. I'm with Edgar and can never be with you.* My breath caught, and realization hit me like a freight train.

Edgar. My phone. That night. Edgar had sent it. He had taken my phone, pretended to be me, and tried to destroy the one good thing I had felt in years. Rage and disbelief surged through me, leaving me trembling. How could I have let him have so much power over me for so long?

I keep reading. To my horror, Damian responded: *"Ok."*

Despite my better judgment, I call him. The music blares around me as I step outside.

Hello?" Damian's voice was calm, cautious, and it sent a shiver through me.

"Damian! Hey, it's Talia," I said, too eagerly, cringing at the sound of my own voice.

He pauses for a moment, and I could feel his hesitation through the line. "What's up?"

"I just... I wanted to explain. That text? Edgar sent it. It wasn't me," I said quickly, holding my breath as I waited for his response.

Another pause, then a soft laugh, tinged with relief. "That makes sense," he said finally. "I thought it didn't sound like you."

The tension in my chest loosened, replaced by a flare of hope. "So... I was wondering. Do you want to meet me in Vegas? I'm going in February."

There was a beat of silence, and then he chuckled. "Vegas? I love Vegas. And my birthday's in February."

My lips curved into a smile, my heart pounding. "Perfect. I'll send you the details."

"Okay. Talk to you later," he says before we hang up.

As I hung up, I couldn't stop smiling, my heart racing with a mix of nerves and exhilaration. I did it, something new—something just for me. Edgar was gone. Damian wasn't out of reach. And I believed that maybe, just maybe, I could finally start over.

Nine

January truly feels like a new beginning—a quiet, welcome calm settling over my apartment now that I have it all to myself. Edgar is finally out of the house. Lindsey and I have worked out that I'll still take Bella regularly, but without Edgar involved. The arrangement feels like a breath of fresh air—a sense of control I hadn't realized I missed.

Work is picking back up now that everyone's back from the holidays, and I've been put in charge of helping plan the annual Vegas trip.

"Talia, where are we with the hotel booking? Did you find us a big enough suite for the planning sessions?" my boss, Sara, asks.

"Oh yes, I emailed you the options, but I think the Bellagio is our best choice with the separate dining spaces," I answer, hoping she agrees.

"Perfect. Yes, just book it," she says decisively. "And go ahead and make reservations at Nobu and Craft Steakhouse," she adds without hesitation.

"Okay, will do," I respond, feeling a little like a personal assistant but biting my tongue. No way am I risking a visible eye roll.

A text from Maya flashes on my screen: *Yes, Talia, and book our yoga class this week as well.* I can't help but smile at her teasing.

The meeting ends, and I jump back on the phone to make the reservations before I forget—or worse, before the spots are booked and I end up on the receiving end of my boss's irritation.

As I hang up after finalizing the reservations, my phone rings—Maya. I answer, still smiling from her message.

"You're trying to get me fired," I joke.

She laughs. "Never! But seriously, are we going to yoga this week?" She pauses, probably expecting me to fall back into my usual pattern of excuses.

"Yeah, let's do it! How about Thursday?" I answer, feeling a small rush of excitement at finally saying yes to something I'd been avoiding.

"Really?" she asks, surprised.

"Yes, really. See you there," I reply before hanging up.

Her surprise lingers in my mind, reminding me that I still have work to do with my friends and family after the years of pushing them away. Saying yes to yoga with my sister feels good—like I'm back to choosing myself again.

At the end of the day, I walk downstairs to pour myself a much-deserved glass of prosecco. As I take a seat out on the patio, my phone lights up with a message from Damian.

Damian: *So… when am I seeing you again?*

Talia: *Depends… are you prepared to behave yourself?*

Damian: *Nope. Not even a little.*

Talia: *Good. Then Vegas—the first week of February.*

Damian: *Good. I'm in.*

I smile down at my phone, completely wrapped up in the exchange, so much so that I don't even see Jenni walk up.

"Umm, excuse me, what are you so smiley about?" she asks, yanking my phone out of my hand and grabbing my glass off the table in one swift move. She takes a sip, her eyes widening as she reads the screen.

"Ooooh, Vegas huh? Sounds sexy," she teases, taking another sip like she's savoring the details.

"It will be," I say, giggling as I snatch my phone back. "Keep that glass—I'll grab another one," I add, already halfway inside the house, grinning to myself.

I return with another glass and the bottle in hand. Jenni holds out her glass, ready for the refill.

"So… Vegas? For real? You two are really going to meet up?" she asks, her tone full of curiosity and just enough mischief to make me smirk.

"You saw the message. Sounds like he's in," I answer, feeling a stupid grin spread across my face. Just the thought of seeing Damian again gives me a rush.

"Oh, he's *into* something," she teases, raising one eyebrow as she looks me up and down.

"He's so hot," I say, my voice filled with desire, my pulse picking up. "And that kiss..."

"Yeah, yeah—it's gonna be hot!" Jenni cuts in, rolling her eyes like she's already heard the steamy details.

"What about you? How's Jeff?" I ask, steering the conversation her way.

"Ew, no. Jeff is *donezo*." She waves her hand like she's swiping at a fly. "I'm *staying single* for at least a month." She places her hand on her heart like she's swearing off carbs. "No more drama, no more mixed signals. Just me, my work and wine nights."

I raise an eyebrow. "Mmm-hmm. Sure."

"I *am*!" she insists, pointing her finger at me like I'm about to file her dating profile myself. "You watch."

"Okay, okay," I say, raising my hands in surrender.

Jenni launches into a dramatic rant about how guys are like socks—always disappearing when you need them or showing up as mismatched pairs. Halfway through, she reenacts a conversation with Jeff, complete with exaggerated voices and fake tears. I'm laughing so hard I nearly choke on my drink, clutching my stomach as tears prick at my eyes.

Before we know it, the bottle is empty. Jenni stands, wobbling slightly with the giddy buzz and endless giggles.

"Text me if you need me!" she calls out in her best fake-serious voice as she stumbles back to her apartment.

I smile to myself as I gather the empty glasses, still feeling that warm, happy buzz—the mix of prosecco, laughter, and the thought of Damian lingering in my mind like an unspoken promise.

I meet Maya in the parking lot outside the yoga studio, her smile brightening the dreary afternoon. It's been a while since we've done this — too long, really — and as we walk inside together, I feel a surprising sense of comfort.

"Feels good to be back," Maya says, stretching her arms above her head. "I forgot how much I needed this."

"Me too," I admit.

The soft scent of lavender greets us as we step inside, the faint hum of calming music floating through the air. We unroll our mats in the back corner, and for the first time all day, I try to clear my head.

But it doesn't take long before my mind wanders — straight to Damian. Especially when my phone buzzes just before class starts.

Damian: *Good morning, beautiful. How's your day going?*

I smile, warmth blooming in my chest.

Me: *Hey! It's going well — would be better if it were February already.*

I tuck my phone away and attempt to focus, but my mind keeps drifting — back to him, back to *us*. When class ends, I barely say goodbye to Maya and make it to my car before I'm checking my phone again.

Damian: *Soon enough. I can't wait for Vegas.*

Me: *For what...? I tease.*

Damian: *To be with you. No distractions. Just us. So I can kiss you and...*

Me: *And what?*

Damian: *You know...*

His unfinished sentence lingers in my mind like a spark, igniting something deep inside me. That "..." is a promise — a whisper of all the things we haven't said but both feel. It sends flashes through my mind — the way his lips felt on mine, the way my body leaned into his without thinking, the heat of his hand sliding down my back.

Me: *You're going to have to be more specific...*

Damian: *If I tell you, you won't sleep tonight.*

I bite my lip, his words hitting me low in my stomach.

Me: *Maybe I don't want to sleep.*

Damian: *You don't play fair.*

Me: *Neither do you.*

For the rest of the day, our messages continue to intensify, laced with something more dangerous. Something hotter.

Damian: *I keep thinking about that dress you wore that night at Molotov... I couldn't stop looking at you.*

Me: *Yeah? I noticed. You couldn't keep your eyes off my legs.*

Damian: *Because I wanted them wrapped around me.*

I sit back in my office chair, phone warm in my hand, breath shaky.

Me: *I can't wait for Vegas.*

Damian: *Me neither... but waiting makes it better, don't you think? Builds tension.*

Me: *You're trying to kill me.*

Damian: *Maybe a little.*

Each text feels like a new spark, the heat between us rising to something undeniable. I can practically feel his hands on me — the slow drag of his fingers down my arm, his mouth just barely brushing mine.

When his shift ends late that night, I'm already curled up in bed, phone in hand, waiting for him to call.

"Hey," he says softly when I answer, his voice warm and low — the kind of sexy that makes me forget how tired I am. "You still awake?"

"Barely," I reply, smiling despite the sleepiness tugging at my eyes. "But I wasn't going to miss this."

Our late-night conversations are slower, softer — filled with laughter, sleepy murmurs, and the kind of honesty that only comes when the world is quiet.

"I keep thinking about you," he admits, his voice quieter than usual. "You know... that night at Kiss Fly when you invited me over after that kiss."

My breath catches. "Yeah?"

"I should've gone," he says. "I should've come over, should've..." He trails off, but I know exactly where his mind is going.

"Why didn't you?" I ask, my voice barely a whisper.

"Because if I had..." He pauses, and I swear I can hear his breath catch. "I wouldn't have been able to stop."

The air feels heavier, warmer. My pulse thrums in my throat. "I wouldn't have wanted you to."

"I know," he says, his voice low and rough. "That's what scares me."

I clutch my phone tighter, my body aching with the need to close the impossible distance between us. "I can't stop thinking about it either," I confess.

"Now you are trying to kill me," he mutters, and I can practically hear his smile. "But Vegas..."

His words linger in my mind long after we hang up. The sound of his voice stays with me as I drift to sleep, the warmth of it curling around me like a blanket.

By the time February rolls around, the anticipation has reached a fever pitch. The countdown to Vegas feels like it's moving in slow motion, every day stretching unbearably long. But I know it'll be worth every second.

Because when I finally see Damian again... I won't be able to hold back. And I don't think he will either.

A week before the trip, Jenni and I hit the mall. We make a beeline for Victoria's Secret and Nordstrom—I need *outfits*. Afterward, we grab lunch at our favorite Mexican restaurant, complete with Dos Equis and endless chips and salsa.

"So, what are you getting him for his birthday?" Jenni asks, squeezing her lime into her beer. "I mean besides that sexy little number we just found at Victoria Secret."

I freeze mid-bite. "I... haven't thought about it. His phone is always breaking and acting up, though. Maybe I should get him a new one?"

Jenni raises an eyebrow. "I mean, that's a *nice* gift," she says, her tone laced with caution.

"Nice as in... too much? Because we're just talking?" I ask, already knowing the answer.

"Well, yeah, it's super nice. But also, you just got that bonus from work, so maybe go for it!"

Jenni's not the type of friend to talk me out of crazy ideas. If anything, she encourages them. I spend the next week looking for a phone to buy.

Ten

The Vegas trip is jam-packed with planning sessions, fancy dinners, and shows. I know I won't have much free time, but I've already carved out moments when I can slip away undetected — moments I've planned carefully, knowing exactly when I'll see Damian.

Maya and I ride to the airport together, and the thought of being with Damian soon sends butterflies fluttering through my stomach. I try to stay calm, laughing along with Maya's chatter, but my mind keeps drifting — to his smile, his voice, the way his hand felt on my waist that night by my car.

We breeze through security and find a restaurant near our gate to grab a glass of wine. While we sip, Maya decides to pick up a book for the flight, giving me the perfect opportunity to call my friend Jess and wish her a happy birthday.

Jess and I met back when I was working as a hostess at Barton Creek Resort during college. She was the lead hostess — serious about her role and known for her quirky yet oddly endearing rules. The first rule? Highlight the reservation names *perfectly* inside the box — no coloring outside the lines. The second? Pour a glass of champagne flawlessly, filling it right to the top without spilling a drop. I still remember her scolding me after my first failed pour — her voice sharp but her smile soft. Somehow, her perfectionism never felt intimidating; it made me respect her more. Those quirks are what drew me in, and we became fast friends.

We don't see each other often these days, but we never miss each other's birthdays.

When her call goes to voicemail, I grin and leave a playful message. "Happy Birthday, gorgeous! Sorry I'm missing it, but I can't wait to get together soon. Drinks on me!"

I hang up, still smiling. As I slip my phone back into my bag, I can't help but let my mind wander again — back to Damian, back to Vegas, back to all the things that feel so dangerously close yet so impossible to resist.

We settle into our rooms and call it an early night, knowing the days ahead will be packed with meetings, events, and endless socializing. I crawl into bed, but my mind refuses to quiet down.

I know why.

Tomorrow, Damian will be here.

The thought sends a wave of nervous energy rolling through me — excitement tangled with something deeper. I can't stop imagining what it will be like when we're finally alone. When our whispered promises will be brought to life. The way he's been talking to me, the heat in his words, the tension that's been building for weeks — it's all been leading to this.

I close my eyes and picture it — his hands exploring me, his mouth tracing the curve of my neck. I wonder what it will feel like to have his skin against mine, no more teasing or restraint — just us, lost in each other. My pulse skips just thinking about it.

The next afternoon, after a team lunch at the Bellagio, my phone buzzes.

Damian: *There's maintenance needed on the plane. My flight is delayed until 9 p.m.*

I exhale slowly, both relieved and frustrated. The anticipation is killing me. *No big deal,* I tell myself. I'll slip away after the Elton John concert and meet him at the Excalibur, where he's staying.

Our meetings wrap up for the day, and we indulge in an incredible dinner at Craft Steakhouse. My boss knows her fine dining.

Afterward, we pile into a stretch limo bound for the concert. My boss pops a bottle of champagne, her smile radiant as she raises a toast to the team.

The concert is incredible — Elton's voice filling the theater, the red piano on stage — but I can barely focus. I keep trying to lose myself in the music, to let the magic of the performance sweep me away. But it's no use. My mind keeps drifting to Damian, to the way I imagine his hand sliding across my waist, the way his breath will feel warm against my skin.

By the time the show ends, I'm a bundle of nerves. I fake a yawn, tossing out a convincing "I'm so exhausted" act to my team, and slip back to my room.

Once inside, I waste no time. I toss off my heels and wriggle out of my dress, swapping it for something far more intentional — a fitted black dress with delicate purple ruffles that hug my curves just right. My silver pointed-toe heels click against the marble floor as I gather my things.

Inside my bag, his birthday gift waits — a sleek new silver Blackberry phone I'd picked out last week, knowing he'd been grumbling about his old one giving him trouble. Tucked beside it is something just for me — a carefully chosen set of lingerie from Victoria's Secret: black lace over soft pink satin.

I hesitate for a moment, fingers brushing the delicate fabric. It's barely anything — thin straps, soft cups, sheer lace tracing every curve. Sexy, but still soft… still me. My heart races, equal parts excitement and nerves. I zip up the bag and head downstairs to the lobby.

Me: *I'm on my way.*

Damian: *Finally! I am at the blackjack tables*

Outside, I hail a cab, barely noticing the glittering Vegas lights or the busy hum of tourists spilling onto the Strip. The cab ride to the Excalibur felt like an eternity, my heart pounding with every passing second. I kept smoothing the fabric of my dress, my palms damp with nerves.

Tonight isn't just another night.

Tonight, I know I'll be his. And even though it scares me, I know I've never wanted anything more.

Walking through the casino, my eyes scan the crowded room until they land on him. He's leaning casually against the blackjack table, effortlessly confident, a navy blue polo stretching perfectly across his broad chest and hugging his arms in a way that does dangerous things to my focus. His jeans fit just right, accentuating strong legs, and the way he carries himself—relaxed yet completely in control—only adds to his appeal.

Then, as if sensing me before even seeing me, he lifts his head. Our eyes meet, and that familiar sexy grin spreads across his face, slow and knowing. He gives me a once-over, his gaze dragging just long enough to make my skin heat.

That smile…

He steps away from the table and closes the space between us without hesitation, without question.

"Took you long enough," he murmurs, his voice low, teasing as his fingers skim the curve of my waist before pulling me into an embrace.

"You look incredible," Damian says, his gaze locking onto mine with a hunger that steals my breath. His fingers trail down my arm, his touch spreads like a slow burn beneath my dress, a promise of everything to come.

"Could say the same about you," I reply, my voice unsteady. His presence is intoxicating, magnetic.

His lips brush against my neck, igniting a delicious thrill down my back, before finding mine in a kiss that's slow, deep, and filled with longing. His hands on my waist, his touch, the way he looked at me like I was everything he had been waiting for—it all felt like a quiet kind of magic, a soft rebellion against everything that had ever hurt me.

With a teasing smile, he pulls back, his hand lingering on my waist. "One more hand," he murmurs, his voice low and velvety. I watch, still catching my breath, as he returns to the table. His focus is sharp, every move deliberate, and when he finally cashes out, his eyes meet mine again, full of promises yet to come. "Let's go," he says confidently, grabbing my bag from me, his hand resting on the small of my back as he leads me to his room.

The elevator ride is a blur of nervous excitement. All of the built-up tension fills the air. As the doors open he pauses and looks at me to be sure. I walk through the doors pulling him by the hand as if to say yes.

At the door, he swipes the key card, and we step inside. The door clicks shut, sealing us into the room, into the night we've been teasing for weeks. He holds me against the wall and claims my mouth with a fierce, hungry passion. I have to pull away to catch my breath.

"Wait. I'll be right back," I say, slipping into the bathroom to change.

He gives me a look of both intrigue and questioning.

In the mirror, I adjust the delicate lingerie, the corseted apron hugging my waist, cinching me in with subtle elegance before flaring out, the lace teasingly sheer and inviting. The silky pink ribbon is tied just above the curve of my ass, its playful bow adding a touch of sweetness to the seductive design. I linger for a moment longer, studying my reflection—not with doubt, but with something new. Confidence. A slow-burning desire that flickers in my eyes, making the hazel flecks stand out like gold in the dim light.

I inhale deeply, steadying myself as nerves and anticipation twist together in my chest. Then, with one final glance, I turn and step into the room.

He's sitting on the edge of the bed, elbows resting on his knees, shoulders tense like he's barely holding something back. When he turns to face me, the air shifts — heavier now, charged with something that crackles between us. The playful smirk he wore at the blackjack table is gone, replaced by something darker... hungrier.

His gaze travels over me, slow and deliberate, like he's memorizing every detail — the curve of my waist, the rise and fall of my chest, the way I'm standing there, breathless and burning beneath his stare.

I reveal the small, wrapped box hidden behind my back. His eyebrows lift in surprise.

"Happy birthday," I say, holding it out to him.

His gaze softens, something warm and genuine passing over his features as he takes the gift. "You didn't have to do that."

"I wanted to."

He tears open the wrapping paper, his eyes lighting up when he sees the phone. "You didn't!"

"Of course I did. You wouldn't stop complaining about your old one."

He laughs, the sound deep and rich. "I like that you listen. Thank you."

Slowly, he rises to his feet, each step deliberate, until I feel like I might break if he doesn't touch me.

He stops just inches away, his breath warm against my skin — close enough that I feel the heat of his body without him even touching me. Still, he waits, letting the tension build until it feels like a live wire between us.

His hands find my waist, firm but unhurried, fingers sliding along my curves like he's tracing a map. He trails upward, brushing over my ribs, pausing at my jaw. His thumb ghosts over my lower lip, and I swear I forget how to breathe.

Then — *finally* — he kisses me.

Soft at first, teasing, tasting, like he's savoring the moment. But when I sigh into him, when my fingers curl into his shoulders and tug him closer, his control unravels.

His lips crash into mine, and I taste whiskey and heat — raw, intoxicating, and dangerously close to need.

I arch into him, my body molding to his, but then — he slows.

His hands drift down, tracing the delicate lace that hugs my hips. His fingers follow the curve of my body — slow, deliberate, excruciating. He finds the satin ribbon at the small of my back and pauses — his breath warm against my collarbone.

"Don't stop," I whisper, voice barely a breath.

With a single, gentle pull, the ribbon slips free.

His mouth moves lower — slower — his lips brushing that delicate spot just below my ear. My pulse stutters, and I feel my knees weaken beneath me. Heat blooms low in my stomach, sharp and undeniable.

"I've imagined this," he murmurs, his voice low, rough, devastatingly sure. "Every... single... detail."

His words skim over my skin like a spark, and I gasp, my fingers tightening around his arms.

"Damian..." I start, my voice shaking.

"Shhh..." His fingers tilt my chin until I'm looking up at him, and his gaze locks with mine — dark, smoldering, filled with promises I already feel sinking into my bones.

"We've waited this long," he murmurs, lips hovering just above mine. "What's a few more minutes?"

Minutes?

The teasing edge in his voice sends a fresh wave of anticipation curling through me — sweet and torturous all at once.

I reach for him, fumbling with the button of his jeans. The zipper slides down in one smooth motion, and he lets out a low chuckle — but it's cut short when I push the denim down his hips.

The air thickens. His shirt is gone in an instant, revealing broad shoulders and a sculpted chest, every muscle carved like stone. Ink winds down his ribs and across his hip — dark lines that seem to beckon my fingers to follow.

I trace them, letting my fingertips drag slowly over his skin, feeling the tension and his heat growing beneath the surface. His eyes burn hotter — fierce and unrelenting.

"Now," I whisper, breathless. "No more waiting."

He lowers me onto the bed, his body hovering just above mine, tantalizingly close. My legs part instinctively, and I feel the pressure of his hips settling between them — just enough to leave me aching for more. His other hand braced against the mattress beside my head.

His mouth finds mine, hard and demanding — his kiss no longer a tease, but a promise of everything he's about to give me. His body presses closer. His lips trail down my throat, lingering where my pulse races beneath my skin. He pauses at the thin strap of my lingerie, his teeth grazing the fabric before his fingers slide it down.

"You're so beautiful," he murmurs against my shoulder, his voice low and wrecked.

His hands skim down my back, fingers expertly unfastening the clasp. The delicate fabric falls away, forgotten, as cool air brushes against my bare skin — but then his mouth finds a new part of me.

His lips close around my nipple, his tongue flicking, teasing, sending sparks racing down my spine. I arch beneath him, desperate for more, but he's in no hurry.

He takes his time — learning me by touch alone.

Lower.

Slower.

His fingers skate along the inside of my thigh, barely touching me — enough to leave me restless, aching, desperate.

I don't even realize I'm holding my breath until his lips return to mine, stealing what little oxygen I have left.

His hands cradle my face, his forehead resting against mine. For a moment, everything is still — just our breathing, the heat between us, the undeniable pull that's been building for so long.

His eyes — dark, searching, knowing — lock with mine. It's like he's branding me into his memory. Like he already knows we'll never be the same after this.

I pull him closer, my legs wrapping around his waist, guiding him into place.

His body sinks into mine in one slow, steady thrust, and I swear I forget everything — my name, my breath, the space between us — gone.

I gasp, my fingers digging into his back, holding on like I might fall apart. He stills, breathing hard, his forehead pressed to mine.

"Okay?" he murmurs, his voice strained.

"Yes," I whisper. "More."

His control falters as he starts to move — his rhythm builds, slow at first, each thrust deliberate, each drag of his body against mine sending sharp, spiraling heat curling low in my stomach.

I meet him movement for movement, tilting my hips to take him deeper, to pull him closer. Every roll of his body drives me higher, tension winding tighter, until I feel like I'm burning from the inside out.

His hand drifts up my spine, palm flattening between my shoulder blades as his other hand fists the sheets beside me. He's losing control, his breath ragged, his rhythm faltering, and the sheer desperation in the way he grips me — like he's afraid to let go — unravels me completely.

I press my hands to his chest, feeling the frantic thrum of his heartbeat beneath my palms.

In one swift motion, I push him back, flipping us over. He lands beneath me, breathless, his gaze hooded and dark as I straddle him.

For a heartbeat, I pause — hovering just above him, taking him in. His chest rises and falls in sharp, uneven breaths. His hands slide up my thighs, fingers curling tightly around my hips, holding me like he's afraid I'll disappear.

"God…" he rasps, his gaze dragging over me savoring every detail. "You're incredible."

His fingers slide higher, tracing the curve of my waist before curling around my breasts — reverent and possessive all at once. The heat of his touch sears through me, leaving me gasping as a shiver ripples down my spine.

I tip my head back and move — a slow, intoxicating winding of my hips that leaves him groaning beneath me. His fingers grip tighter, his nails digging into my skin, dragging me harder against him.

"Damian…" I moan, my voice breaking as the tension coils tight — so tight I can barely breathe.

"Don't stop," he growls, his voice thick, wrecked.

I don't. I can't.

The pressure builds — higher, hotter, sharper — until it finally breaks. The rush of release crashes over me in waves, pleasure so fierce and consuming that I swear I forget where I end and he begins.

His name spills from my lips again — a whisper, a gasp, a surrender — and I feel him follow, his body tensing beneath me before he shatters completely.

I collapse against him, my heart racing, my body trembling — spent, breathless, and utterly undone.

His arms wrap around me, pulling me closer, and I melt into him — warm, safe, and whole.

Damian lets out a contented sigh, his fingers lazily tracing up and down my back. "Well, damn."

I smile against his skin, still wrapped in the afterglow. "Oh yeah?"

He chuckles, his grip tightening around me. "Yeah. Definitely worth the build-up." He presses a lingering kiss to my hair, and I can feel the smile against his lips.

I tilt my head up to look at him, my fingers drawing slow, absentminded patterns on his chest. "Worth the build-up, huh? Is that what we've been doing?" I tease, my lips curving into a soft smile.

He smirks, brushing a loose strand of hair from my face, his fingers lingering. "I don't know what we've been doing... but I really, really like what we just did."

I pretend to consider, tapping a finger lightly against his chest. "Hmm. Well, lucky for you, I really liked it too."

His expression shifts, the teasing fading into something deeper. His thumb strokes my cheek, his gaze holding mine like he knows I am his. "Good," he murmurs, his voice quiet but sure.

My heart flutters, warmth spreading through me, making it impossible not to smile. I tuck myself in closer, breathing him in, my body melting into his as if this was where I was always meant to be.

"Stay here tonight," he whispers, his lips brushing against my forehead.

I sigh, already feeling the pull of sleep. "I have early meetings," I protest weakly, though my body makes no move to leave.

His arms tighten around me. "Call in sick," he murmurs.

I giggle, my eyes already drifting closed. "Mmm, tempting."

"Sleep first, decide later," he says, his voice a low, soothing hum.

And with his warmth wrapped around me, I do just that.

The harsh buzz of my alarm drags me from sleep, cutting through the warmth of the moment. I groan softly, reluctant to move, but reality is already creeping in. Carefully, I slip out of bed, the cool air making me shiver as I reach for my clothes.

Before leaving, I pause at the door, glancing back at Damian. He's still asleep, his breathing slow and steady, one arm sprawled across the empty space where I just was. The sight tugs at something deep inside me—something that makes it even harder to walk away.

With a quiet sigh, I turn and slip out of the room, heading back to my hotel to get ready for another long workday. But even as I leave, I already know—I'll be thinking about him all day.

I walk into the suite, coffee in hand and a barely concealed smile on my face. My sister, Maya, immediately eyes me with curiosity the second I step through the door.

"Where have you been? And why do you look… happy?" she asks, like it's some kind of mystery that needs solving.

I take a casual sip of my coffee, forcing my expression to stay neutral. "I got great sleep. These beds are ridiculously comfortable," I say, which isn't *totally* a lie.

She narrows her eyes, clearly suspicious, but thankfully, she doesn't press further. Before she can, our boss steps to the front of the room, kicking off the meeting with the financial report and sales goals. This is our last planning session of the trip, and I sink into my chair, pretending to focus — but I'm still tangled in the warmth I left behind this morning, my skin remembering the press of Damian's body before I slipped away.

To my delight, my boss announces she has an urgent client meeting, which means we'll be wrapping early before dinner. Relief bubbles in my chest as I grab my phone and quickly type out a message to Damian.

Me: *Meet me at the Bellagio casino at 3:00.*

I barely contain my smile when his reply pings back.

Damian: *Can't wait.*

I tell Maya I'm going to walk around the Strip for the break, but the moment I step outside the suite, my heart is already racing. I head downstairs to meet Damian, excitement and nerves twisting inside me.

When I spot him near the entrance, my pulse stumbles — hard. He's leaning casually against a pillar, hands tucked into his pockets, radiating that effortless, sexy confidence that never fails to undo

111

me. His shirt fits just right, sleeves pushed up to his forearms, and the faint shadow of stubble along his jaw makes him look dangerously good.

Grinning to myself, I come up behind him, slipping my hands over his eyes.

"Guess who?" I tease, my voice light and playful.

Before I can finish laughing, his fingers wrap around my wrists, firm and warm. He pulls my hands down, turning in one smooth motion — and then suddenly, I'm against his chest, his arms locked tight around me.

"Hey, beautiful," he murmurs into my hair, his voice low and full of something that makes my stomach flip.

I melt into him, my face pressed to his chest, breathing him in — warm skin, faint cologne, and just a hint of whiskey lingering on his shirt.

We duck into a quieter corner of the casino near the slot machines. It's cozy and dimly lit — just enough privacy to let his hand rest lightly on my thigh. We chat, spinning the slots between conversations. A woman behind us suddenly erupts in a joyous scream — she'd just hit a jackpot. Damian and I both laugh, he grips my thigh tighter as we watch her celebrate.

"My favorite part about you is your chin," he says out of nowhere, his fingers gently brushing along it.

I blink, caught off guard. "My *chin*?" I laugh, unsure whether to feel flattered or confused but the warmth in his gaze shifts something inside me. The way he looks at me, like I'm *worth* paying attention to, makes my heart skip. My smile falters, replaced by something deeper, something that feels rare — almost too good to be true.

"I don't know…" he murmurs, that playful grin teasing at the corner of his mouth. "I just like it." And then he leans in, lifting my chin and capturing my lips in a kiss that's soft and slow.

We linger like that, caught in our own little world, until I spot movement from the corner of my eye — my team.

"Shit! My boss!" I hiss, panic surging through me. I shove Damian behind a nearby slot machine just in time.

I smooth my hair, plastering on a surprised smile as I step forward to greet my team.

"Oh! Hey!" I say, too brightly.

"Talia," my boss says with a smile, eyeing me suspiciously. "We're heading to the bar for a drink before dinner. Want to join us?" Her gaze sweeps over me — taking in my jeans and casual top — clearly unimpressed. Dinner at Nobu requires something far more polished.

"I was just on my way upstairs to change," I say with an apologetic smile. "I'll meet you there in thirty."

The moment they're gone, I rush back to Damian. I steal one more kiss — quick but lingering — and whisper, "I'll see you later."

Back in my room, I pull out a coral satin dress that hugs my curves just right. I slip into sleek heels, fix my hair, and refresh my makeup. When I meet my boss and the rest of the team at the bar, they're just finishing their glasses of wine. My boss gives me a once-over, this time with a slight nod of approval.

Thank God.

Dinner at Nobu is exquisite — delicate slices of sushi so fresh it practically melts in my mouth, and flavors that seem to dance on my tongue. But no matter how incredible the food is, I keep looking at the time, wishing the dinner would end.

"Got a hot date or something?" Maya teases, leaning in close. "Why are you so antsy?"

"Oh am I?" I ask, feigning surprise as I try to play it off. "I must be tired. It's been a long week."

She thankfully agrees.

By the time dinner ends, the rest of the group is winding down — their minds already on the morning flight back to Austin. But me? My night is just beginning.

Damian meets me back at my hotel, and together we step out into the neon-lit night. The air is cold against my skin, but I barely feel it. The city's energy buzzes around us — tourists spilling onto the streets, flashing billboards flickering above us, laughter echoing from all directions. The night feels alive, buzzing with possibility.

"Let's play some blackjack," Damian says, his grin wide and inviting.

"I've played before," I admit, "but I don't really know all the rules."

"Perfect," he says, sliding his fingers through mine and tugging me gently forward. "I'll teach you."

We weave through the crowded Planet Hollywood casino floor until we find a blackjack table tucked near the back. The lights are dimmer here, quieter, with just enough of a buzz to keep the energy alive. We slide into two seats, and Damian leans in close, his arm brushing against mine.

"Okay," he says, his breath warm near my ear. "Watch the cards. You want to hit when you're under sixteen. Stand when you're at seventeen or higher. And..." his fingers tap the table softly, "...always keep an eye on the dealer's card. That's your advantage."

I nod, biting my lip as I place my first bet. His hand rests on my thigh — casual, warm, yet enough to send a slow curl of heat through me.

"Now for the fun," he murmurs.

"Yes," I whisper back, heart racing.

The cards come — first the king of spades, then the ace of hearts. Blackjack.

"I won!" I squeal, half in disbelief.

"Beginner's luck," I add quickly, laughing as Damian shakes his head with a grin.

"No," he says, his voice low and sure. "You're good at this." His fingers tighten on my leg, sliding just a little higher. "Trust me."

We keep playing, and I let Damian guide me — whispering when to hit, when to hold. Each time he leans closer, his lips brush my ear, his voice smooth as silk. His hand never leaves my thigh, his thumb tracing lazy circles against my skin, each stroke drawing me closer to him.

Before I know it, there's $100 stacked neatly in front of me.

"You did awesome!" Damian's grin is pure pride, his excitement lighting up his face. Without thinking, I turn toward him, and in an instant, his arm slips around my waist, pulling me flush against him.

His mouth finds mine — hot, firm, and tantalizing. The kiss is quick but deep, his lips parting mine just enough to make my head spin.

The dealer clears his throat, clearly amused, and Damian reluctantly pulls back. His hand lingers on my waist, fingers flexing like he's not quite ready to let go.

"I should meet you in Vegas more often," he whispers.

When we step back outside, we're both flushed from excitement — and maybe the tequila shots Damian convinced me to take. The Strip hums around us, glowing in colors that feel brighter somehow — like the whole city is vibrating with possibility.

"I'm not ready to say goodnight yet," Damian says, his fingers twining with mine. His voice is low and rough, like he's barely holding something back.

"Me neither," I admit. My pulse quickens when he stops and tugs me closer.

His free hand slides to my waist, fingers curling just enough to make me stumble slightly into his chest. I let out a breathless laugh, but it's swallowed when he seizes my mouth with a hunger that matches my own.

His lips move against mine with purpose, deliberate and teasing. His hand exploring down my satin dress with ease, his fingers pressing firmly at the curve of my hip, anchoring me to him. My body leans into his instinctively, craving the solid heat of him. When his teeth graze my lower lip, a soft sound escapes me — part sigh, part moan — and I feel him smile against my mouth.

"Let's get out of here," he murmurs, his voice warm against my skin.

We weave through the crowd, fingers still locked, him leading the way.

We barely make it back to his room. The moment the door clicks shut, Damian's hands are on me, his gaze dark and hungry. He steps in close, fingers sliding over my shoulders to grasp the thin straps of my dress.

He pushes them down slowly, his eyes locked on mine, his touch deliberate and intoxicating. The silky fabric slips from my shoulders, gliding over my skin before pooling at my feet. I'm left standing before him in nothing but black lace and desire.

"God, Talia…" His voice is thick, wrecked. His hands grip my hips, lifting me effortlessly. My legs lock around his waist, arms wrapping around his neck as his mouth claims mine, fierce and urgent.

He carries me to the bed, our bodies already straining toward each other with an urgency that makes my pulse race. The heat of his skin presses against mine, but it's not enough. I need all of him.

His hands glide down my sides, fingers hooking into the delicate black lace stretched across my hips.

"Tell me you want this," he rasps, his voice wrecked and raw.

"I do. God, I do."

He slides my panties down, eyes darkening as he tosses them aside. His hands move to the clasp of my bra, unhooking it with a precision that leaves me breathless. When he strips it away, his gaze turns ravenous.

"Beautiful," he murmurs, his mouth trailing fire down my neck, over my collarbone, lower. My back arches into his touch, the intensity of his mouth against my skin making me tremble.

Then, he pulls back, rising to his feet to unbutton his shirt. One button. Then another. Slow, deliberate, as if he knows it's driving me insane. I watch, my breathing shallow, skin already tingling from his touch.

The shirt falls to the floor, revealing the sculpted planes of his chest, muscles flexing as he unbuckles his belt and pushes his pants down. His eyes never leave mine, the heat between us thick and heady.

When he returns to the bed, it's with a ferocity that leaves me gasping. His body covers mine, his mouth claiming me with a hunger that steals my breath. His hands are everywhere—gripping, caressing, demanding.

"Damian..." I moan, his name torn from me as his fingers explore, teasing and tormenting until I'm writhing beneath him.

He slides inside me in one smooth thrust, and the pleasure is so sharp and sudden I cry out. There's nothing slow or tentative about the way he moves, nothing controlled. It's raw and consuming, our bodies crashing together in a frenzy of need.

The intensity builds, his name spilling from my lips over and over, my body arching against him as he drives me relentlessly toward the edge. I shatter beneath him, pleasure ripping through me so fiercely I forget how to breathe.

My climax seems to pull him over the edge, his own release following with his body tensing and trembling against mine. The sensation of him surrendering to the moment leaves me feeling deliriously satisfied.

He collapses beside me, chest heaving, his arm pulling me close. His lips brush against my shoulder, tender and possessive.

"Fuck, Talia," he breathes, his voice wrecked and satisfied. "You're everything."

I smile, the aftershocks still rippling through me. "I didn't even know I could feel like that…"

He tightens his hold, his breath warm against my skin. "You can. With me."

As sleep claims me, I know he's right. He's awakened something inside me that I can't silence. And I don't want to. The steady rhythm of his heartbeat is the last thing I hear before I drift off — warm, safe, content.

When I wake, sunlight spills across the room, washing the sheets in soft gold. The morning light dances over Damian's bare skin, tracing the lines of muscle along his shoulders and back. He's still asleep, his arm heavy around me, his fingers curled loosely at my hip.

This. Him. I think to myself a smile growing on my face.

The gnawing voice in the back of my mind whispered: *Why does today have to be the last day? What happens next? What happens when the magic of Vegas fades, and the reality of the distance between us sets in?* My heart aches at the thought.

I shift slightly, and the movement stirs him. He exhales a low sound, somewhere between a sigh and a groan, his breath warm against the curve of my neck.

"Good morning," he murmurs, his lips brushing lazily against my skin, his voice still thick with sleep.

His mouth lingers there, soft and slow, trailing warm kisses along my shoulder — like he's savoring the feel of me beneath his lips.

I smile, turning to face him, my fingers sliding down his arm, tracing the hard muscle and soft warmth of his skin.

"Good morning, indeed," I murmur, leaning in to kiss him — a slow, lingering kiss, one I hope will wake up *all* of him.

His lips curve into a lazy smirk against mine, his eyebrow lifting in that teasing, wicked way of his — as if to say, *Message received.*

Before I can react, he disappears beneath the sheets.

I laugh softly, but the sound falters when I feel the warm press of his mouth trailing down my stomach. His lips move in slow, deliberate kisses, each one lower than the last. My breath hitches when he pauses just below my navel, his tongue finding my skin before he moves to that sensitive space near my hip bone.

I jolt, startled by the unexpected tickle, and a burst of laughter spills from me.

"Damian! That tickles!" I gasp between uncontrollable giggles, twisting beneath him.

"Oh, this?" he teases, grinning wickedly before pressing another playful kiss to the same spot — lingering just enough to make me squirm.

"Yes!" I gasp, wiggling in protest, barely able to breathe through my laughter.

"Oh no," he murmurs, voice low and mischievous. "I *like* this."

With a burst of strength, I grab his shoulders and try to pull him back up, but instead of moving, he shifts lower. His lips trail along the sensitive skin inside my thigh, his stubble scraping in a way that's both maddening and intoxicating.

"Damian…" I whisper, my voice breaking on his name — half warning, half plea.

His fingers slide beneath the lace of my panties, drawing them down slowly, deliberately — like he's savoring the moment. His mouth follows the path, brushing soft kisses along my inner thigh until I'm trembling beneath him.

And then his tongue glides against me — soft, warm, deliberate — and I forget how to breathe.

My fingers tangle in the sheets, my head falling back as the pressure builds. His tongue moves in slow, teasing circles, dragging pleasure through every nerve in my body. He takes his time — no rush, no urgency — just deep, languid strokes that make my thighs tremble.

"Please…" I gasp, lifting my hips toward him.

He groans softly, the sound vibrating against me, and his grip tightens on my thighs as he buries himself deeper. His tongue flicks faster now, sharper, more focused — and I'm unraveling, splintering apart beneath his mouth.

The pressure crests, sharp and overwhelming, and I break — pleasure crashing over me in hot, breathless waves. My fingers tighten in his hair as I shudder beneath him, my breath catching in a shaky moan.

He presses one last lingering kiss against me before sliding back up my body. His lips find mine again — hot, possessive — and I taste myself on his tongue.

"You're incredible," he whispers, voice rough and wrecked.

I barely manage to catch my breath before I feel him — hard and ready, pressing firmly against my entrance.

"Damian..." I whisper again, my fingers curling around the back of his neck, pulling him closer.

He presses into me slowly, his body stretching and filling me until there's no space left between us. My breath stutters and for a moment we just stay like that — still, caught in the quiet intimacy of being completely tangled together.

Then he moves — slow, deliberate — each thrust dragging pleasure through my body in slow-burning waves. His mouth finds mine again, his kiss matching the steady rhythm of our bodies. Every roll of his hips leaves me breathless, each deliberate stroke winding the tension inside me tighter.

"God, Talia..." he groans, his voice rough as his fingers tighten on my hips. His breaths come faster, each one ragged and strained, the deep grunts of pleasure spilling from his lips sending heat coursing through me.

I lift my legs higher, wrapping them around his waist, pulling him deeper. The tension coils, sharp and unbearable, winding tighter with every urgent movement, every sound he makes. When his release crashes over him, the guttural groan that tears from his throat is pure, unrestrained bliss.

The sound shatters my control, pushing me over the edge. Pleasure rips through me, hot and consuming, my body arching against his as the waves crest and break, leaving me breathless and trembling in his arms.

His head drops to my shoulder, his body still shuddering from the intensity of it all. For a moment, we're both suspended in the quiet, tangled together, lost in the afterglow. Both wanting to stay in the spell Vegas has put us in.

"I could stay like this all day," he murmurs, his voice softer now — almost sleepy.

"Me too," I whisper, closing my eyes and letting the warmth of his body pull me under once again.

We finally make it out of bed and decide to take a slow stroll through the Venetian, our steps falling in sync as if we've been moving together forever. The elegant arches and soft golden light create a dreamlike glow around us, but my attention is locked on him— on the way his fingers thread effortlessly through mine, on his easy smile that makes my heart stutter.

We find a hidden lunch spot to stop, Rubio's, and grab some lunch.

"Alright," Damian says, squeezing my hand lightly. "I have a very important question for you."

I glance up at him, amused. "Oh yeah? Let's hear it."

"If you could only eat one meal for the rest of your life, what would it be?" His tone is playful, but there's a curiosity behind his eyes that makes me want to give a real answer.

I pretend to think. "Hmm. I should probably say something sophisticated, right? Like filet mignon or sushi?"

He chuckles. "You *should*, but you won't."

I grin and point down to my plate. "Fine. Tacos. Hands down."

He laughs, pressing a hand to his chest in mock relief. "Thank God. If you had said something like plain chicken and rice, I would've had to reconsider everything."

I nudge him playfully. "Oh, because *you're* such a refined eater?"

"Actually, yeah," he says with a smirk. "See, that's my problem. I *love* food too much to ever choose just one meal. I could eat fresh pasta one day, then perfectly spiced Thai curry the next. Sushi, street tacos, and don't even get me started on a perfectly seared steak."

I raise an eyebrow. "Wow. Somebody knows his food."

He grins. "What can I say? Life's too short for bad meals. Every bite should be an experience."

I shake my head with a laugh. The conversation flows effortlessly. Everything about this moment feels impossibly easy, we just *fit*.

The cab hums softly beneath us as it makes its way to the airport. I glance over at Damian, his gaze distant, lost in thoughts I can't reach.

"What's on your mind?" I ask, my voice quiet, the question tentative.

"Just... this. Us."

"Us?" I turn to face him fully, searching his eyes for answers.

"Yeah." He hesitates, his fingers tracing absent patterns against his knee. "It's just... complicated."

I study him, trying to read the unspoken words tangled in his expression. It's like he's trying to solve a puzzle with too many missing pieces.

"I'm willing to figure it out if you are." My voice is firmer than I expect, the truth of it steady and sure.

His eyes meet mine, something shifting there — a mix of relief and something deeper. "I want that." His smile is soft, almost shy, a vulnerability I'm not used to seeing.

"Good." My throat tightens, but I press on. "Because I'm not ready to let you go."

He reaches for my hand, his fingers lacing through mine with a gentleness that feels like a promise. The words hang between us, heavy and uncertain, but also full of possibility.

As Damian's flight is called, he leans in for one last kiss, his arms wrapping around me like he didn't want to let go. I clung to him, savoring the moment. I watched him disappear into the crowd at the airport and my chest tightened, the weight of it hitting me all at once. I was falling for him—hard and fast, like I couldn't stop myself even if I wanted to.

Eleven

Back home, I'm still riding the high from Vegas. Memories of Damian cling to me like a second skin—his kisses, his touch, the way his voice curled around my name. I wake up smiling, my body still buzzing from the weekend. My house feels quiet—too quiet. Peaceful, yet strangely empty.

My eyes drift open, and out of habit, I reach across the bed for him. My fingers brush against cold sheets. *Dang it*, just a dream. I sigh, flopping back against my pillow, a grin still tugging at the corners of my mouth. I can't wait to see him again.

My phone rings. It's him. My heart jumps.

"Hey," he says, his voice low and warm.

"Hey," I breathe back, my voice barely above a whisper.

"Vegas was..." He trails off, but his tone says everything.

"Yeah... Vegas was..." I echo, my mind flashing back to stolen kisses and fingers tangled in bed sheets.

"I want to see you again," he says, his words slow and deliberate.

My pulse stumbles. "Well, I guess you need to come back to Texas for a visit," I tease, my voice light but hopeful.

"Yeah... I guess I do," he replies, that familiar smile practically woven into his words. "How about next month?"

"Deal," I say, unable to hide the excitement bubbling up inside me.

I hang up, grinning like an idiot, my heart racing. Next month suddenly feels way too far away.

Later that evening, Jenni pushes through the patio door, bottle of wine in one hand and a mischievous grin on her face.

"Okay," she says, kicking off her shoes before I can even say hello. "I need details. Start talking."

I laugh and follow her into the kitchen. "About what?" I ask innocently, though I know exactly what she's after.

"Vegas! Duh!" she exclaims, flopping onto the couch like she's about to watch a movie. "I want *all* the details."

I grab two wine glasses and join her, pouring us both a drink. "Well... let's just say it was *hot*." I take a sip, smirking over the rim of my glass.

Jenni's eyes go wide. "Don't you dare stop there! I want details. Who made the first move? How was the kiss? And don't you dare skip the spicy parts!"

I burst out laughing, sinking deeper into the couch. "Let's just say... Damian may be back in Texas sooner than expected."

Jenni gasps, clapping her hands like a kid on Christmas morning. "I *knew* it! Oh my God, Talia! Spill!"

We talk late into the night, laughter filling my apartment.

To make use of my spare time (and earn a little extra cash), I take on a second job at a spa. The slower pace of weekday shifts is a nice contrast to my chaotic weekends—weekends that are now a whirlwind of new bars and restaurants with Jenni and Thomas. Fun? Absolutely. But also a little hard on the wallet.

In between late nights and endless laughs, I'm still taking on a more active role in Bella's life—picking her up from preschool when Lindsey needs help or keeping her for the weekend. Our "Bella and Talia time" has become sacred. Lindsey was right—this little girl has a piece of my heart, and I want nothing but the best for her. Those moments of cuddles, cartoons, and Bella's sweet giggles feel like the calm in my busy life.

Life feels calm and beautifully balanced. I'm falling in love—with my freedom, my routine, and even the chaos of it all. For the first time in a long time, I feel like I'm steering my own life instead of reacting to it.

The only shadow is Edgar. He's still trying to push his way back in—occasional drunk texts and voicemails filled with ramblings about "just talking" or begging me to take him back. His messages blur between pleading and anger, but I do my best to ignore them, offering polite but brief replies when absolutely necessary.

But things shift when Edgar starts working at Perry's and makes friends with Rodney and another server, James. When Rodney casually mentions that Damian and I are together, Edgar's fury explodes. My phone becomes a constant buzz of nasty, manic messages and late-night visits that leave me feeling on edge.

"I know you're with him! You're disgusting!" one message screams.

Moments later, another follows:

"I miss you. Please take me back. I'm different. I'll get help."

The words lurch between rage and desperation, and I can't help but worry about what he will do next.

But instead of giving in, I find something stronger inside me—a protective instinct for the life I've built. I refuse to let him drag me back into his chaos. I delete his messages without reply, silencing his voice one text at a time. Each time I hit 'delete,' it feels like a small victory—a reminder that I am choosing my own peace, my own happiness.

I start saying yes to things again—like reconnecting with friends.

My friend Jess is hosting one of her incredible parties this weekend, the kind that usually draws at least fifty people. I haven't seen her in a while, and since I wasn't there for her birthday, I know I can't miss it.

As I walk up to her house, I can already hear the party in full swing—laughter, music, and the familiar buzz of conversation spilling from the backyard. Instead of going through the house, I decide to take the side gate. As I step into the backyard, a familiar voice calls out over the noise.

"Talia!"

It's Jess, weaving her way through the crowd toward me, her usual energy radiating even before she speaks. This month, her ever-changing hair is jet black, making her eyes pop in a striking shade of teal. It suits her—though, to be fair, I've yet to see a hair color that *doesn't* suit her.

"I'm so glad you came!" she exclaims, pulling me into a tight hug, her excitement buzzing between us like static electricity.

"Of course! I wouldn't miss it," I reply with a smile.

"Let's get you a beer," she says, grabbing my hand and leading me toward a cluster of coolers. She hands me a Dos Equis and a lime. In unison, we squeeze the lime into the bottle, press our thumbs over the opening, and flip the bottle upside down to push the lime to the bottom—a ritual we've performed countless times since our nights out downtown. We both take a sip, laughing as we make our way back to the party.

In true Jess fashion, she introduces me to at least fifteen people in rapid succession. I know I'll never remember all their names, but I smile and nod, doing my best to keep up. Eventually, we find seats by the firepit, and she turns to me, eyes gleaming with curiosity.

"So, what's new?" she asks, leaning in.

I take a deep breath, deciding to keep it short. "Well, Edgar and I are done... and I'm in love with someone else."

Jess almost spits out her beer. "What?! Holy shit! Where have I been?"

I let out a laugh before reassuring her. "Nowhere, it's just been a crazy time," I say with a shrug.

"Okay, well, yay for no more Edgar! But tell me everything about this new guy," she demands, eyes wide.

"His name is Damian. We met a couple of months ago."

I proceed to fill her in on all the details, from the flirting at Jenni's birthday party to the almost kiss and then the real kiss. By the time I'm finished, Jess is staring at me like I've grown a second head.

"Well, I have to meet this guy. Obviously," she says finally, her tone decisive.

"You will definitely meet him, he is actually coming next week" I assure her. "Besides, you two practically share a birthday—you're only two days apart."

"You know how I love an Aquarius," Jess jokes, laughing with excitement. "Oh shoot, wait—I'll be out of town next week for work," she says, her excitement fading into disappointment.

"This won't be his only visit," I say, more confidently than I expect. "I hope, anyway," I add with a nervous smile.

Jess nudges me with her elbow. "It better not be." Jess pauses, swirling her drink thoughtfully. "You know," she says, her voice quieter now, "I was worried about you for a while. After you met Edgar... it's like you disappeared on me, Tal. And that's not like you."

Her words hit me like a punch to the gut. She's not wrong. I'd pulled away, buried myself in survival mode. "I know," I admit, my voice thick. "I just...didn't want anyone to worry or have to deal with his drama."

"I get that," Jess says, her expression softening. "But I missed you. I missed my friend. And I was scared you'd never come back." Her voice cracks, just slightly, and it tugs at something deep inside me. "

"I'm here," I promise. "And I'm sorry. For pushing you away."

"Just don't do it again," she says, forcing a smile. But there's something else in her eyes — something that looks a lot like doubt.

Jess has always been strong, quick to laugh, quicker to defend her friends. But I can see the hurt I caused her, the lingering fear that I'll retreat again.

"I'm trying," I say. "I really am."

"Good." She clinks her glass against mine.

We spend the rest of the night chatting, laughing, and having the best time, just like old times. I let myself sink into the energy of the party—the hum of conversation, the warmth of friends I haven't seen in too long, and the simple comfort of feeling like myself again.

Twelve

It's just two days before Damian's arrival and I am in a full frenzy. I'm cleaning, organizing, and doing everything I can to make my house perfect. My mind drifts back to Vegas—to the way his hands explored me, the intoxicating pull of his lips against mine. Those unforgettable kisses, the way our bodies moved together like we were made for each other, replay in my mind like a perfectly choreographed dance. Especially at night, when I'm alone in my bed, the memory lingers, igniting something deep inside me that refuses to fade.

The day finally arrives and as I stand in my closet, sifting through my options, an idea creeps into my head—bold, daring, and so far outside my usual playbook that it sends a delicious thrill through me.

Should I?

The thought alone makes my skin heat. It's reckless. It's cheeky. It's something the old me would have never even considered. But with Damian, I feel different—bolder, more alive. A slow, wicked smile tugs at my lips as I make my decision.

I slip into a classic trench coat, the belt cinching at my waist, and… nothing else. The silky lining kisses my bare skin, every movement a teasing reminder of what I'm about to do. The anticipation buzzes through me, a heady mix of nerves and excitement, making my pulse quicken.

By the time I slide into the driver's seat and head to the airport, my heart is racing—not just with nerves, but with pure exhilaration. I've never done anything like this before, but for once, I'm not overthinking. I'm letting desire lead the way. And God, it feels intoxicating.

When I pull up to Southwest arrivals, there he is. He's here.

I hop out of the car, unable to hide my excitement. He wraps me in a hug, and our lips meet in a kiss that's both familiar and electric. As I pull back, his eyes catch a fleeting glimpse of what's under my coat or rather *not* under my coat. His eyebrow arches, a mischievous grin spreading across his face.

We get into the car, and his hands are instantly on me. They slide up my thigh, tugging at the edge of the coat as I try—unsuccessfully—to focus on the road. His hands continue exploring between my legs confirming his suspicions— there is nothing between his hand and my bare skin.

"This isn't working," I mutter breathlessly.

"Pull over," he says, his voice low and urgent.

I veer into an empty parking lot, headlights casting long shadows across the pavement. I barely get the car into park before his lips crash into mine again—harder, more desperate. His fingers knot in my hair, and before I know it, I'm climbing over the console, straddling him in the passenger seat. The confined space only makes it hotter—his hands push the coat off my shoulders, his fingers exploring my bare skin with a teasing slowness that drives me wild.

His mouth trails down my neck, leaving my skin burning everywhere he touches. I tilt my head back, a soft moan escaping my lips as his fingers dig into my hips, pulling me tighter against him.

"I need you," he groans against my skin, his voice raw.

My coat falls open, and his eyes flicker with heat as he takes in the sight of me—bare, vulnerable, and aching for him. The tension between us thickens, urgent and undeniable. In one swift motion, he tugs his sweatpants down, and I don't waste a second. I shift my hips, sinking onto him, feeling him fill me completely.

The rhythm between us builds fast—his hands gripping my hips as I ride him, the air thick with heat and desperate whispers. Each movement is frantic and raw, a perfect storm of tension unraveling into pure need. Time blurs—each gasp, each moan, dragging us closer to the edge until we fall together, breathless and tangled.

I collapse against his chest, my heart pounding in time with his. For a moment, we just sit there, our breathing heavy, bodies still intertwined. Then, laughter bubbles out of me—light and breathless, like I can't believe what just happened.

"Think we can make it home now?" Damian teases, his voice low and playful, his fingers lazily tracing circles on my thigh.

"Barely," I reply, grinning as I slide back into the driver's seat, still breathless and completely wrecked in the best way possible.

The rest of the drive is a blur—a mosaic of stolen glances, secret smiles, and anticipation thickening with every mile. The tension between us hasn't lessened; if anything, it's only grown, coiling tight like a spring ready to snap.

When we finally pull into the garage, the quiet hum of the car engine is the only sound. We climb out, Damian grabbing his bag from the trunk as I unlock the door. The moment we step inside, his presence is magnetic, pulling me into his orbit. I feel his lips grazing my neck as we move through the doorway, his breath hot against my skin. My resolve crumbles under his touch.

I try to head upstairs, but he catches me, his arms wrapping tightly around my waist. He presses his lips to my neck again, this time with more urgency, more need. The kisses shift from soft and teasing to insistent and demanding, each one igniting a fire that spreads through me. The coat I'm wearing slips to the floor, forgotten in the heat of the moment. His bag follows.

His hands explore my body, fingers tracing the stiff peak of my nipple, sending a jolt of pleasure coursing through me. His touch travels downward, sliding between my legs. My body responds instinctively, my wetness an undeniable invitation. Without a word, I lean forward, bracing myself against the stairs as anticipation vibrates with tension.

He presses against me, sliding inside with one smooth motion. His grip on my waist is firm, commanding, grounding me even as the intensity of his thrusts sends me spiraling. Each stroke pushes me further into a haze of pleasure, my moans escaping without restraint. Damian matches my every sound with a deeper rhythm, his movements driven and unrelenting. The pace quickens, our bodies locked in a dance of passion until the simultaneous rush of ecstasy crashes over us, leaving us breathless and trembling.

Later, as we lie tangled in bed, the glow of satisfaction lingering, we laugh and talk, sharing secrets and stealing kisses. His eyes hold mine, and for a moment, the world feels impossibly small, like nothing exists outside this room. It's as if we're suspended in time, weightless and completely lost in each other.

But the illusion shatters with a sudden, loud pounding at the back door. "Talia!" The sound echoes through the house, jolting us out of our reverie. I freeze, my breath caught in my throat, it's Edgar. The pounding comes again, more insistent this time.

Damian sits up, his eyes narrowing as his playful demeanor vanishes, replaced by sharp focus.

"I know you're in there! I can see the lights on. I know he's there with you!" Edgar yells, his slurred words slicing through the stillness.

Damian stood, his fists clenched, ready to confront him, but I grabbed his arm, my voice trembling. "Please, just stay here," I whispered, panic tightening in my chest. "He'll leave."

Terror grips me as I remember the front door is unlocked. Luckily, Edgar's too drunk—or too stupid—to try it.

"How the hell did he know I was here?" Damian asks, his voice sharp with frustration.

"I don't know," I say, rubbing my temples. "He's crazy and probably drunk."

Every second felt like an eternity as we waited, the tension so thick I could barely breathe. When the pounding finally stopped and the sound of his car faded into the distance, I collapsed onto the bed, my hands shaking. The relief was fleeting, though, replaced by the nagging fear of what he might do next.

We fall silent for a moment before Damian speaks again. "Why is he still coming here?"

"I honestly don't know," I reply, hoping this won't become a bigger issue. We eventually drift off to sleep in each other's arms, though I can feel the tension lingering in the air.

The next day, we meet Jenni for brunch at her favorite spot, Moonshine. It's a trendy café tucked in a vibrant corner of downtown Austin, where eclectic art lines the shiplapped walls and the hum of the city mixes with the buzz of conversation. Moonshine is famous for its bottomless mimosas, served in tall, chilled flutes with a splash of fresh-squeezed juice, and spicy bloody marys with just the right kick— garnished with pickled okra and a smoky rim of seasoning.

The patio outside is full of people enjoying the mild weather, and the sounds of live acoustic music from a nearby street performer add to the energetic vibe of the place.

"Damian Bunny!" she squeals, wrapping him in a hug.

"I missed you! I'm so happy you're here," she says, beaming. "I knew you two would get together," she adds, proud of herself as if she were our personal matchmaker. To her credit, she *was* the reason we met.

We sit down, and she launches into a dramatic recap of the office gossip as the mimosas start flowing. Jenni, ever the overachiever, has been leading in sales since she started. But apparently, her coworker Tammy is jealous and has been trying to sabotage her. Tammy accused Jenni of creating false referrals to earn bonuses.

"Now, I *may* have talked people into putting my name down as their referrer," Jenni admits with a sly grin, "but if they agreed, how is that my problem?"

She waves it off, but the story is building toward a tense meeting with her boss on Monday.

The brunch turns into an afternoon of bar hopping. That evening, we end Damian's visit at *The Hideout*, a quirky indoor-outdoor bar Jenni discovered. It's a perfect spot—laid-back and full of character. We're having a blast when Damian gets a message from Rodney asking where we are. Damian sends him the details, and Rodney shows up shortly after, drink in hand, sliding into a seat at our table.

The conversation is light and fun until Rodney casually mentions Perry's restaurant and Edgar.

Apparently, James—one of their mutual friends— spends a lot of time with Edgar. And, as Rodney sheepishly admits, he might have mentioned to James that Damian was coming into town this weekend.

"That's how he knew!" I exclaim, turning to Damian.

Rodney and Jenni look at me, puzzled.

"He came to the house," I explain, trying to sound nonchalant. "He was banging on the back door like a psycho."

Jenni rolls her eyes. "He is so ridiculous," she mutters as she gets up to grab another drink.

Rodney raises his eyebrows, clearly uncomfortable.

"Maybe don't share details about Damian and me with James anymore?" I say my tone firm but polite.

Rodney nods in agreement, and the conversation shifts to lighter topics. That night, after the last round of drinks and the hugs goodbye, Damian and I head back home. The drive is quiet but comfortable, his hand resting on my thigh, fingers tracing lazy circles that make my skin hum. The night air feels cooler now, and I shiver as we step inside.

"Come here," Damian murmurs, pulling me close. His lips brush against my forehead, soft and warm. We head upstairs, but instead of undressing and curling up for sleep, we collapse onto the bed, still in our clothes. My head rests on his chest, his heartbeat steady beneath my ear.

Neither of us speaks for a while, and I realize I don't want the night to end. "I don't want you to leave," I whisper, breaking the silence.

"I don't want to leave either," he replies, his fingers weaving gently through my hair.

We stay like that for hours, talking in whispers, sharing quiet thoughts we hadn't dared say before. Damian tells me about his years running track — the early morning practices, the endless drills, and how hurdles became his obsession. "I loved the rhythm of it," he says, his voice soft with nostalgia. "There's this perfect moment when you're in the air, like you're flying — just you and the next hurdle ahead."

"That's why you have the tattoo," I say, tracing the hurdler inked on his neck with my finger.

He chuckles. "Yeah… reminds me to keep moving forward."

I smile, resting my chin on his chest. "I get that," I say quietly. "I used to swim — competed for United States Swimming through my freshman year in high school. I wanted to go to the Olympics."

"You serious?" His voice perks up. "You never told me that."

I shrug, my fingers absently playing with the hem of his shirt. "I was good — really good — but I pulled the two main muscles in my abdomen. Just like that, it was over."

"Damn," he mutters, his hand tightening around mine. "I'm sorry."

"It's okay," I say, though a faint ache still inside me. "I guess I just had to find a new dream."

His fingers squeeze mine a little tighter. "Well… for what it's worth, I'm glad you did."

Laughter drifts through the room like a warm breeze, wrapping us in something safe and familiar. When the first streaks of light creep in through the window, Damian's arm tightens around me.

"Look," I whisper, pointing to the horizon. The sky is painted in soft oranges and dusky pinks, the city stirring beneath the glow.

"It's beautiful," he says, but his gaze stays locked on me.

I can't help but believe that this — *us* — might just be real.

The next morning — or really, the afternoon — I wake slowly, Damian's soft snores buried in the pillow. I linger in bed for a few more minutes, listening to his steady breathing before I carefully slip away. I pull on one of his shirts — soft and oversized — before heading downstairs to make coffee. The rich scent fills the kitchen as I step onto the patio, mug in hand. The air is warm now, the afternoon sun shining down from a cloudless sky.

I sip my coffee, feeling the quiet settle inside me like a weight I can't quite shake. Damian's leaving today. The thought curls inside my chest, tugging at something fragile.

"Morning," Damian's voice calls softly from behind me. I turn to see him standing barefoot in the doorway, his sweatpants hanging low on his hips. He's blinking sleep from his eyes, and I swear my heart stumbles at the sight of him.

"Morning," I say with a soft smile. "Or… afternoon, I guess."

He steps outside, wrapping his arms around me from behind, his chin resting on my shoulder. For a long moment, we just stand there in silence, watching the neighborhood quietly hum with life.

"This weekend was great and too fast," he murmurs into my neck, his voice low and rough with sleep.

"I know," I whisper back, leaning into him.

Eventually, we head upstairs, where Damian starts packing his bag. I sit cross-legged on the bed, sipping the last of my coffee while he folds his clothes with deliberate slowness, as if dragging out the moments will somehow make time pause.

As he pulls one last shirt from his pile, his eyes flick to me. "You know," he says, smirking, "I'm going to need that shirt back."

I smile lazily, stretching out across the bed. "Oh yeah?"

"Yeah," he says, walking over to me. With one smooth motion, he grabs the hem of the shirt and tugs it up and over my head, leaving me bare beneath him. He grins. "But..." he pauses, stepping back to hook his thumbs into the waistband of his blue sweatpants. "I'll leave these here if you want something of mine."

I bite my lip, grinning. "I think I want something else of yours first."

He doesn't need more of an invitation. Damian crawls over me, his mouth finding mine in a slow, lingering kiss. My hand cups his face to bring him closer. His body presses against mine, and the afternoon — melts away in a haze of heat and skin until we are breathless and content. Damian presses a kiss to my forehead and murmurs, "I really don't want to leave."

"I know," I whisper, trailing my fingers along his chest. "I could visit you next month in California," I say, lifting my head to read his expression.

He nods in agreement and kisses me again. I can tell he's thinking about something, but he doesn't say anything more.

We stay like that for a while longer before reality forces us to move. Damian finishes packing his bag, and we head to the airport — my hand tightly wrapped in his the whole way there.

"Can I play something for you?" Damian asks, his voice low, a hint of something unspoken between us.

"Of course," I reply, offering him a smile that feels too fragile for the moment.

The soft, yearning notes of Justin Nozuka's *After Tonight* drift through the car, the melody tender and full of longing. Damian reaches for my hand, his fingers grazing mine before intertwining effortlessly, like they were always meant to fit. We sit in quiet sync, the world outside the car fading into the background as the song wraps around us, cocooning us in its warmth.

As the lyrics whisper about no longer needing to wish for love *after tonight*, I steal a glance at Damian. The way his thumb traces slow, absentminded circles on my skin makes my heart flutter. It feels like a love letter—unspoken, but there, in the way he holds me, in the song choice. Maybe he doesn't need words. This moment says everything.

Before we know it, we're at the airport. Damian pulls his bag from the trunk, but neither of us moves. We lean against the car, time stretching impossibly—like we've been standing there for both an eternity and just a heartbeat. My face rests against his chest, breathing him in, feeling the steady thrum of his heartbeat under my cheek, and his head gently resting atop mine. The weight of the moment hangs heavy, and Damian pulls me into a kiss—soft and lingering, as if we both know this is our last for now.

"I had an amazing time. I'll call you when I get in," he whispers against my lips, his words a promise.

He pulls back, looking at me one last time before turning to walk away. He pauses at the door, looking over his shoulder, and mouths, "April."

I nod, my heart aching, and wave, holding back the emotions that threaten to spill over.

As I drive home, the melody lingers, echoing in my chest. For the next month, I find myself replaying it, wishing I could rewind time—wishing I could be back in his arms, where everything feels right.

Thirteen

I can't believe how quickly April arrived. One minute, I am dropping Damian off at the airport, watching him disappear into the crowd with a kiss that lingered long after he was gone—and now I'm zipping up my suitcase, heart pounding for a whole new reason.

It feels like I blinked and the weeks between us vanished, lost in a haze of midnight calls, flirty texts, and memories that replayed like a favorite movie. Every time we talked, it felt like we were building something—something intense, magnetic, *real.*

And maybe that's what scares me.

Because somewhere along the way, without meaning to, I started falling in love with him.

And now I need to know if he feels the same.

Jenni's perched on the edge of my bed, tossing travel minis into her makeup bag like she's done this a thousand times. Her suitcase is already by the door— hot pink, hard-shell, and completely overpacked.

"I'm so pumped for this trip," she says with a grin. "A girls' weekend *and* a romance reunion? Come on. Plus, a hotel by the beach? Yes, please."

I laugh, sitting beside her. "You just want an excuse to drink cocktails in a cabana."

"Obviously. But also, I'm here for moral support. And I couldn't pass up staying in Costa Mesa—Damian said it's where all the action is, right?"

I nod. "Yeah. He mentioned it when we were planning. Said there were great spots nearby, fun restaurants, beaches..."

She raises a brow. "Not gonna lie, I *love* that he picked a location that makes the trip feel like a vacation. That's how you do it."

I smile, thinking about how excited and sweet he was in planning the trip with us, sending me links and ideas. I'm finally going to see him again. That's when the nerves kicked in.

Jenni nudges me with her shoulder. "Okay, what's that look?"

"What look?"

"The one where you're overthinking something."

I laugh, caught. "I guess I'm just nervous."

"Because?"

"Because I really like him," I admit. "More than I expected to. And the time we spent together before... it felt like something out of a dream. Magical. Intense. And now I'm going back into that dream and—I don't know—I guess I just want to know if he feels it, too."

Jenni softens. "You're brave, T. Not everyone would fly across the country for love."

I smile at her. "Well, not everyone has you for backup."

"Damn right."

On the plane, Jenni orders us Bloody Marys before I can say no.

"To love and beachside hotel rooms," she says, holding her plastic cup aloft.

I can't help but laugh, clinking mine against hers. "To not overthinking everything."

We sip, and the tomato tang and vodka heat help settle my nerves. Jenni scrolls through Yelp reviews for brunch spots near the hotel Damian had sent us while I stare out the window, watching the clouds part over the California coast.

"God, this is going to be *so* fun," she says. "We are going to eat, drink, tan, and maybe you'll get laid by the ocean. Iconic."

I choke on my drink, laughing. "Oh my God."

"What? I'm manifesting for you!"

And for a moment, I let myself lean into it—into the fun, the sunshine ahead, the butterflies in my stomach that I secretly love. I let myself believe that maybe this trip will be everything I've hoped for.

As the plane begins its descent and the Pacific sparkles in the distance, I feel it—hope, wild and heady, pulsing beneath my ribs.

Damian picks us up from the airport, and the moment we slide into the car, Dream's new album starts playing. Smooth beats and soulful lyrics fill the space, instantly setting a laid-back, sun-drenched vibe. The California streets roll past us—palm trees swaying, golden light spilling through the windows— as we head toward the hotel to check in before dinner at Sharkeez.

Sharkeez is a lively, seaside spot with a beachy, carefree energy. It's the kind of place where the salty ocean breeze dances through an open-air patio, mixing with bursts of laughter and the clink of glasses. Bright murals of palm trees and sun-kissed waves cover the walls, and the air is thick with the scent of sizzling seafood and tangy lime.

We decide to share one of their signature fishbowl cocktails—one of those ridiculously oversized drinks served with a bouquet of neon straws and a tiny piñata donkey perched on top. We burst into laughter the moment it hits the table.

Jenni grabs the little donkey and makes it "dance" in front of us, bobbing it to the beat of the music. "He needs a name," she declares. "I'm thinking Jorge."

Damian chuckles. "Definitely Jorge."

We're a perfect trio—effortlessly happy, feeding off each other's energy. For a moment, it's just laughter and sunlight and sweet, spiked sips from the fishbowl. Our own little bubble of joy in the middle of the crowded restaurant.

When we leave, still light from the drinks and the laughter, Damian starts patting his pockets for his car keys. That's when I notice something.

"Wait… is the car on?" I ask, my voice tinged with disbelief but also a hint of amusement.

"Oh my God," Jenni chimes in, catching on at the same time.

We all burst into uncontrollable laughter. Damian had left the car running the entire time we were inside. The absurdity of it is too much, and we can't stop laughing, barely managing to catch our breath as we climb into the car. We're still giggling when we finally make it back to the hotel, and I can't help but think how easy and fun this trip has been so far.

After a quick change in the room, we head straight for the hot tub. The warm water is a perfect contrast to the cool evening air, and the gentle hum of conversation from nearby guests blends with the soft rhythm of the jets. Jenni, slightly tipsy, can't resist asking the question that's been lingering in the air.

"So, what are your intentions with my Talia?" she asks, her tone playful but also probing, as if she's testing the waters. "Don't get me wrong the jet setting life is great but…"

Damian smirks, clearly trying to act coy. "I don't know. I like her a lot," he says, his fingers brushing mine under the water.

I laugh nervously and give him a quick kiss on the cheek, my heart skipping a beat. "We're just having fun," I add, though it feels almost too casual for how my heart is thumping in my chest.

Jenni's attention shifts as a couple of random guys join the hot tub, leaving Damian and me alone in our little bubble. Beneath the surface of the warm water, our hands find each other again, fingers tracing soft patterns, and our kisses grow deeper, more urgent. There's something thrilling about it—like we're in our own secret world, one where nothing matters but the quiet intimacy we're building.

Later, back in the hotel room, Jenni heads to bed, but Damian and I linger. The dim light of the bedside lamp casts shadows across the room, making everything feel intimate, almost fragile. The quiet between us is heavy, filled with unspoken things.

"I'm really falling for you," I blurt out, my voice a whisper but thick with emotion.

His eyes soften, and for a brief moment, I feel a rush of relief. "Me too," he says, but there's something in his tone that feels uncertain.

I swallow hard, the weight of my feelings pressing down on me. "I mean... I'm falling in love with you, Damian," I clarify, the words leaving my mouth before I can take them back. My heart pounds in the silence that follows, each second stretching out like an eternity.

He shifts, his gaze moves down to his hands, and then back at me. "Oh... okay," he says, his words careful, like he was stepping around something fragile.

The sting of his response was immediate, sharp, and unexpected.

"Okay? So, do you feel the same way?" I asked, my voice rising, raw with hurt.

He sighed, running a hand through his hair. "I really like you, Talia. I can see myself falling in love with you, but I'm not there yet."

His words landed like a cold splash of water, and I could feel the fragile hope inside me shatter. "Then what are we even doing?" I asked, my voice cracking.

"I just... I need time," he pleaded, his tone soft but firm. "Can't this be enough for now?"

I nodded, but my heart felt heavy, the doubts I'd been trying to ignore suddenly impossible to push aside.

I fall silent, the weight of his words settling like a stone in my chest. Back in the bed, I pull the covers up to my chin but can't sleep. My mind races with questions, doubts. Did I just tell Damian I love him, and he didn't say it back? What am I doing? I just got out of a serious relationship—why do I always rush things?

The next morning, we all pretend like nothing happened. We're off to Santa Monica Pier for sushi, but the chilly wind makes me realize I forgot to pack a hoodie.

"Are there any stores around here?" I ask, my voice a little strained as I shiver against the cool breeze.

We wandered through shop after shop, turning the search for a hoodie into an inside joke that spiraled out of control. "How about here? Do they have a hoodie?" Jenni asked, her mock-serious tone making Damian and me burst into laughter. It was silly and ridiculous, but for a little while, it felt like the weight in my chest wasn't there—like I could just exist in the moment.

We end the day on the beach, lounging on a blanket, letting the waves crash nearby, the golden hour sun casting everything in a soft, melancholy light. There's an unspoken sadness in the air, the quiet ache of knowing we'll be leaving in the morning, but we don't say anything—just soak in the fleeting beauty around us.

Even as Damian kissed me goodbye at the airport, his arms wrapping around me like he didn't want to let go, a quiet unease settled in my chest. I wanted to believe this was enough, that we were enough. But his hesitation, and the distance between us all felt like cracks in something fragile, threatening to break if I pushed too hard.

As the plane lifted off, I stared out the window, the California coastline fading into the distance. Jenni was beside me, flipping through a magazine, but my mind was miles away, stuck on Damian. His hesitant words replayed in my head: "I really like you, but I'm not there yet."

The weight of it pressed down on me, heavier with every passing mile. What were we doing? Was I chasing something that wasn't really there? And yet, despite the doubts swirling in my mind, I couldn't deny the ache in my chest—the quiet, desperate hope that this was real, that it could become everything I wanted it to be.

Jenni breaks the silence with a question that catches me off guard.

"Do you think it's weird we didn't see his apartment?" Jenni asked, her tone casual but laced with curiosity.

My stomach tightened as I forced a laugh. "No, no," I said quickly, the words tumbling out before I could think. "He has a roommate and sleeps on the couch, so there wasn't really a reason to go there."

Jenni shrugged, accepting the answer, but the question stuck with me, gnawing at the edges of my mind. Was it weird? Why hadn't he wanted to show me his space? Was he hiding something, or was I just overthinking it? The doubt settled like a quiet weight in my chest, growing heavier the more I tried to dismiss it.

Fourteen

Back at home, everything feels quieter than usual—too quiet, like the calm before a storm. Jenni's work drama had been escalating for weeks, but nothing could've prepared me for what happens next.

The patio door swings open with a sharp bang, and Jenni storms inside, her shoulders stiff, her face a storm of rage and disbelief.

"Talia!" she calls out, her voice thick with emotion.

"I'm in my office! Coming down!" I yell, dread already curling in my stomach.

I hear the fridge door open, the sharp *crack* of a beer being opened echoing through the house. By the time I reach the bottom of the stairs, Jenni is pacing, her anger radiating like heat.

"What's wrong?" I ask, my heart sinking.

"They freaking fired me!" she spits, her voice breaking as tears brim in her eyes. "Tammy took that bullshit to corporate and got me fired."

"What? No. That's—no. That's insane," I say, stunned. "You're their top sales associate! How could they—?"

"They believed *her* story over mine," she says bitterly, swiping at her eyes. "I gave that job everything."

I wrap my arms around her, trying to anchor her even though I feel just as unsteady.

"And now," she adds, pulling away, "I have to move out of my apartment by the end of the week. Where the hell am I supposed to go, Talia?"

The panic in her voice hits me like a gut punch. Without hesitation, the words tumble out: "Move in here. I've got the extra bedroom. I'll move my office downstairs, and when Bella visits, she can crash with me. Easy."

Jenni stares at me, the fight in her eyes softening just slightly. "You'd really do that?"

"Of course," I say. "We'll figure the rest out."

"Thank you," she breathes, taking a long pull of beer. "This is all just so... fucking insane." She shakes her head. "I need a cigarette."

I grab two more beers and follow her out to the patio. The evening air is cool, still, the kind of night that holds its breath. Jenni lights up, the cigarette ember glowing in the shadows.

We sit for hours—talking, venting, drinking. Her frustration slowly unwinds, but the weight of everything doesn't leave. It just settles in deeper.

160

Eventually, she sighs and stands, brushing ash off her jeans. "Guess I should head back and start packing."

"We're still on for this weekend, right?"

"Yeah," she nods. "I'll start job hunting tomorrow. Thanks, Talia. I don't know what I'd do without you."

"You never have to find out."

She gives me a tired smile, waves, and disappears into the night.

I head back inside, emotionally drained, but I try to shift back into work mode. I sit at my desk and open my laptop—only to end up doom-scrolling Facebook like a zombie. That's when I see it.

Damian is online.

But... he's supposed to be at work.

My stomach tightens.

Me: *Hey, thought you had to work?*

The reply comes almost immediately.

Damian: *Who is this?*

My blood runs cold.

Me: *Wait... who is this? Damian?*

Damian: *No. This is his girlfriend, Nicole. Why are you messaging him?*

His *girlfriend?*

My lungs stop working. My heart hammers against my ribs as the words blur on the screen. My entire body goes still.

Me: *Girlfriend? He told me you two broke up when he moved back to California.*

Nicole: *Well, we didn't. Stop messaging him.*

I feel her typing again, the bubbles mocking me. Then—

Nicole: *How long have you been talking to Damian?*

Me: *We met in Austin. We've been talking since February. I'm sorry… I didn't know.*

Nicole: *Am I supposed to believe that? Just leave him alone. We're going to work this out and be together.*

I stare at the screen, stunned. Shaking.

Then anger hits—fast and hot and wild.

Me: *I talked to your girlfriend, Nicole. You're a fucking liar.*

I throw the phone down, grab a cigarette from Jenni's stash, and step onto the balcony, trying to breathe through the betrayal tearing through me.

Two hours later, my phone starts buzzing nonstop. Calls. Texts. Voicemails. Damian.

I finally pick up.

"What?" I snap, my voice cold, shaking with emotion.

"Talia, please—just hear me out," he says, his voice frantic. "It's not what you think."

"Really?" I bite back. "Because Nicole is on your computer, answering your messages, calling herself your girlfriend. So go ahead—tell me what I'm *supposed* to think."

"We're broken up," he insists. "We've been done for months. She just won't accept it."

"You *live* with her."

"I had no choice," he says, his voice strained. "Neither of us could afford to move out yet. That's all it is. I swear."

My chest tightens. "So *that's* why we never saw your place while we were there. That's why you suggested a hotel near the beach and acted like it was just for fun. You planned that—because you didn't want me anywhere near your reality."

He's quiet for a beat. "I didn't know how to explain it without ruining everything."

"Because it would've ruined everything," I say, the hurt slicing through me like glass. "What if I had asked to come over? You would've lied to my face."

He doesn't respond, and his silence is answer enough.

"You *would've* lied," I say again, this time more to myself than to him. "That's the worst part."

"I didn't want to lose you," he says softly. "Talia... I love you. I was scared. I made a mistake— one I wish I could undo."

The words hit hard—but they don't land like they should.

"You say you love me, but you let me sleep next to you, kiss you, make plans with you—knowing the whole time you were keeping this massive secret."

"I didn't mean for it to go this far without telling you. I thought I'd have it figured out by the time you came out. But it didn't happen, and then you were here, and everything felt so good, and I didn't want to wreck it."

"But you did," I whisper. "You already did."

A long silence stretches between us, heavy and unbearable.

"I just need time," I finally say, voice barely steady. "I need to think. I need space."

"Talia—please."

But I don't give him a chance to say more. I hang up.

My phone drops to the floor beside the bed, and I pull the covers over my head, numb and shaking.

I'd wanted to fall in love with him.

Now I'm just falling apart.

I barely sleep that night.

Every time I close my eyes, it replays—Nicole's messages, Damian's voice, the sickening moment when the truth hit me like a punch to the gut.

By morning, the sun is up, but I'm still curled in bed, hollow and heavy, the weight of it all pressing down like wet cement.

I cancel my meetings. Leave texts unanswered. I don't even brush my hair. I just exist—barely. Thinking to myself, *and we are here again, awesome.*

Jenni texts mid-morning:

Jenni: *Want me to bring breakfast over? I found the perfect greasy hangover burrito.*

I stare at the message for ten minutes before replying:

Me: *No thanks. Not hungry.*

She sends a gif of someone dramatically eating pancakes anyway, but I don't laugh. I don't even smile.

By the time evening creeps in, I still haven't moved from my bed. I feel distant from myself, like I'm watching my own life from the outside.

It isn't until I hear the patio door open that I even remember Jenni has a key.

"T?" Her voice calls out, cautious but not unsure. She's already halfway up the stairs. "You home? I brought some stuff over, thought I would get a head start on the move. Plus, wine of course!"

I stay quiet, part of me hoping she'll leave. But of course, she doesn't. She's Jenni.

She finds me in the dark, curled under the blanket like I'm trying to disappear.

"Jesus, Talia," she mutters, flipping on the lamp. "You look like I did yesterday."

I don't answer. I don't even flinch. I just keep staring at nothing.

She sits on the edge of the bed and looks at me, really looks at me. "Okay. Who do I need to kill?"

That almost makes me smile. Almost.

After a beat, she softens—just enough. "What happened?"

I open my mouth, but nothing comes out. The words are thick and sticky and raw. But Jenni waits. And finally, I say it.

"He lives with his ex."

Her whole face shifts. "*What?*"

165

"Nicole. She answered his messages. That's his *roommate*." I choke out a laugh that doesn't sound like me. "I flew across the damn country to see a man who couldn't even tell me the truth."

Jenni goes dead quiet for a second. Then—"That motherfucker."

I nod, eyes stinging. "He said they broke up. That it was just temporary. That they couldn't afford to move out yet."

Jenni scoffs. "Bullshit."

"And that's why we never saw his place," I whisper. "That's why he pushed the hotel. He knew. He planned it. And if I had asked to see his house? He would've lied."

Jenni's jaw tenses, her fists clenched. "I swear to God, we need to go full Thelma and Louise on these people. Just drive off a cliff and flip everyone the bird on the way down."

I let out a broken laugh.

She grabs the blanket and pulls it off my head. "Look, the world is clearly broken right now. I got fired for doing my job. You got lied to by a man you were falling in love with. Honestly? Fuck everything."

She locks eyes with me, fierce and certain. "But we are *not* going down like this. You hear me? It's you and me now. You and me against the damn universe if we have to. And we're gonna be okay. We always are."

I blink at her, the words hitting harder than any comfort could.

"Do you want me to delete his number?" she asks, deadly serious.

"No," I whisper, smiling weakly. "Not yet."

Jenni grins like a wolf. "Okay. But the offer's on the table."

Then she crawls into bed with me, pulling the blanket over both of us like we're kids again hiding from the world. And for the first time all day, I let myself exhale.

Jenni moves in over the weekend, her life packed into a blur of boxes, takeout containers, and mutual emotional chaos. Neither of us has our lives together, but at least we have each other.

It's late, and the apartment is dimly lit, soft shadows stretching across the walls. I'm rummaging through my dresser when I spot them—Damian's blue sweatpants, the ones he left when he was here last.

For a moment, I just stare at them.

The memory rushes in, uninvited: him standing barefoot on the patio, those sweats slung low on his hips, a sleepy smile on his face. The way he kissed my forehead like it was the most natural thing in the world.

I hate how much I miss him.

Even though I'm angry. Even though I feel betrayed.

I grab the sweatpants and tug them on anyway, the fabric soft and familiar. It hurts—more than I expect—but I can't help it. I want to feel close to him, even in this small, pathetic way.

When I walk into the living room, Jenni's already on the couch, barefoot, wine bottle open, oversized pink hoodie half-swallowed by the blanket draped over her.

She looks up and smirks. "Are those *his* sweatpants?"

I shrug, not ready to talk about it. "They were clean."

She doesn't push. Just hands me a glass of wine.

"Well," she sighs, "this isn't exactly how I pictured my mid-twenties. But hey, at least I don't have to deal with Tammy's two-faced ass anymore. Small wins, right?"

I manage a weak smile as I take the glass. "Yeah. Small wins."

My phone buzzes on the table—**Damian.** My stomach twists. I reach for it, then stop myself. I hit *silence* and flip the phone over, face-down.

Jenni narrows her eyes. "So... still ignoring him?"

I sigh, sinking deeper into the couch. "Not ignoring. Just… not answering."

"That's literally ignoring," she says, raising a brow.

I give her a look and swirl the wine in my glass. "He keeps calling, texting, trying to explain. And part of me wants to believe him, but…"

"But you don't want to be stupid," she finishes.

"Exactly."

Jenni pulls her knees up under her, resting her glass on her thigh. Her voice softens, but there's still that fire underneath. "Look, I get it. You're scared of getting hurt again. And you should be. People suck. Life is messy. But if there's even a piece of you that believes him... what's really stopping you?"

I bury my face in my hands. "What if I'm just some placeholder? What if he's not over her and I'm just the distraction until he figures his shit out?"

Jenni scoffs. "Girl, no. Damian's *obsessed* with you. He looked at you like you were the last person on earth who mattered. But yeah, this whole thing? It's a mindfuck. If it were me, I'd be spiraling too."

I let out a shaky breath. Her words comfort me, but they don't make it easier. Not really.

"I just..." My voice catches. "I really thought this was it. That he was different."

Jenni scoots closer and rests her head against my shoulder. "I know," she says quietly. "I know."

The silence that follows isn't peaceful. It's thick, charged with everything I don't want to say out loud. I keep replaying every moment—how safe I felt with him, how certain I was that this time was real. The way he touched me like I was the only thing that mattered. And now? I feel like an idiot for falling for it.

"I let myself believe I wasn't going to get hurt again," I whisper. "And I did. Bad."

"Stop right there," Jenni says, lifting her head, her tone sharp. "You can't blame yourself for that. You believed in something good. You let yourself feel something real. That's brave, not stupid."

"It *feels* stupid," I choke out. My glass clinks as I set it down on the coffee table, my hands shaking too much to hold it. My vision blurs as the tears finally break free.

"I just... I loved him. I *love* him."

Jenni doesn't say anything right away. She wraps her arms around me, holding me tight as I fall apart. The sobs shake me, deep and raw, like the grief is pouring out of places I didn't know could hurt.

"I don't know what to do," I whisper through the tears.

Her voice is low but solid. "You don't have to know right now. You just have to survive it. We both do."

I nod against her, the ache in my chest pulsing like a bruise. I feel hollow. Like something essential has been ripped from me and nothing will ever fill the space it left.

Then, my phone buzzes again.

I glance at it. **Damian.**

Damian: *Talia, please. I know you're upset, but I need you to call me back. I swear I can explain. Just... please let me fix this.*

The words hit like a punch to the gut.

We sit there for a while longer. The wine doesn't taste like anything. The room doesn't feel like home. Everything's quieter than it should be. Duller.

Jenni finally stands and stretches, her voice gentler than before. "Just think about it, Talia," she says as she heads toward her room. "I know he cares about you. And I've never seen you light up the way you do when he's around."

Her words hang in the air long after she's gone.

I stare at Damian's message, my thumb hovering over his name.

Should I forgive him?

Could I?

To complete the trifecta of disaster, now my job is on shaky ground. A co-worker recently quit and filed a complaint, claiming we were being treated as employees instead of contractors. If the investigation goes badly, the entire company could be in jeopardy.

I'd been thinking about leaving for months, but now that it feels like the decision might be made for me, I'm not so sure. Between the stress at work, Jenni's upheaval, and the mess with Damian, my brain feels like a crowded room—no windows, no doors, no way out.

I crave clarity. All I have is chaos.

My phone rings. **Damian.**

For reasons I don't understand, this time... I answer.

"Hi," I say softly.

"Hi," he replies, cautious, but hopeful. "I do love you, and I don't want to lose you," he begins. "We agreed on the roommate situation right before I moved back—before I knew where things were going with us. After Vegas... I didn't know how to tell you. I didn't want to ruin everything."

"I believe you," I say, surprising us both. "But it's still a lie, Damian," I add, my voice firmer.

"I know," he says, regret thick in his voice. "I want to be with you. I'll start looking for another place. Immediately."

My heart stutters. "You told her about me?"

"Yes," he replies without hesitation. "She knows it's over. She knows about you. She knows we're together."

His words come in a rush, like he's afraid I'll hang up before he finishes. I can hear it in his voice—the desperation, the rawness. I can almost see him pacing the room, running his hand through his hair, trying to hold everything together with nothing but a thread and a prayer.

"I know I should've told you sooner," he says, voice cracking. "But I need you to believe me when I say I love you. I'll prove it. I'll fix this. Just... please don't give up on me."

I exhale slowly, trying to absorb it all. My chest feels too small for the weight pressing down on it.

"So... what now?" I ask.

"I'm coming to see you," he says, voice steadier now. "I need to see you. In person."

"When?"

"Two weeks," he says. "I'll be there in two weeks."

I hesitate, but then: "Okay. Two weeks."

There's a pause on the line—soft, full of unspoken things—before he says gently, "I love you, Talia."

I close my eyes. His words land like a warm ache in my chest.

"I love you too, Damian," I whisper.

"Besitos," he says softly, but I can hear the smile in his voice.

"Besitos," I echo, the word tender, heavy, and fragile.

We hang up, and I step outside onto the balcony. The city lights shimmer in the distance, cool night air brushing against my skin. I light a cigarette and watch the smoke curl skyward as his voice replays in my mind.

I love you.

I want to believe him. I do. But that stubborn little voice inside me—the one that's been burned before—whispers, *What if it's another lie? What if you let him in again just to watch him walk away?*

Two weeks, I remind myself.

Two weeks to find clarity.

Two weeks to find courage.

I grab my journal, hoping to bleed some of the noise from my head. My handwriting is shaky as I begin:

March 18, 2009

I don't know what to do. My heart's a mess. I want to believe Damian—God, I want to—but I don't know if I can. What if I let him back in just to watch him leave again? What if trusting him is the thing that breaks me all over again?
I hate that this doubt is eating away at the love I know I feel.
He says he loves me.
And I think I believe him.
But what if loving him isn't enough?
What if trusting him... is the mistake?
I pause, gripping the pen, forcing myself to keep writing.
Two weeks.
That's what I told myself.
Two weeks to figure out if I can be brave enough to believe in love again.
Two weeks to decide if my heart can take the risk.
Two weeks to decide if I can trust him...
or if I need to learn how to let go.

Fifteen

The next two weeks are a slow burn of anticipation—
equal parts tension, tenderness, and questions I'm still
not ready to answer.

Damian and I talk almost every day now. Some
conversations are short and careful, like we're still
tiptoeing through the fragile edges of trust. Others
stretch deep into the night, his voice low and warm in
my ear, the way it used to be.

One afternoon, my phone lights up with his
name. Damian.

I hesitate only a second before answering.

"Hey," I say.

"Hey," he replies, voice steady, familiar. "I wanted
to tell you something."

I wait, the beat between us hanging quietly.

"I moved out," he says. "I'm staying with my
friend Mark from work until I can get my own place.
I didn't want to wait anymore. I needed to show you I
meant what I said."

A breath escapes me—long, slow, something I hadn't even realized I was holding.

"You didn't have to do that for me," I say, my voice soft.

"I did it because I should've a long time ago," he says. "But yeah… you're part of the reason. I told you I love you, Talia. And I meant it. I still mean it."

His words don't feel like a Band-Aid. They feel like a promise.

And something in me shifts.

The wall I've been holding up begins to lower, just a little. Just enough for the warmth to sneak back in.

After that call, everything starts to feel lighter. Easier.

The tension between us begins to dissolve. Our texts fill with teasing again. Inside jokes resurface. The late-night calls stretch longer. Deeper. Flirtier.

One night, he texts:

Damian: *You know I'm going to kiss you the second I see you, right?*

I grin at my screen, my fingers already moving.

Me: *And…? I'm going to need more than just your kisses.*

His reply is instant.

Damian: *Kisses and… I want your body.*

My breath catches, heat blooming low in my stomach.

That spark. That fire. The thing that made falling for him feel inevitable in the first place is there but so is the fear.

On Thursday, I meet Maya for yoga at the studio. It's warm out—humid, spring air sticking to my skin as we unroll our mats in the far corner of the class. The lights are dimmed, soft music plays in the background, and the scent of eucalyptus drifts in the air.

Our instructor, Sanieya, begins class with a slow, grounding breathwork sequence. She stands at the front, her voice calm and soothing.

"Today," she says, "we honor the strength of the lotus. A flower that grows only in the mud, pushing through the darkness to reach the light. In yoga, the lotus represents the soul's journey to rise through pain and chaos toward clarity... toward enlightenment."

I close my eyes. The words hit me hard.

She continues, her tone like a soft chant. "And at the center of this journey is the *Om*—the vibration of peace. Of presence. Of connection to self."

That's it, I think. That's what I've been trying to find again—*me*.

The version of me I fought so hard to reclaim after Edgar. The one who pieced herself back together, who learned how to stand on her own, how to breathe without needing someone else to catch her breath.

I had her—strong, grounded, whole.

But then love came again. Beautiful. Intoxicating. I let it sweep me up, and somewhere in the whirlwind of Damian's touch and promise and possibility, I lost her again. Not completely, but enough to forget that *I* was the thing I needed most.

Now, I see it clearly.

To truly love him—to truly love anyone—I have to return to her. To myself. I have to rise from the mud and choose peace. Not the kind someone else gives me, but the kind I carry within.

That's the tattoo. That's the symbol I want on my hip. A lotus rising from the mud. An *Om* at its heart.

After class, Maya loops her arm through mine as we walk to the juice bar next door. "You okay? You were super still during Savasana."

"I'm good," I say, feeling strangely steady both physically and emotionally. "Her class was amazing! This magical blend of exercise and spiritual enlightenment."

Maya nods in agreement while she sips her juice.

Later that night, I'm curled up in bed, the familiar hum of *Sex and the City* playing in the background for the hundredth time, its dialogue blending into white noise as I fight to stay awake for Damian to finish his shift. My eyelids grow heavier with each passing minute, my body surrendering to exhaustion, when suddenly— My phone vibrates against the pillow, and my heart jolts awake before the rest of me does. It's him.

The familiar notes of *Kiss Me Through the Phone* by Soulja Boy play—his designated ringtone, a private joke between us after one too many late-night calls filled with playful teasing. Smirking, I reach for my phone, already feeling the exhaustion fade.

"Hey, stranger," I murmur, my voice thick with sleep but threaded with warmth.

"Damn," he teases. "Did I wake you?"

"Maybe," I admit, rolling onto my side. "But I forgive you."

And just like that, the miles between us don't feel so far.

"I'm getting a tattoo."

"Oh?" His voice perks up. "What kind?"

"A lotus with an Om in the center. On my hip."

There's a pause, and then his voice drops an octave. "That's sexy."

I laugh. "It's symbolic."

"Even better."

"I want you there," I say, surprising even myself. "At the appointment."

His response is instant. "Of course, I'll be there."

Something warm blooms in my chest.

This tattoo isn't for him. It's for *me*. But I want him to witness it—to see the woman I'm choosing to become, not despite the pain, but because of it.

"I can't wait for the weekend," he says, his voice earnest, full of longing.

"Me neither. Can this week just hurry up?" I respond, smiling to myself, imagining the moment when I'll see him again.

"I hate this long-distance thing. I mean, the buildup is nice," I smile at the implication, "but I don't like being apart," he confesses, his honesty catching me off guard and making my heart skip.

That statement jolts me awake. "Oh, really? You want to move back to Texas?" I ask, half-joking but secretly hopeful. My mind races with the possibility.

"No, Texas wasn't for me..." he trails off, his voice quieter, as if unsure whether to say the words that are lingering between us. The unspoken implication is clear, though: maybe I could move to California.

"Well, things are getting weird at work with this complaint. Maybe I should look for jobs in both Austin and Orange County and see which one comes through first," I say, testing the waters, half-joking but with a hint of seriousness beneath it.

"I like that idea," he replies quickly, his enthusiasm clear in his voice.

We shift our focus to planning his visit for the weekend, but the conversation lingers in the air, thick with unspoken possibilities. After we hang up, I lay in bed, staring at the ceiling as Damian's words echoed in my mind: "I like that idea." The thought of moving to California felt both exhilarating and terrifying. Could I really leave everything behind—my family, my friends, my life in Austin—for the possibility of something more? What if it didn't work out? What if I regretted it?

But then I thought about Damian—the way he made me feel seen, valued, wanted in a way I had never felt before. Maybe this wasn't just about him. Maybe it was about me, about finding a new version of myself. The idea lingered, equal parts thrilling and daunting.

The next morning, a meeting is called at work, and it doesn't take a genius to sense that bad news is coming. My boss strides to the front, her perfectly coiffed blonde bob gleaming under the fluorescent lights. Her tan slacks and crisp white satin blouse are immaculately tucked, cinched at the waist with a sleek gold belt. When she speaks, her words come out in a polished, rehearsed cadence—more like a legal disclaimer than a genuine expression of concern.

"We want to be open and honest about the situation at hand... We won't be able to keep the company going much longer with the complaint. We want to give you enough time to find something else and understand if you decide to leave as soon as you secure another position..."

As she drones on, her words fading into a dull hum, I felt a strange mix of emotions. Fear, yes, but also a spark of something else—relief? For months, I'd felt stuck, my days a monotonous loop of resumes and recruitment calls. Maybe this was the push I needed to finally make a change. But what kind of change? The idea of moving to California both thrilled and terrified me, like standing on the edge of a cliff, unsure if I'd fall or fly.

My sister, Maya, calls me as soon as the meeting ends. "What the hell are we going to do?" she exclaims.

"I don't know," I reply, the weight of the situation settling heavily in my chest. "Maybe I'll look for jobs outside of Texas. I need a change."

"What are you talking about, Talia?" she asks, clearly confused by the sudden shift in my mood.

"I don't know. Don't listen to me. It's been a crazy week," I say, trying to brush it off.

But the idea of California—of change—won't leave me alone. It lingers, soft but persistent, like a whisper I can't quite silence.

We're not even fully back together. I'm still trying to figure out how I feel—about him, about everything. Part of me is thrilled at the thought of starting over. California. Sunshine. A new chapter. A chance to be with Damian.

But then there's the other part—the part that remembers why I had to forgive him in the first place. The lie. The hurt.

I wonder if it's foolish to dream of something so big, so soon. To let myself hope again.

Still… it feels like a sign. Like the Universe is holding out its hand, daring me to leap.

I decide to wait. To see how I feel when we're face-to-face. If being with him still feels like home. If the trust I'm rebuilding can hold the weight of something this big.

Until then, I need to prepare—for him.

And I need to see how he fits into my world… not just mine into his.

I reach for my phone and send Jess a quick text:

Me: *Hey—Damian's coming to town this weekend. I want you to meet him.*

Her response is immediate.

Jess: *UM YES. Finally! I've been waiting for this moment.*

I smile at the screen. That's all I say—nothing about the fight, nothing about Nicole. I want her to meet *this* version of us. I want her to see him as the man I chose—again—after everything.

Sixteen

When the weekend finally arrived, I was buzzing with anticipation, my pulse thrumming with excitement.

And then I saw him.

Damian stepped through the airport doors, his presence hitting me like a jolt of electricity. He looked the same, yet different—more confident, more grounded, more *real.* His eyes locked onto mine, and for a split second, everything else—the noise, the movement, the distance that had weighed on us— faded away.

Then he was in front of me, closing the space between us in two long strides. His arms wrapped around me, pulling me tight against him, like he was afraid to let go.

I inhaled deeply, breathing in his scent—fresh, warm, unmistakably *him.*

"God, I missed you," he murmured into my hair, his breath hot against my skin. "I missed *this.*"

I squeezed him tighter. "You have no idea."

He pulled back just enough to look at me, his eyes dark and hungry. "Oh, I have an idea."

My stomach flipped. I knew that look.

He grabbed his bag, slinging it over his shoulder as he laced his fingers through mine and led me toward the exit. "Come on. We've got a lot of catching up to do."

The moment we were in the car, Damian's hand found my thigh, his grip firm, possessive. He hadn't stopped touching me since he landed, and I didn't want him to.

"Tell me," He said, glancing over at me as he maneuvered onto the highway, "how bad was it?"

I sighed dramatically. "*Torture.*"

A slow smirk spread across his lips. "That bad?"

I leaned closer, running a hand down his arm, feeling the tension there. "Worse."

His fingers inched higher on my leg, his thumb tracing slow circles on my inner thigh. "You should've picked me up sooner, then."

I turned, arching a brow. "Pretty sure your flight had something to do with that."

Damian chuckled, but his grip on me tightened. "Do you remember the last time you picked me up from the Austin airport?"

A wave of heat rolled through me. Oh, I remembered.

Judging by the way his hand was creeping up my leg now, he remembered too.

"Damian," I warned, my voice shaky.

His lips quirked up. "What?"

I shot him a look. "You know *what.*"

He exhaled, shaking his head. "I swear, if we didn't have somewhere to be…"

A delicious thrill shot through me. "We *do* have somewhere to be," I teased, biting my lip. "At least my ass will be out while I get my tattoo."

He groaned, shifting in his seat. "I do love your ass."

I laughed, but my pulse was racing. The tension between us was thick, heavy, *dangerous.*

As we approach the exit, I begin feeling nervous, but determined. Damian holds my hand sensing my nerves.

Inside the shop, the artist preps the stencil. I explain it quietly—the lotus rising from the mud, the Om symbol in the center. My journey. My peace.

I try to act brave, but when the needle starts, I flinch. Damian squeezes my hand, murmuring, "You've got this."

Halfway through, I grit my teeth, tears brimming in my eyes.

"You okay?" he asks, voice low.

I nod. "It hurts. But it's worth it."

And it was. It was perfect, exactly as I imagined it.

After, we head to a nearby bar for a celebratory beer. But halfway through my drink, the room tilts.

"Whoa," I mutter, gripping the table.

Damian is at my side instantly. "Let's get you out of here and get you some juice."

Before we can even make it to the door, the bartender intercepts us, eyes narrowing as he takes in my wobbly step.

"Hey—if she's drunk, you two need to go. I'm not risking a liability."

"I'm not drunk," I mumble, but my voice is weak, my legs unsteady.

Damian steps in smoothly, calm but firm. "She just got a tattoo. She's lightheaded from the pain and adrenaline. We were already on our way out to get her some juice."

The bartender studies me for a second longer, unconvinced but unwilling to argue. He gives a curt nod. "Alright. Just—take care of her."

"Always," Damian says without missing a beat, guiding me toward the door with a protective arm around my waist.

By the time we reach the gas station, I'm trembling, lightheaded, and trying to will the room to stop spinning. Damian runs inside and returns within minutes, a cold bottle of orange juice in hand. He cracks the cap and hands it to me like it's a lifeline.

I take a long sip—and the effect is almost immediate. The sugar hits my bloodstream like a warm rush, flushing through me. The chill in my fingers fades, replaced by a spreading heat, like my body is slowly waking back up. The fog lifts. The spinning slows. My muscles unclench one by one, the weakness in my knees giving way to steady ground again.

"You okay?" he asks gently, brushing a strand of hair from my face.

I nod, taking another drink. "Better," I whisper, almost in disbelief. It's like nothing had happened at all—just a bad moment, erased.

We stay in the parking lot for a moment, his hand in mine. The ache in my hip is throbbing, but my heart feels... full.

He finally breaks the silence. "Your ass did look good."

"Oh yeah?" I laugh, leaning in for a kiss. "You'll have to be gentle tonight," I whisper against his mouth.

"I'll do my best," he murmurs, his fingers slipping behind my neck and pulling me into a deeper kiss, his tongue finding mine.

My phone buzzes. It's Jenni—she's headed to Shooters, where we're supposed to meet her.

Damian drives us there, but his free hand stays on my thigh, roaming slowly upward.

By the time we pull into the parking lot of Shooter's Billiards off Anderson Mill, I am feeling fully recovered. He parks, and his fingers linger on my skin for just a second longer before he exhales and shakes his head.

"Do we have to go in?" he asks, his lips brushing mine—teasing, taunting.

"Yes, we do," I say, my voice low, seductive. "But later... I'll make it up to you."

Inside, Jenni is already waiting at a high-top table with three giant Dos Equis in front of her. The buzz of the place is alive with laughter and the clinking of glasses.

"Holy shit, you're here! Let me see it!" she calls out across the bar.

I lift the hem of my dress, revealing the bandaged tattoo, then show her a picture on my phone.

"It's awesome! I love it!" she says, then turns to Damian. "What do you think?"

"I love it," he replies, wrapping his fingers around mine.

We take our seats and raise our glasses, picking up exactly where we left off—like nothing had changed, and yet everything had.

As we sit down and start drinking, thankfully this beer doesn't make the room spin. The conversation turns to my job. With newfound courage, I blurt out, "Well, since the complaint is moving forward and they basically told us to start looking for new jobs, I've decided—I'm going to apply to jobs in both Austin and California. Whichever place offers me something first, that's where I'll go!"

Jenni and Damian cheer in unison, their excitement heightened by the tipsy haze of the moment. The world feels a little lighter, I feel a spark of possibility—of adventure.

We play some air hockey and pool before we say goodbye to Jenni outside Shooters, but it's more like a smirk and a wave.

"See you at the house. I am going to stop for smokes," she says, giving me a wink before hopping into her car.

The drive home is thick with tension—the kind that wraps around you and makes it hard to breathe. His fingers drift over the inside of my thigh with maddening slowness, igniting a low, aching need in my core. By the time we pull into the driveway, I'm already squirming.

Inside the house, it's quiet. Jenni's room is across the hall, so I head to the bedroom first and put on some music. A sensual playlist fills the space, soft and rhythmic, just enough to cover the sounds I'm pretty sure I won't be able to suppress.

Damian leans against the doorframe, watching me. "Trying to hide how loud I'm gonna make you?"

My breath catches. I shoot him a look over my shoulder, trying to stay composed. "Just being considerate."

He moves into the room, closing the door behind him. "That's sweet of you," he says, his voice dropping as he reaches for me. "But I like when you're loud."

His hands slide down my sides, his fingers teasing the slit of my dress before slipping under it. "Tell me if anything hurts," he murmurs, lips brushing the shell of my ear. "I'll be gentle."

And he is. Torturously so.

He lays me down like I'm made of glass, kissing around the edges of the tattoo, his lips grazing my inner thighs but never quite giving me what I crave. His fingers dance over my skin, skimming, trailing, circling places that make me gasp—but never staying long enough to satisfy.

I arch under him, my body on fire, aching.

"Please," I whisper, breathless. "Damian."

He looks up, his eyes dark with desire, a slow smile tugging at his lips. "Please what?"

"Please... come inside me," I breathe, my voice trembling.

His lips brush mine, his tongue sliding into my mouth with a kiss that steals the last of my restraint.

"This?" he whispers, and finally, finally, he gives me what I need.

It's slow at first—deep, steady, aching. His hands cradle my face like I'm precious, but his rhythm builds with every moan, every whispered plea. The contrast—his gentleness, my desperation—makes it all the more intense. My nails dig into his back as the pleasure crests and crashes over me in waves.

I feel his release, his body tensing as a deep groan moves through him.

He kisses my temple and whispers, "You okay?"

I nod, too dazed to speak, my body still trembling in the aftermath. "Perfect," I finally manage, my voice a ragged whisper.

He pulls me closer, his arms wrapped tight around me.

I'm his.

I wake up to soft kisses on my shoulder and the scent of coffee drifting in from the hallway. Light filters through the blinds, casting golden stripes across the bed, and Damian's arm is still wrapped securely around my waist.

"Morning," he murmurs against my skin.

I hum in response, too comfortable to speak. My muscles ache in all the best ways. He runs his hand slowly down my side, stopping just above my hip.

"Can I see it?" he asks.

I nod and roll onto my back, lifting my shirt slightly so the tattoo is exposed. He sits up beside me, eyes soft as he takes it in.

"It's healing nicely," he says, brushing a fingertip gently near the edge of the bandage. "Time to clean it?"

I nod again, sitting up as he heads to the bathroom and returns with a warm washcloth, some mild soap, and a fresh bandage. He kneels in front of me, hands steady and careful.

The way he tends to me—gentle, focused, completely present—makes my heart ache in the best way. He washes around the ink, dabbing softly, his touch reverent.

"You're really good at this," I say, watching him.

"I've never had a reason to be," he says, glancing up at me with a small, crooked smile. "You bring out new things in me."

Once he's finished, he leans in and kisses my hip. "What's on the agenda today, beautiful?"

I stretch and yawn. "We're meeting my friend Jess later—at Sherlock's Irish Pub. She's been dying to meet you."

He raises an eyebrow. "A pub? Afternoon drinks?"

"More like late afternoon. She'll want to talk, grill you a little. She's protective."

"I like her already."

We head to the kitchen together. I scramble some eggs while Damian butters toast and brews a second pot of coffee. Just as we're sitting down to eat, Jenni comes bounding down the stairs in an oversized sweatshirt and fuzzy socks, her hair in a messy bun and a smug grin on her face.

"Well, good morning, lovebirds," she teases, grabbing a mug from the cabinet.

I freeze with a bite of eggs halfway to my mouth. Damian just smirks.

Jenni pours her coffee and leans against the counter, smirking like she knows *exactly* what went down last night.

"I mean, the music was a nice touch," she says, taking a sip, "but the walls aren't *that* thick."

I groan, hiding my face in my hands. Damian just laughs and shrugs unapologetically.

"I did say I like when she's loud," he quips.

Jenni nearly chokes on her coffee, cackling. "Okay! TMI, but also... respect."

I glare at both of them, cheeks burning. "Can we not?"

She waves a hand and grins. "Relax, I'm happy for you. And I heard Sherlock's, by the way. I'm coming. I need a beer and some girl time."

"You mean a beer and maybe find a cute cowboy time." I tease.

She grins and flips me off as she heads to the fridge. "You don't know me."

Damian leans over and kisses my cheek. "I love your chaos," he whispers.

I smile, feeling full—in every way that matters.

Later that afternoon, we all head out to Sherlock's. We find a cozy booth and grab a few beers from the bar. The place is buzzing with the usual weekend crowd, but in here, tucked away in our little corner, it feels easy.

Not long after, I spot Jess walking in. I wave her over, and her face lights up as she makes her way across the room.

We hug, warm and familiar, and for a moment I feel grounded—like everything is falling into place.

Then I turn toward Damian.

"Jess, this is Damian," I say, grinning—though there's a flicker of nervous energy beneath my smile.

"So nice to finally meet you," Jess says, pulling him into a friendly hug. Damian smiles and introduces himself, and soon the two of them are chatting like old friends. Their laughter mixes with the lively hum of the pub, and I can't help but smile.

"He's awesome!" Jess whispers in my ear, giving me an approving nod.

I nod back, warmth blooming in my chest. It's such a relief to see my friends genuinely like him. For so long, moments like this were laced with tension—wondering what my boyfriend might say, or if my friends would quietly hate him. But tonight feels different. It's light. Easy.

As I lean into a conversation with Jenni, Jess turns back to Damian, a curious smile playing on her lips.

"So," she says casually, "are you thinking about coming back to Texas?"

Damian shakes his head. "No. I want to stay in California."

Jess tilts her head. "Long-distance?"

He pauses, then glances toward me before answering. "I don't want to do long-distance. I want to be with Talia. I'm hoping maybe she'll come to California."

Something flutters in my chest—equal parts excitement and nerves.

Jess gives him a slow nod, her expression softening. "You know she's been through hell and back, right?"

"I do," he says quietly. "And I'm not here to make it harder. I just want a chance to be what she deserves."

My heart catches. I wasn't supposed to hear all of that—but I did. And I can't stop replaying it in my mind.

Jess smiles at him—warmer now, less protective. "Good. Because if you mess this up, you're gonna have more than just her to answer to."

Jess heads out to another party, but before she leaves, she gives me a look—a glowing, joyful kind of look that says, *you deserve this.* That one glance is all I need.

The hours slip by in laughter, clinking glasses, and easy touches beneath the table. Jenni disappears with a flirty cowboy from the bar for a while, but Damian and I barely notice. We're tangled in our own world of stolen kisses and playful banter.

"You know," he murmurs, brushing a strand of hair from my cheek, "your eyes give everything away. It's like they tell on you before you even speak."

I tilt my head at him. "Is that a compliment or are you making fun of me?"

"Oh, definitely a compliment. It's dangerous, though," he adds, grinning. "I could get addicted to it."

I laugh, and he leans in, his lips brushing mine— soft, slow. The kiss deepens, and I feel my heart flutter in my chest, a thousand unsaid things rushing between us in that single, captivating moment.

When Jenni finally returns, cheeks flushed and eyes sparkling, she spots us cuddled close and gasps dramatically. "Hold that pose!" she says, pulling out her phone.

"Jenni, no—" I protest, laughing.

"Shush. This is gold," she says, snapping a few photos. "For memories. And possibly your wedding slideshow."

Damian pulls me closer and kisses my cheek just as she clicks again, making me blush.

It's 2 a.m. now and we find ourselves at a classic late-night diner, craving breakfast to cap off the night. Jenni is half-laying in the booth, lazily feeding herself French fries with a dazed grin plastered on her face. Damian and I share a plate of fluffy buttermilk pancakes and perfectly golden hash browns.

The food is comforting, satisfying, and grounding. As I take another bite, I feel a quiet sense of peace. The restlessness that's swirled inside me for so long seems to settle, if only for this moment.

The cab ride home is a blur of roaming hands and deep, lingering kisses, the urgency between us growing with every mile. Jenni, oblivious to it all, has already passed out against the window, her soft snores providing an unintentional soundtrack to our stolen moments. Every touch, every heated glance makes the ride feel endless, the anticipation coiling tight between us.

By the time we finally pull up to the house, we're both barely holding back the need to rush inside. But just as I step out of the cab, my stomach lets out a loud, ominous gurgle—a sharp, gut-churning reminder of all the greasy food we'd just inhaled.

Damian pauses mid-step, giving me a wary glance. "Uh… that didn't sound promising."

I force a smile, waving him off. "I'm fine. Totally fine."

Jenni mumbles something incoherent before stumbling off to bed, while Damian disappears into the upstairs bathroom. I make my way downstairs to the powder room, but with each step, nausea creeps up like a slow-moving nightmare. And then, suddenly, it's not creeping anymore.

Oh no.

Within minutes, my worst fear is confirmed— food poisoning. And judging by the very distinct groans echoing from upstairs, I'm not the only one suffering.

What had been shaping up to be a night full of fun and sexy promises quickly turns into a race to the bathroom, both of us making frequent, miserable trips, alternating between dramatic suffering and weak laughter.

At one point, we both crawl back into bed, completely drained. Damian flops onto his back, clutching his stomach like a man on the brink of death. "Well," he rasps, a small, pained smile tugging at his lips, "that's *one* way to bond."

I groan, rolling onto my side to face him. "If we can survive this, we can survive anything," I say, my voice still hoarse from the ordeal.

He chuckles, eyes half-lidded with exhaustion. "Nothing like simultaneous food poisoning to really solidify a relationship."

The night had been messy, ridiculous, and absolutely *not* the romantic reunion I'd envisioned. But as I drift off to sleep with Damian's arm draped over me—our battle wounds still fresh—I realize something.

Perfect moments are overrated.

The real magic is in this—the chaos, the imperfection, the way we can still find laughter even when everything goes sideways. Because at the end of the day, we're in this together. And that's all that really matters.

Seventeen

It's Monday morning, and the remnants of the weekend fun with Damian linger in the form of a mild, slightly embarrassing hangover. I take a deep sip of coffee, hoping the caffeine will jumpstart my brain. Curled up at my desk, I tuck one leg beneath me, the other perched up on my chair as I settle into my usual work-from-home position. I'm dressed in my go-to comfy-but-cute outfit—soft, fitted joggers and an oversized off-the-shoulder sweater that drapes just right. My hair is piled into a messy bun, loose strands framing my face in a way that looks effortless, even though it took me three tries to get it right.

With a quiet sigh, I open LinkedIn and type "Recruiter" into the job search bar, filtering results for both Austin and Orange County. The soft glow of my laptop screen illuminates the room as the page populates with listings, each one holding the potential for something new. I lean forward, fingers hovering over the keys, meticulously combing through each post, my mind already running through the possibilities. I apply to a few Recruiting roles before opening the search back up to general jobs.

One particular job catches my eye: a swim coach position at Westwood Country Club. It's not full-time, but it's perfect for some summer income while I search for something more permanent. Swimming has always been close to my heart—I was a competitive swimmer for ten years and taught swim lessons and coached from the time I was fourteen until my early twenties. The idea of getting back to the pool, especially working with kids again, excites me.

Without hesitation, I apply and send a quick email introducing myself. The following day, I receive a response inviting me to meet the Head Coach at the club.

The interview takes place poolside under a bright Texas sun. As we talk, it's clear we click. He asks about my experience, and I dive into stories of coaching summer league swim teams and the joy of teaching beginners their first strokes. Before the meeting ends, he offers me the job on the spot. I leave the club with a bounce in my step, thrilled to be back in a space I love.

But that's just the beginning. Before the week ends, an email lands in my inbox. It's from a physician recruiting firm based in Dana Point, California. They're interested in interviewing me for a full-cycle recruiting role. My stomach does a flip as I read the email. This isn't just a step forward; it's a leap.

The phone interview is scheduled quickly, and when I speak to the owner, he walks me through the job responsibilities. It's a full-cycle role, which means I'll be handling every aspect of recruitment: finding physicians, initiating contact, scheduling interviews, and extending offers. While I've only ever been involved in sourcing candidates, I project confidence, assuring him I'm ready for the challenge.

Then we discuss compensation: a lower base salary than I currently make, but with significant earning potential through incentives. I mull it over as he explains the structure, but I can't deny the allure of moving forward with this opportunity. By the end of the call, we agree I'll come out for an in-person interview during the first week of June. When I hang up, the reality of it all begins to sink in. This is happening—and quickly.

I call Damian to share the news.

"I have an interview in California!" I announce, my voice buzzing with excitement.

"That's amazing!" he exclaims. "When are you coming out?"

"The first week of June," I reply. "But…I was thinking we could make a little trip out of it. Maybe head down to San Diego afterward?"

"Absolutely. We'll make a whole thing of it," Damian says, and I can hear the smile in his voice.

It's Thursday, and I have plans to meet my sister, Maya, for yoga with Sanieya again. I am excited to see what spiritual beauty awaits us.

When I walk into the studio, the scent of lavender and eucalyptus instantly calms me. I find a spot in the back row and lay out mats for both of us. Maya arrives a few minutes later, dropping into a seated stretch beside me.

"So," I start, excitement bubbling in my voice, "I have an interview with a recruiting firm in California in June!"

Maya lifts an eyebrow, her expression amused. "Oh wow, so the *California thing* wasn't just a weird phase then?"

I shake my head. "Nope. I want to go somewhere new, do new things, figure stuff out on my own."

She tilts her head, giving me a knowing look. "You mean *with* someone new?"

I bite my lip to keep from grinning too hard. She knows me too well.

Instead of answering, I shift the conversation. "How about you? Have you found a new role yet?"

She exhales, rolling her shoulders. "Not yet. I don't know… maybe I'll become a yoga instructor," she says, half-joking, half-serious.

I glance at her, my expression turning approving. "Honestly? You'd be great at it."

Before I can respond, Sanieya walks in, her presence instantly commanding the room. She moves with an effortless grace, her energy both calming and powerful. The soft hum of meditative music fills the space, and the class instinctively quiets, settling into focus.

She begins class as she always does, with a message. Today's is about discomfort.

"We are wired to avoid discomfort," she says, her voice smooth, steady. "The moment things get hard, we retreat. We tell ourselves the challenge is too much, that we aren't ready. But growth doesn't happen in ease. It happens in the moments we want to give up—but don't."

Her words settle over me as we transition into pigeon pose. The stretch is deep, almost unbearable. My hip flexors scream, my breath turns ragged, but Sanieya's voice anchors me.

"Breathe into it," she instructs. "Notice where your mind goes. Does it tell you to escape? To shift out of the pose? Stay with it. Let the discomfort teach you something."

My muscles tremble, the ache intensifies. And yet, I stay.

How many times have I turned away from something hard? How often have I chosen familiarity over the unknown, comfort over growth? The questions stir something deeper than I expect, threading through past choices, unspoken fears, roads I never dared to take.

I exhale slowly, releasing more than just tension.

As we finally lay in savasana, her words are still echoing in my head, they linger in my mind like an invitation—one I'm finally ready to accept.

I grab a quick bite to eat before heading to the pool for my first day coaching. Coaching the swim team reminded me of something I'd almost forgotten—the joy of making an impact, of helping others find their potential. And now, with the recruiting job on the horizon, I felt like I was finally piecing together a life that was both fulfilling and exciting. California wasn't just about Damian—it was about rediscovering who I was and what I wanted.

The weeks fly by in a blur of preparation and anticipation. I dive into swim coaching, spending afternoons at the pool with kids who remind me how much I love the sport. Their laughter and determination inspire me and give me a sense of purpose as I wait for what's next. It's also not a bad way to get my tan back.

Before I know it, the day arrives. I'm on a plane bound for California, a mix of nerves and excitement bubbling in my chest. First, I have my interview, and then we're heading down to San Diego for the weekend. On the plane, I practice my interview answers and review my résumé. I feel ready.

When I arrive at John Wayne Airport, Damian is there to pick me up. I'm already dressed and prepared for the interview, so we can head straight to the office. Damian gets out of the car to give me a hug and grab my bag. When he embraces me and gives me a kiss, I can't explain the feeling. It's like home—safe, loved, and exactly where I'm supposed to be.

"How was your flight?" he asks.

"It was good—nothing too crazy," I reply with a smile.

It's a quick drive to Dana Point where the office is, and I'm right on time for my interview.

"Good luck, babe. You've got this," Damian says, encouraging me.

"Thanks," I say, crossing my fingers.

The interview lasts about an hour and goes as well as I could have hoped. The team is warm, welcoming, and genuinely eager to teach. There's an energy in the room—one of excitement, of possibility. They're interested in what I can bring to the table, and for a reason I can't explain, I feel like I belong in this space.

"This will be new for you. How confident are you that you can learn the role quickly?" the owner asks, his tone curious but measured.

This will *all* be new for me. New job, new boyfriend, new state. The thought bubbles up, but I push it back. I won't let doubt speak for me.

"Yes, it will be," I admit, meeting his gaze. "But I've had great mentors at my current firm who have taught me so much. I know I'll learn a lot here, too. More than anything, I'm excited about the work and ready to put in the effort to grow into this role."

He nods, considering my words, and I catch a brief, approving smile.

By the time I step out of the office, the weight in my chest has lifted. The nervous energy that followed me here has transformed into something lighter—something that feels a lot like hope.

I leave with a smile on my face, the kind that lingers.

Damian is waiting for me in the car.

"How'd it go?" he asks.

"It went really great. I think I got it," I reply confidently.

"That's awesome. Are you ready to go?"

"Yes, let's do this!" I say, excited for what's next.

The hour-and-a-half drive to San Diego feels like it lasts only minutes as Damian and I sing along to our favorite songs, letting the music carry us through the scenic route. There's a certain magic in the way we effortlessly talk about everything and nothing—laughing at inside jokes, sharing random thoughts, and dreaming about the future. His voice is a steady, comforting presence beside me, and I feel like everything is right in the world.

"You know," Damian says as we approach the city, glancing at me with that mischievous smile I can never get enough of, "I think this weekend is going to be perfect. It has to be better than the last visit."

"Yes it will, just no diners this time," I reply, shaking my head. I glance at him, and for a moment, everything outside the car fades away. There's only Damian and I—together.

When we finally reach San Diego, Damian pulls into the charming streets of the Gaslamp District. He parks the car, and I look up to see the quaint, yet stylish façade of the historic boutique hotel, The Sofia. It's everything I imagined and more—its vintage charm with modern touches speaks to our shared love for the little, cozy spots that feel both intimate and special.

"How cool is this hotel!" I say, my eyes lighting up as I take in the surroundings.

"I thought you'd like it. Let's check in, and then I've got something fun planned for tonight." His wink makes me smile, and I can't help but feel a rush of excitement.

We step inside, and the hotel has this cozy, old world vibe. We drop off our bags in the room, which has a view of the lively street below, and then head down to the bar. Damian orders us a couple of cocktails—his favorite Seven and Seven, and I go for a Mandarin and 7 —we find a quiet corner.

"To us," Damian raises his glass, his eyes locking with mine. "To this weekend, to new beginnings, and to whatever comes next for us."

"Cheers," I say, feeling a deep warmth spread through me. I clink my glass with his, savoring the moment as I meet his gaze. The world seems to slow down as I feel a wave of love and contentment wash over me.

After drinks, we wander through the vibrant streets of San Diego, strolling hand in hand, finding little hidden gems along the way—charming shops, cozy cafés, and of course, the beach. We make our way to the water, the waves crashing gently against the shore, their rhythmic lull blending with the cool evening breeze. The city lights shimmer in the distance, but here, under the stars, it felt like we were in our own little world. Damian's hand in mine was warm and steady, grounding me even as my thoughts soared with dreams of what could be. In that moment, the future didn't feel so daunting—it felt wide open, full of possibility.

"This feels like one of those moments we'll talk about for years," Damian says, his voice low and thoughtful.

I nod, my heart swelling with affection. "It's perfect," I whisper back. "Just like you."

We walk barefoot along the beach, the sand cool beneath our feet as we share stories, dreams, and laughter. There's something undeniably magical about these moments—simple, yet filled with such meaning.

When we reach the front of the hotel, Damian spots a statue of a man pointing toward the entrance. Without missing a beat, he mimics the statue's pose and starts singing, "Hey you there... I see you over there." It's a line from one of our favorite songs that we've been playing on repeat all weekend. I can't help but laugh, and Damian's infectious grin only makes it worse. I quickly pull out my phone and snap a picture of him mid-performance, capturing the moment for us to laugh about later. We both burst into laughter, the sound echoing around us as we walk through the doors of the hotel, feeling lighter and more connected than ever.

We are still giggling until we reach our hotel room door. I lean casually against the door while Damian looks for his key. Our eyes meet and his hand finds my waist as we embrace in a kiss.

The door clicks open, and he leads me backward through the dimly lit hall, his hands never leaving me. We stumble into the room, laughter melting into something deeper, something electric.

Damian drops onto the lounge sofa overlooking the city, the neon lights painting his features in shades of blue and gold. I feel his gaze on me, hot and possessive, as I let the straps of my dress slip from my shoulders, the satin whispering against my skin before pooling at my feet. Beneath, I'm wearing a fitted cream satin bodice that hugs every curve, the delicate matching thong peeking just below.

His eyes darken, his hunger palpable. "You're stunning," he breathes, his voice thick with desire.

I step forward, unbuttoning his shirt one button at a time.

I sink to my knees before him, my hands gliding over his thighs as I undo his belt, tugging it free before removing his pants. I keep my eyes locked on his

My lips find his abdomen, trailing kisses along the ridges of muscle, tasting the salt of his skin. I wrap my hand around him, teasing the edges with my

210

mouth, my tongue tracing slow, deliberate circles. His breath stutters, his fingers threading through my hair, guiding me with a desperation that only fuels my own.

"Talia..." he groans, his voice a broken plea. His head falls back, his breath quickening, a low growl escaping his throat.

Before I can push him further, he pulls me up and onto his lap, his mouth crashing into mine with a fervor that steals my breath. His hands grip my hips, pulling the delicate cream thong to the side, he guides me as I lower myself onto him, the sensation so intense I can't help the gasp that escapes my lips.

I start to move, rocking my hips against him, our bodies aligning perfectly. His hands clutch me harder, his fingers digging into my skin like he can't bear the thought of letting me go. I set the pace, slow and deliberate, teasing him as I roll my hips until his breath comes faster, his control unraveling.

"God, you feel..." His words trail off, lost to the heat building between us.

I lean forward, my hands braced against his chest as I ride him, my rhythm growing desperate and wild. His eyes never leave mine, his gaze filled with so much want it's almost overwhelming.

His hands slide up my back, pressing me closer until our mouths meet in a kiss that's all heat and hunger. His body tenses beneath me, with each relentless movement, pulling us closer to the edge until there was nothing left but warmth and the sound of our tangled breaths.

The following days are a blur of romance—sunny mornings spent wrapped in each other's arms, lazy breakfasts at the hotel's café, and endless conversations over candlelit dinners. Damian has this way of making every moment feel special, like the world outside doesn't matter. Every time he touches my hand or pulls me close, I can't help but feel like this is exactly where I'm meant to be.

On our last night, we take a slow walk back to the hotel after a delicious dinner at a rooftop restaurant with stunning views of the city. The air is crisp, laced with salt from the ocean and the faint hum of city life below. Damian stops me at the entrance, his hand entwining with mine before he pulls me into his arms.

"This weekend has been incredible, Talia," he murmurs, his breath warm against my ear. There's a fire in his voice, an urgency threaded with hope. It's like he's already picturing our future here, together.

"It has been," I say softly, looking up at him, my heart full and brimming with certainty. "And I know there's more to come." For once, my words aren't clouded by doubt or hesitation. I feel it — this is where I'm meant to be. With him.

"I can't wait for the next chapter with you," Damian says, brushing a lock of hair from my face, his eyes searching mine for assurance. "I want you here, Talia. With me. Every day. I love you."

The words hit me like a rush of warmth, flooding my chest with something I can't contain. "I love you, too," I whisper, my voice trembling with equal parts joy and relief. Saying it feels right. More than right. Like something I've been holding back for far too long. "And I think… no, I know this is where I belong." I can feel the truth of it settling into my bones. I'm ready to make this work, to build something real with him.

On Sunday, Damian drops me off at the San Diego airport. The goodbyes feel heavier this time, but not with doubt — with anticipation.

"Next time, it's going to be you moving down here," he says with a smile, but there's no uncertainty in his tone. Just hope and determination.

"Oh yeah?" I tease, my own excitement spilling over. "Well, hopefully, I get the offer tomorrow, and we can be together here in California." My voice is light, but the promise beneath it is solid. I'm leaving this up to fate, but my heart is already here. With him.

His grin widens, eyes glinting with relief and something deeper. "I'm holding you to that." His fingers squeeze mine, a silent vow between us.

As I walk away, my heart feels impossibly full. I don't glance back — not because I'm afraid, but because I know where I'm headed. This isn't an ending. It's the beginning of everything I've been waiting for.

Monday morning arrives, bringing an offer from Carver Reed to join the team. I'm moving to California. It's happening.

As I read the offer email one more time, a strange mix of emotions wash over me—excitement, fear, and something deeper: pride. I'd spent so long feeling stuck, unsure of my next step, but now, I was taking control. This wasn't just a move to California. It was a move toward the life I wanted, the life I deserved. I wasn't afraid of what came next.

I picked up the phone with shaking hands and dialed Damian.

"Babe! I got the offer," I said, my voice trembling just slightly. "I'm coming to California."

"Wait—really? You're really coming?" His voice sounded groggy, confused, half asleep.

"I am."

He let out a sleepy laugh, that low, warm sound I already loved. "Talia, that's amazing. I knew it would happen."

"I know," I breathed, and then sighed. "Now I just have to tell my parents... and my friends. That should be interesting."

He was quiet for a beat. "Yeah... same here. I haven't told my family yet either."

"Oh?" I asked, surprised.

"I wanted to be sure before I said anything." he admitted with a nervous chuckle. "Still—you're coming. That's all that matters."

We both laughed—nervous, giddy, and a little scared

As I hung up, the knot in my stomach tightened. My parents had always been my biggest supporters, but they were also fiercely protective. I could already hear my dad's voice, laced with concern: "California? That's so far from home? Are you sure about this, Mija?"

But beneath the anxiety was a quiet strength—a determination to show them I was ready for this. I wasn't running away; I was running toward something, toward someone, and for the first time in a long time, it felt like I was exactly where I needed to be.

Eighteen

Telling my parents about my plans to move to California feels like something that should be done in person, so I plan a weekend trip and make the three-hour drive to their high-rise apartment in downtown Dallas.

Their apartment is a small but luxurious two-bedroom space, with ultra-modern features that make it feel sleek and sophisticated. The open-concept living area boasts floor-to-ceiling windows that offer a stunning view of the Dallas skyline, and the kitchen gleams with stainless steel appliances and marble countertops. The furnishings are minimalist yet elegant, with plush gray sofas and vibrant artwork adding pops of color to the space. The building itself feels exclusive, and the parking garage is filled with expensive cars—sleek sports cars and luxury SUVs that seem to speak of success and ambition.

I've told my mom about Damian in passing, but my parents have never met him, and I know this news will be a shock. When I arrive, we decide to walk over to our favorite brunch spot, Breadwinners. It's one of those places that always feels warm and welcoming, with the smell of freshly baked goods wafting through the air.

My mom looks young for her age, with a small frame, fair skin and brunette hair streaked with blonde and gray highlights that catch the sunlight as we walk. Her green eyes are sharp yet kind, a feature that always gives her an air of approachability. Beside her, my dad is tall and handsome, his Hispanic heritage evident in his warm brown eyes and beautiful white-gray curly hair that frames his face. His kind demeanor and easy smile make him the type of person who can put anyone at ease, and I've always admired the way he seems to radiate warmth.

We place our orders, and as our drinks arrive, my dad and I clink our bloody mary glasses together.

"Salute," we both say in unison, smiling as we take a sip. My mom raises her water glass. She has never been a drinker.

"So, how are the interviews going?" my dad asks, setting his glass down.

I take a deep breath. "Well, you know I went to California for that interview with the physician recruiting firm," I begin. "They offered me the job." I take another sip, bracing for their reaction.

My parents exchange a glance—proud, yet concerned.

"That's great. Congrats," my dad says, his tone steady but measured.

"Does that mean you're taking it? Are you for sure moving to California?" my mom asks, her voice carefully neutral but tinged with worry.

"I want to take it. The only downside is the commission-based pay. It's a little scary," I admit, addressing the exact concern I know she'll raise next.

"Yes, that's something to think about," she replies, her brows knitting slightly. "Especially with how expensive California is."

I nod. "I know, but...I've never moved away from home. I was supposed to go to Boston or New York for college, but I couldn't afford it back then." My voice softens as I continue. "I want a fresh start. Something new and different," I say, my voice steady but carrying the weight of all the reasons I haven't yet spoken aloud—the years I spent stuck in a cycle of bad relationships, the dreams I put on hold, the version of myself I'm still learning to love.

My dad leans back in his chair, his thoughtful brown eyes meeting mine. After a moment, he smiles kindly, the kind of smile that always made me feel like no problem was too big to solve. "We get that, sweetie. We just want you to do what makes you happy." His reassurance means everything.

My mom, on the other hand, stays quiet for a beat too long, her fork hovering above her plate. "I just hope you're not rushing into anything," she finally says, her tone soft but pointed. "You've been through so much already. I just don't want you to get hurt again."

The words land harder than I expect, like a pebble hitting the surface of a still pond, sending ripples of doubt through me. I force a smile, trying to ignore the small voice in the back of my mind that wonders if she's right.

"I know, Mom," I say, keeping my tone as reassuring as I can. "But worst case, I go, I hate it, and I move back. It's not forever."

She nods, her lips pressing together in that way she does when she wants to say more but decides against it. The silence that follows feels heavy, but I let it linger. I've already made up my mind.

As the silence stretches between us on the walk back to their apartment, I can feel my mom's thoughts brewing. Finally, she clears her throat. "So, what about Damian?" she asks, her tone casual, but her eyes scanning me carefully.

My heart skips, though I keep my expression neutral. "What about him?" I ask lightly, but her question lingers like a challenge.

"Well, will you two be living together?" she presses, her voice soft but firm, like she's testing the weight of the idea.

I stop walking and turn to her. "Yes, Mom, we will." My voice is steady, but I feel the unspoken tension building between us. I've rehearsed this in my head, yet now, standing in front of her, I suddenly feel like a teenager breaking curfew.

She hesitates, her lips pressing into a thin line. "I just worry you're moving too quickly," she says gently, her concern apparent. "I mean, I don't want you with Edgar—God knows that wasn't healthy—but we don't really know Damian. We've never even met him."

Her words sting more than I expect, and doubt bubbles to the surfaces again despite myself. "I know, Mom," I say, my tone softening. "But you'll meet him soon. I promise."

She studies me for a moment, her gaze searching my face for something. "You're sure about this?" she asks, almost pleading.

I nod, swallowing the lump in my throat. "I am. And again worst case, if it doesn't work out, I'll come back. But I have to try, Mom. I need this."

The finality in my voice seems to quell her questions, though I can still see the worry etched in her expression. She offers a small, tentative smile. "Okay, sweetheart. I just want you to be happy."

After leaving my parents' house, I stop by my sister Esme's place to see her and my niece and nephew. She recently moved to Dallas, and I haven't had much time with them. When I walk in, she's in full mama mode, juggling a toddler and a baby. While she feeds the baby, I play dress-up with my niece, laughing as she teeters around in her mama's high heels, giggling with every wobbly step.

"You ready for one of these?" Esme nods toward the baby, a knowing smile on her lips.

"One day." I return her smile, warmth spreading through me at the thought. I've always wanted to be a mom—there's never been a question in my mind. And now, with Damian and the move to California on the horizon, that dream feels closer. More tangible.

"Mom and Dad still processing the news?" Esme asks, her tone teasing but her gaze curious.

I let out a laugh. "Yeah, I think so. They're happy for me. Worried, of course. But I think they can see how much I want this."

"They'll come around," Esme says, her voice gentle. "They always do. Especially when they see you're happy."

"I am happy." And I mean it. The decision to move to California feels right. More than that—it feels like a step toward everything I've been longing for.

Esme shifts the baby to her other arm and gives me a knowing look. "And who knows? Maybe you'll be over here chasing little ones of your own soon enough."

The thought sends a flutter of excitement through me. "Maybe," I say, the word laced with hope.

We share a smile before my niece tugs on my hand, demanding my attention once more. I let myself be pulled into her tiny world of princesses and glitter, before I have to head back to Austin.

I call Damian on my drive home, the sound of my tires humming along the highway filling the silence before he picks up.

"So, how did it go with your parents?" he asks, his voice warm, but I can sense the slight tension in his words.

I take a deep breath, my fingers tapping lightly on the steering wheel. "My family isn't really sure what to think, to be honest," I admit, the truth feeling heavier than I expected.

He's quiet for a moment, then I ask, "Have you talked to your mom and dad about us?"

I can sense his wince at the question. "I don't really talk to my dad like that, to be honest. He knows I'm seeing someone though," he says, the words a little more clipped than I expected.

Damian's voice softens, and I can almost picture him squinting his eyes, the way he always does when he's thinking. "Now, my mom is another story," he continues. "She's a little upset about Nicole. I guess Nicole called her the night of the Facebook incident."

I frown, my grip tightening on the phone. "I didn't realize they were still talking like that." The thought stings more than I expect, but I keep my voice steady, trying not to show how hurt I feel.

He lets out a quiet sigh, and I can sense him shifting. "My mom just wants me to be happy, but she's not sure about meeting anyone new until I'm sure," Damian says, his words slower now, as though he's choosing them carefully. "But now that she knows we're moving in together, I think it'll be OK."

"Oh…OK," I reply, trying to keep the disappointment out of my voice, but I can feel it creeping in. I know he's being honest with me, but somehow, it still stings. "I mean, I guess that makes sense."

There's a long pause before Damian speaks again, softer now. "Talia, I know it's complicated, but I want you to know that I'm serious about us. I want you to move here with me."

I swallow hard, forcing a smile even though he can't see it. "I know, Damian. I know."

The words linger between us as the miles stretch on, the silence almost comfortable now, but still, a quiet ache settles in my chest.

Damian and I settle on a July 1st move date. By then, I'll have finished coaching the summer swim team and can get out of my lease. Damian takes charge of finding us an apartment, which I'm more than happy to leave in his capable hands.

Not wanting to haul my entire apartment across state lines, I start selling furniture and other belongings on Craigslist. It's bittersweet but freeing to let go of things I've held onto for years.

Jenni has a new job at another apartment complex just down the road and will be moving there over the next few weeks. I'm excited for her, proud even—but underneath the happiness is a sadness I can't shake. Our short time as roommates is coming to an end far sooner than either of us wanted.

One afternoon, we're sitting cross-legged on my bedroom floor, surrounded by piles of clothes, a half-empty bottle of prosecco between us.

"Keep or toss?" Jenni holds up a glittery crop top she wore exactly once to a New Year's Eve party.

I squint at it. "Toss. To disco."

Jenni cackles and tosses it into the donation pile. "Fair."

Just as I'm sorting through a stack of jeans, my phone buzzes with a message from Damian: *"I think I found it. Check this out!"*

Attached are several photos. I swipe through them, my heart skipping.

"Oh my God," I say, holding the phone out to Jenni. "Look at this!"

She leans in, cradling her prosecco like it's sacred. "Ohhh… that's cute. That patio? I can already see string lights and wine nights."

"I have to call him." I step out into the hallway and press Damian's name.

"Damian, it's perfect!" I say, my voice bubbling with excitement.

"Right?" he says, clearly grinning. "It's a mile from your new office and two miles from the beach. We could ride our bikes on the weekends. What do you think?"

"I think I'm already imagining us there," I reply softly, picturing us sipping coffee on that little patio in the mornings, filling the space with laughter, building something new together.

He laughs, and it sends a flutter through my chest. "I knew you'd love it. I'll lock it down tomorrow."

The thought of this place being ours feels surreal. "This is really happening," I whisper, more to myself than to him.

"It is," Damian says, his voice full of quiet certainty. "And I can't wait for you to get here."

I return to the bedroom, still clutching my phone like it's something fragile and glowing. Jenni's trying on one of my old jackets in front of the mirror.

"So? Is it the one?" she asks.

"It's the one," I say, falling back onto the pile of clothes.

She turns around, her smile soft. "I'm so happy for you, T. Like, *really* happy. But damn, I'm going to miss this."

I nod, a lump forming in my throat. "Me too. It's all happening so fast."

Jenni flops down next to me, topping off our glasses. "Well, at least now I have a beach to visit whenever I want."

I grin. "And you better visit. Like, often."

"Oh, I will. And you better believe I'm throwing you the most epic goodbye party this town has ever seen. Drinks. Dancing. Karaoke. Maybe a mechanical bull."

I laugh, wiping the corner of my eye. "God, I love you."

"I know," she says with a wink, clinking her glass to mine. "Now drink up—we've got memories to pack."

Things are really falling into place—the job, the apartment, the life I've only dreamed of. But with every step forward, the goodbyes are getting harder.

Next, it's time to tell my sweet Bella that I'll be leaving. I've been dreading this conversation, knowing how hard it will be. Lindsay and I already planned for me to pick Bella up after school and have her for the weekend.

As I walk into the school to sign her out, there's a new person at the front desk. She asks for my ID, so I hand it to her.

"Oh, are you her mom?" she asks, her tone curious.

"Oh no, I'm her Talia," I reply, as if that explains everything.

The confusion on her face is obvious.

"Yes," she continues, "she says the same thing, that you're her Talia."

She laughs a little, still trying to piece it together.

"I used to be with her father, and her mother and I are good friends. I take care of Bella like a third parent," I explain, hoping to make it simpler.

"Oh, I see," she says, the realization sinking in.

I've never liked the word "stepmother"—it never felt right for our relationship. Bella and I have something special, something uniquely ours.

Bella walks out, her arms wide open, yelling, "Talia, you're here!"

I scoop her into a big hug, her joy contagious. We walk out to the car together, and I get her settled in her car seat before handing her her favorite snack.

"Can we go to Target?" she immediately asks, her face lighting up with excitement.

I giggle. "Yes, we'll go to Target this weekend. I promise. But first, tonight we'll do one of our movie nights," I say.

She smiles and nods eagerly. Later, as we snuggle up in bed, I pass her some popcorn before starting the movie.

"So, Bella," I begin gently, "you know things have been a little different lately."

She nods solemnly, her big eyes fixed on me.

"I know it's been hard that your dad and I aren't together anymore, but I hope you know how much I love you."

"I love you too, Talia," she says in her sweet, unwavering voice.

I take a deep breath. "Well, I have a new job. I'm going to be moving to California," I say, holding back tears.

"California? Like Disneyland?" she asks, her face lighting up at the idea.

"Yes, California like Disneyland," I confirm, smiling at her enthusiasm.

"Can I come visit you and we go to Disneyland?" she asks.

"Of course," I say, surprised and relieved by her excitement.

"I'm so excited to go to Disneyland," she says, turning back to find the remote and pressing play to start the movie.

I watch her for a moment, marveling at her resilience and her ability to find joy even in the midst of change. She's such an amazing little girl, and I feel so grateful to have her in my life.

I head downstairs to grab some more popcorn, heart still tender from the conversation, when the doorbell rings. I glance at the clock—too late for deliveries. My stomach tightens as I open the door.

It's Edgar.

He stands on the porch, hands shoved into his pockets, eyes flicking past me as if searching for something.

"I knew Bella was here," he says. "Lindsay told me you were picking her up."

Before I can respond, a joyful voice calls from the stairs behind me.

"Daddy!" Bella runs past me and throws her arms around his waist.

He scoops her into a hug, smiling down at her like nothing in the world has changed. But it has. All of it.

I cross my arms. "Edgar, you can't just show up like this."

"I just wanted to see her." He looks back at me with a shrug, but I can tell there's more behind it.

"Talia is moving to California!" Bella announces proudly. "And I get to go to Disneyland when I visit her!"

I see it the moment the words hit him. His expression shifts—his smile falters, and his eyes harden.

"Bella," I say gently, "go finish the movie, sweetheart. I'll be up in just a minute, okay?"

"Okay!" she says, skipping back toward the stairs, completely unaware of the storm brewing behind her.

As soon as she's gone, Edgar turns to me. "You're really leaving?"

"Yes. I got a new job there."

He takes a step closer, his voice low and urgent. "Talia, please. Don't go. I've changed. I'm not the man I was. If you'd just give me a chance... we could make this work. We could be a family again."

The words sting more than I expect. Once, I would have done anything to hear them. But not anymore.

"I can't," I say, my voice steady but quiet. "I'm moving forward. I'm building something new. And this... whatever *this* is? It's not what I want anymore."

His jaw clenches. "But Bella."

"I'll always be part of her life," I say softly. "But not with you. You need to go. I don't want her to hear us and get upset. I won't let her feel confused or caught in the middle."

He hesitates, clearly torn, then slowly nods. But as he turns to leave, he looks back over his shoulder. "Just... think about it, okay? Please."

I close the door gently behind him, leaning against it for a moment as I breathe through the ache in my chest. Some things aren't meant to be reclaimed—no matter how badly someone wants them back.

Upstairs, Bella's laughter floats down the hall. And I remind myself: I'm choosing the life I want.

The next day, around the usual time I'd expect to hear from Damian, there was nothing. No call, no text. I tried sending him a quick message and even called him, but there was no answer. A knot of worry started to form in my stomach, its grip tightening with every passing minute. Damian was usually so reliable, so this silence felt deafening and out of character.

An hour later, my phone buzzed. I lunged for it, relief surging until I read the text: "I wrecked my car. I'll have to call you later—trying to deal with this."

My heart sank, a wave of dread washing over me as I quickly typed back, "Oh no! Are you okay? Please call me when you can."

A few minutes later, another message came through: "Yes, I'm okay. I'll call you later."

Relieved but still anxious, I spent the next few hours pacing my living room, checking my phone every five minutes, the silence only amplifying my worry. When Damian finally calls, his voice is sharp, a far cry from the warm, steady tone I'm used to.

"Hey," I answer quickly. "Are you okay?"

"I'm fine," he replies, the words clipped and mechanical. "The car's totaled, though. It's a mess."

I hesitate, unsure how to navigate his mood. "I'm so sorry, Damian. What happened?"

"Some idiot slammed into me," he mutters, his frustration boiling over. "I don't even know how I'm going to afford a rental, let alone a new car."

His irritation is palpable, and I feel the tension radiating through the phone. "You'll figure it out," I say softly, though my words feel inadequate.

"Well, it doesn't feel like that right now," he snaps.

The sting of his tone catches me off guard. My throat tightens, but I try to stay calm. "I know it's hard, but you don't have to do this alone," I offer, hoping to reassure him.

"I just need to figure this out," he says flatly. "I'll call you later."

Before I can respond, the line goes dead.

I stare at the phone in my hand, a knot of worry twisting in my stomach. This version of Damian is unfamiliar, and it leaves me unsettled. I tell myself it's just the stress of the situation, but a quiet voice in the back of my mind wonders if there's more beneath the surface. I knew he needed space to process, but I couldn't shake the gnawing ache of wanting to comfort him, to bridge the gap that had opened between us. I just wished I could find the words to ease his frustration and make him feel a little less alone.

The next day, Damian seemed mostly back to his normal self. My going-away party was that night—a grand sendoff meticulously planned by Jenni and my sisters. They pulled out all the stops, organizing an epic farewell that began at my older sister's cozy, inviting house and spilled into a wild night of bar hopping downtown.

The house thrummed with energy as friends gathered, each holding a drink, their laughter and chatter filling the air. The backyard glowed with string lights that cast a warm, golden hue over the scene. A taco bar was set up on the patio, brimming with colorful toppings, freshly grilled meats, and warm tortillas that filled the air with a mouthwatering aroma. Inside, the aroma of my sister's famous cashew queso dip mingled with the scent of margaritas being blended in the kitchen. My nieces raced around the house, their high-pitched giggles weaving through the music from the playlist my sisters had painstakingly curated. The sounds of old favorites and guilty pleasures added a nostalgic rhythm to the evening.

Oliver, Karina's Australian boyfriend, had come from London for a visit. His sun-kissed skin and easy smile were a testament to the adventurous spirit that had drawn him and Karina together while backpacking through Greece. Karina's face lit up every time she glanced his way, her love for him unmistakable.

Jenni, always the ringleader, stood in the center of the living room, her eyes bright as she raised her glass.

"Here's to Talia!" she announced, her voice ringing out like a celebratory bell. The room erupted in cheers, glasses clinking and toasts spilling over one another.

"To new adventures!" Maya chimed in, winking at me as she hoisted her drink in the air.

"To the beach life!" someone hollered from the back, prompting a ripple of laughter that swept through the crowd.

I laughed along, clutching my glass and taking in the sight around me. This moment felt like a snapshot of everything I cherished about home—the chaos, the warmth, the unconditional love.

My orange strappy dress hugged my figure, the vibrant color highlighting my golden tan from the summer. I caught a glimpse of myself in the mirror and smiled, feeling a rare confidence. Tonight was about celebration, and I was determined to soak in every moment.

When the party transitioned downtown, the energy only amplified. The bars were buzzing, their neon signs flickering against the night sky as we poured into our favorite spot. Despite the crowds, we managed to claim a booth, squeezing in shoulder to shoulder. The drinks flowed freely, and the toasts continued as the night unfolded in a whirlwind of joy.

"To new beginnings," Karina says, her glass meeting mine with a solid clink. Her smile was both proud and bittersweet, her eyes glistening in the dim light.

"And don't you forget us when you're out there living the California dream!" Jess, teased as she threw an arm around me. Her voice was playful, but there was a weight in her words that made my heart clench.

"I could never forget you guys," I assured her, my voice firm but warm. I leaned into her embrace, grateful for her unwavering support.

Throughout the night, old friends I hadn't seen in years made appearances, each one adding another layer of joy and nostalgia.

"You're really doing it, huh?" Thomas asks, shaking his head with a grin as if still processing the news.

"I am," I said, the excitement blooming in my chest every time I repeated it.

As the night wore on, it became a kaleidoscope of hugs, laughter, and promises to visit. At one point, Karina grabbed my hand and dragged me onto the dance floor. Oliver joined in, his charm and rhythm adding to the fun as we launched into one of our legendary Michael Jackson dance-offs. The crowd around us cheered and clapped along, their energy lifting us even higher. Karina's moves were as sharp and exaggerated as ever, her laughter bubbling over as we hammed it up to "Billie Jean."

The whole night felt like an embrace—a jubilant, chaotic, and heartfelt sendoff that reminded me exactly why leaving would be so hard and yet so necessary. It was a celebration of the life I'd built here, the people who had shaped me, and the promise of what lay ahead.

I'm standing on the brink of this new and exhilarating next chapter of my life. As I look around at the people I love, I know I'll carry this night with me, a reminder of where I've been and the incredible future that lies ahead.

The next morning, reality sets in—Damian will be flying in to help with the move in just a couple of days. We've worked out the logistics of getting my car and belongings to California, and it's a bit of a puzzle. My little car can't pull a U-Haul, and we need to get everything there in one trip. Thankfully, my mom agrees to drive her Escalade, towing the U-Haul with all my stuff, while Damian and I follow in my car. Once we're settled, my dad will fly out to California and drive back home with her.

Packing up feels surreal, like I'm closing one chapter and opening another. I take a break from organizing the chaos in the kitchen and decide to post photos from the farewell party on Facebook. As the pictures upload, I scroll through comments and notifications, smiling at all the well-wishes from friends and family.

Then a notification pops up unexpectedly. The bold letters of her name instantly tighten the knot in my stomach.

Nicole.

I hesitate, my finger hovering over the message like opening it might unleash something I'm not ready to face.

Are you really moving to California? the message reads.

Her tone seeps through the screen—accusatory, bitter, dripping with venom. I take a deep breath, resisting the urge to fire back something equally sharp. Instead, I type carefully, choosing my words like I'm defusing a bomb.

Umm, hi. And not that it's any of your business, but yes, I am.

The message sounds more confident than I actually feel, but I hit send anyway. The knot tightens again as her response comes almost instantly.

That's insane. You're nothing but a phase to Damian. We'll be back together soon.

Her words hit like a slap. I take another deep breath. I won't let her get to me.

I'm sorry you feel that way, but I am moving there with him, I reply, adding a touch of humor to soften the blow—for myself, mostly. *Maybe one day, we can all be friends and have a margarita.*

I stare at the screen, unsure if the joke was too much. Her reply is instant:

A margarita? I would never be friends with you!

The sharpness of her response actually makes me laugh—not because it's funny, but because it's so absurd. I close the app, the conversation ending as quickly as it began.

That was… weird, I think, shaking my head. First Edgar, now Nicole. Like ghosts rising for one last attempt to haunt me before I leave it all behind.

I turn back toward the half-packed boxes scattered around my apartment, but something catches my eye—my journal, peeking out from a drawer I thought I'd already emptied. The soft blue cover is worn at the edges, the word *breathe* still etched across the front in quiet gold letters. I thumb through the pages and realize there are only a few blank ones left. Just enough.

I slip out onto the patio one last time.

The late afternoon sun washes everything in amber light, and the breeze carries the familiar hum of the city below. This little slab of concrete has been my refuge more times than I can count. I sink into the chair, light a cigarette, and let the stillness settle in my chest.

Opening the journal, I begin to write.

I remember the night I wrote that I wanted to free myself from Edgar. I didn't know how I'd do it—I just knew I couldn't stay. I was drowning. And somehow, this space, this journal, helped me breathe again. I made it. I reclaimed my life. And now... I'm leaving this place not to escape something, but to step into something new. Something good. Maybe even something great.

I press the cover closed and trace the word *breathe* one last time. It feels like a goodbye. Time for a new journal. A new story.

Just then, I hear the creak of the gate and footsteps on the patio.

"Thought I'd catch you before the U-Haul swallowed you whole," Jenni says, lifting a bottle of prosecco in one hand and two plastic cups in the other.

I smile, already feeling the lump form in my throat. "You always show up right when I need you."

"Damn right I do," she says, settling into the chair beside me. She pops the cork, pours us each a cup, and raises hers. "To new chapters."

We clink. The bubbles fizz between us, the silence stretching for a beat too long.

"I'm gonna miss you," I say quietly.

Jenni nods, staring out over the skyline like she doesn't trust herself to look at me yet. "I know. I'm gonna miss you too."

There's something unsaid in her voice. I can feel it—the ache behind her smile, the way she keeps sipping like it'll make the moment go down easier.

"You know this is what I need, right?" I ask.

She exhales, finally looking at me. "Yeah. I do. You've always been the brave one. I just… I guess I thought we'd keep doing life side by side for a while longer."

"I did too," I admit. "Especially since we just got each other back."

That gets her. Her eyes glisten, and she lets out a breathy laugh. "It's been a wild and fun ten months."

I reach for her hand, squeezing it gently. "It sure was. And it meant everything to me."

Jenni nods slowly. "You and your big, messy, beautiful love story. I'm proud of you, Tal. I really am."

"But?" I prod, giving her a knowing look.

She shrugs. "No *but*. Just... don't forget about us little people when you're living your beachy, happily-ever-after life."

I lean in and rest my head briefly on her shoulder. "Never. You're stitched into all of this. You're part of the reason I even had the strength to go."

We sit there a while longer, sipping prosecco on mismatched patio chairs, holding onto the quiet. Holding onto each other.

Eventually, the sun dips lower, and the breeze cools. Jenni stands first, brushing off her jeans and draining the last sip of prosecco.

She looks around at the scattered boxes through the sliding glass door. "Alright," she says, forcing a smile through the emotion in her voice. "These boxes aren't going to pack themselves. Let's get you packed and ready for Cali."

I nod, slipping my journal under my arm. "Let's do it."

Back inside, the mood shifts. We move with quiet efficiency—wrapping plates, sealing boxes, labeling with Sharpies. There's a rhythm to it, like muscle memory from every late-night move or wine-fueled packing session we've ever done together. She doesn't say much, but her presence is steady. Comforting.

By the time we finish, the apartment feels hollow. The walls are bare, the air still.

"Alright, you call me as soon as you get there and everyday!" She says pulling into a hug.

"I promise." I say, holding back tears.

Jenni rushes out before we both lose it again.

Damian arrives just in time to help me load up. Despite selling so many of my things, it's still a tight fit. The U-Haul is crammed with my bedroom set, kitchen essentials, and clothes—just the basics for a fresh start. I keep telling myself that letting go of so much will make it easier to embrace everything ahead.

As we load the last box, I glance around my now-empty apartment. It feels strange to see it so bare. The echoes of my time here—the time I spent reclaiming myself and my independence—still linger in the quiet space. I run my fingers along the cool counter remembering the first night I stepped into this apartment and gently lay the key down. Look at me, so far from that night and yet on the brink of something just as scary.

But when I turn and see Damian smiling at me, ready for the journey ahead, I know I'm making the right choice.

Nineteen

It's a long but fun two days on the road. On the first day, we head to my aunt's house in Las Cruces, New Mexico, where we plan to stop for the night. After some much-needed rest, we hit the road early the next morning.

Somewhere along a long stretch of empty highway, Damian and I fall into easy conversation—one of those silly, meandering talks that makes the miles fly by.

"I like cleaning the kitchen and vacuuming," Damian says.

"Well, that's good. I hate cleaning the kitchen," I laugh.

What I don't say is that I kind of hate all chores. I can be a little messy—a detail I'm not sure Damian's ready for.

"I can do laundry and the bathroom," I offer.

"Cool. For the bathroom, I usually leave a small towel under the sink. That way you can wipe water spots after brushing your teeth," he says, totally serious.

I half-laugh, half-sob internally. I'm dating a neat freak. Great. Still, it's a one-bedroom apartment—I can manage. And honestly, it feels nice knowing I won't be the only one keeping things together. That alone feels like a huge shift from my past life.

When the "Welcome to California" sign finally appears, I nearly cry. I've never been so relieved to see a road sign in my life. It's just after 10 p.m. when we pull into the apartment complex, and all I can think about is blowing up the mattresses and crashing.

The apartment is even better in person. The living room greets us with cozy charm, complete with a fireplace nestled in the corner. It's not grand or fancy, but it already feels like home. The kitchen-dining combo is compact but functional, with a small island perfect for coffee or late-night takeout.

I wander through the space—the bedroom tucked past the fireplace, the bright bathroom cleverly accessible from both the bedroom and the main area. The sliding closet is massive, cleanly split down the middle. I grin. One side for me, one for Damian.

I step out onto the little patio, the warm California air brushing past my face. Below, palm trees sway over a quiet street. I imagine us out here—coffee in the morning, wine at night, maybe even a plant or two I'll forget to water.

"This is so us," I say, turning to Damian as he hauls in our luggage.

"Right? I knew you'd love it," he says, and in his smile, I see every reason I came.

Then my mom claps her hands. "Okay, lovebirds, mattresses before midnight," she says with a laugh.

We set up quickly. Damian and I take the bedroom; my mom claims the living room. It's late, and none of us have much energy left for organizing. Still, there's a strange calm in the chaos. As Damian and I climb onto the mattress and settle in, I listen to the hum of crickets outside the window.

"Can you believe we're finally here?" I whisper.

He reaches out, tucking a strand of hair behind my ear. "Not really. It doesn't feel real that you're here. With me. In California."

"I know," I say, my voice catching. "I'm happy… really happy."

He kisses me softly, and for a moment, the whole journey feels worth it.

The next day is a blur of unpacking, grocery runs, and setting up our bed properly. My dad flies in that afternoon, so we squeeze in lunch at a cute café nearby before heading to the airport.

Later, we decide to visit the beach to celebrate our first full day in California. The sun hangs low in the sky, casting a golden glow over the shoreline. I leave my purse in the car, figuring we'll just be a few steps away. My mom doubles back to grab something from the front seat—but forgets to relock the doors.

The breeze is warm and salty, the ocean stretching out endlessly ahead of us. We kick off our shoes and walk barefoot along the edge of the waves. I feel light, almost weightless, watching my parents smile together on a blanket. It's hard to believe this is the same family that was once so unsure about all of this.

Maybe I do belong here, I think.

But that illusion shatters when we return to the car.

I reach for my purse—and it's gone.

Panic punches through me. My breath catches, and I feel my heart drop into my stomach.

"No. No, no, no." I frantically check under the seats, inside every crevice, even though I already know. It's not there.

"What was in it?" my dad asks, already pulling out his phone.

"Everything," I whisper. "My ID. Social security card. All the cash from selling my furniture."

Damian rubs the back of his neck, trying to stay calm. "We'll figure it out."

Figure it out? My head spins. That money was supposed to help us settle. Those documents were critical for starting my new job next week.

I try not to cry. I try to breathe. But the weight of it all crashes down like a wave.

Dinner is quiet. We head to The Crow Bar—Damian's restaurant—and I do my best to fake a smile as we walk in. The space is beautiful: warm, stylish, alive. I should be proud. Instead, I feel numb.

This was supposed to be a celebration. A fresh start.

Instead, I feel like I've already failed.

Then, to add to the pressure, Damian's mom—Pam—is meeting us for the first time.

My stomach churns. I remember Damian mentioning her hesitation about meeting me. *What if she hates me?*

"Relax," Damian whispers, placing his hand on my knee beneath the table. "She's going to love you."

Just as I try to smile, Pam walks in—and every anxious thought vanishes.

She's radiant. Her short black curls flecked with gray, her presence warm and steady. She hugs everyone, saving me for last.

"You must be Talia," she says with a smile that wraps around me like a blanket. She smells like warm vanilla. "I've heard so much about you."

"It's so nice to meet you," I say, and for the first time since the purse was stolen, I truly mean it.

Dinner flows with laughter and stories. Pam and my mom bond over motherhood, while my dad and Damian nerd out over beer. The food is incredible—crisp Brussels sprouts, fresh seafood, and perfectly cooked steak.

When Pam orders bread pudding for the table, my dad lights up.

"You're a fan?" she asks.

"More like obsessed," he replies, grinning.

They argue over whether the caramel sauce makes it better or worse, their laughter melting the tension I'd been holding in.

I look at Damian. He leans in, his lips brushing my ear.

"Told you she'd love you."

By the time we step out into the warm night air, the earlier panic has faded—at least for now.

As Damian and I drive back to the apartment, I look out my window watching the waves crash onto the shoreline under the moon, a feeling I can't quite name settles in.

Excitement.

Terror.

Hope.

I'm here. I'm in his world now.

The question is—will I survive it?

Twenty

Our first weekend together in California is the Fourth of July, and Damian has gone all out to make it unforgettable.

"We're heading to Huntington Beach for the surfing competition," he tells me over breakfast, his enthusiasm contagious. "And later, we'll hit up a house party with some of my friends. It's going to be epic."

The moment we arrive at Huntington Beach, I realize this isn't just a surfing event—it's a full-blown summer festival. The air hums with energy. Music blares from speakers, food trucks line the streets, and crowds of people are decked out in red, white, and blue. The scent of salty air mixes with sunscreen and sizzling hot dogs.

Damian takes my hand, weaving us through the sea of sun-soaked bodies. "The pier's the best spot to watch," he says, steering us toward the wooden planks stretching over the ocean.

We find a place halfway down, leaning against the railing as waves roll beneath us. Surfers cut through the water with effortless grace, each trick greeted with wild cheers from the crowd.

"Look at that one!" Damian says, pointing as a surfer launches into an aerial spin and lands it clean.

"That's insane," I gasp, gripping the rail.

Damian grins. "Makes me want to grab a board and get out there again."

"Again?" I raise a brow, smirking. "I'd pay to see that. You think you can hang with the pros?"

"Hey, I've surfed before!" he says, mock-offended.

"Great! You can give me lessons," I tease.

We spend hours soaking in the vibe, sipping icy drinks from a vendor and watching the chaos of California unfold around us—kids with sparklers, DJs on balconies, strangers dancing in the streets. And somehow, in all the noise, I feel a strange calm.

"This is incredible," I say, leaning into him. "I see why you love it here so much."

"It's not bad, huh?" he says, snapping a picture with one arm wrapped around me. "Just wait until tonight—it gets even better."

Later, we hop on bikes and pedal through palm-lined streets to the house party. Damian looks completely at ease. I, on the other hand, feel a flutter of nerves climbing up my throat.

The house is buzzing—music thumps from the backyard, laughter spills through open windows, and the scent of grilled burgers and coconut sunscreen hangs in the air. I grip the strap of my purse a little tighter.

"Most of them are from work," Damian says, sensing my hesitation. "They're great—you'll love them."

I nod, offering a tight smile, but can't shake the anxiety. His world feels cool and effortless. I suddenly wonder if I look too plain, if I sound too awkward, if I belong here at all.

People greet Damian with cheers and high-fives. He fits in so naturally it's like watching a movie I'm not sure I've been cast in. Then the host of the party bounces toward us.

Valentina.

Petite, pretty, with sun-kissed hair and an easy laugh. She playfully punches Damian's arm and flashes me a bright smile.

"So, you're Talia," she says. "Damian has been talking about you nonstop."

"All good things, I hope," I say politely, even though jealousy sparks behind my ribs like a faulty firework.

"Only the best," she says genuinely. "Damian's been counting down the days until you got here."

Damian slips an arm around my waist and kisses my temple. "And now she's here."

Valentina claps. "Oh my God, Damian, you have to try the Flabongo!"

"The what?" I blink.

She reappears with a hot pink flamingo yard ornament—turned upside down into a beer bong. She grins, flips it, and demonstrates like a seasoned pro.

Damian jumps in to try it, earning cheers from the crowd. I laugh, finally letting my guard down. Maybe this isn't a test I have to pass. Maybe it's just a party.

As the night goes on, my anxiety slowly dissolves. Valentina even pulls me aside.

"You're perfect for him," she says sincerely. "I've never seen him this happy."

By the time the fireworks begin, I'm laughing with people I just met, sipping something fizzy, and feeling—miraculously—at home.

Damian pulls me out to the front lawn as the sky explodes into bursts of red, gold, and blue. The colors reflect in his eyes as he watches me.

"You okay now?" he asks, squeezing my hand.

"Yeah," I say, smiling at him. "I really am."

The fireworks crackle above us, and I rest my head against his shoulder.

For a moment, I stop worrying about whether I belong in his world. Because maybe the real question isn't *if* I belong—maybe it's *how* I want to show up in it.

As the final sparks fade and we walk back into the house, I feel it in my chest: this life—this love— might just be worth the risk.

Monday dawns, the coastal breeze filtering through our curtains like a whisper of possibility.

It's my first day at Carver Reed.

I dress carefully—structured slacks, a silky blouse that doesn't cling, a spritz of perfume at my wrists. I want to look like someone who belongs here, even if I don't feel it yet.

The drive to the office is short, and the streets still smell like ocean and sunlight. I park in the small parking beneath the building, heart pounding beneath my tailored layers. The sign outside is modest. The building is even more so—clean lines, small footprint, unassuming. But inside, everything could change.

A woman with curly auburn hair and a cheerful energy greets me as soon as I walk through the glass door.

"Talia! Welcome," she says, her voice warm. "I'm Erica—we're so glad to have you."

"Thank you," I say, managing a smile. "I'm really glad to be here."

Erica leads me through the quiet space—six desks total. That's it. Just Matt, Sally, Alan, Erica, and now… me. It's intimate. Exposed. There's nowhere to hide.

"We're still growing," she says brightly. "But we believe in quality over quantity. And we're betting big on you."

That last part echoes in my head as I sit down at my desk.

They're betting on me. And this is base-plus-commission. Which means the base covers groceries and not much more. If I don't start signing doctors soon, this dream might evaporate faster than California rain.

Matt, my boss, arrives not long after. He's polished, mid-forties, with a firm handshake and kind eyes.

"Welcome aboard," he says. "We've got our Monday meeting in thirty. Need coffee?"

"Desperately," I admit.

He laughs and walks me to the breakroom. It's not much—a Keurig, some mismatched mugs, and a fridge humming in the corner. I can't help but see the potential.

The rest of the day moves in a blur of usernames, passwords, CRM platforms, pitch decks, and paperwork. I keep smiling, keep nodding, keep taking notes. But underneath it all, the pressure doesn't ease—it tightens.

Because this isn't just a job. It's a new life. A new state. A new everything. I need this to work.

By the time five o'clock rolls around, my mind is mush and my heels feel like medieval torture devices. I get in my car and try calling Jenni—desperate for a familiar voice, a joke, something that feels like home.

No answer. Straight to voicemail.

I sigh and stare at my screen, debating whether to just sit in silence for the drive home. But before I can hit play on a podcast, a new call lights up my phone: **Karina**.

"Hey, you," I say, trying not to sound as tired as I feel.

"Talia! How was your first day? Tell me everything."

I exhale, finally letting some of the tension go. "It was… good. The office is tiny—five of us total—but everyone's nice. And it's right near the beach. I can see palm trees from the conference room."

"That actually sounds kind of dreamy," she says, a smile in her voice.

"It is. Kind of. But it's also intense. The base salary is… modest. The rest is commission, so I've got to land clients fast."

"You will," she says, full of big-sister certainty.

"Thanks," I say softly. "But enough about me. What's going on with you? How's Oliver?"

There's a pause. A heartbeat of hesitation.

"I wanted to wait until you were settled to tell you… but we're eloping."

I blink. "Wait—what?"

"We're going to do something really simple here in Austin. Just us. But Oliver's family wants to throw a small reception back in Australia. Nothing huge. Just close friends and family. And… I want you to be there."

A thousand emotions crash into me at once. "Karina, that's amazing. I'm so happy for you."

"I know it's last-minute. And far. And expensive."

I close my eyes. "It's not even about the last-minute part. I just… I don't think I can swing the ticket. I just moved here, I've barely started working, and—"

"You don't have to explain," she says quickly. "I get it. I really do."

My throat tightens. "I just hate the thought of missing it. Missing *you*."

"I'll send a million pictures. And I'll FaceTime you before the reception," she says softly. "It won't be the same, but you'll still be with me."

I smile through the ache in my chest. "I love you, Karina. I am so happy for you both!"

"I love you too. I am so happy—Oliver is everything. No drama, no guessing games. I feel... peaceful. Like I can finally breathe."

I stare out at the ocean in the distance, the sun dipping low. "That's all I ever wanted for you."

We talk a few minutes more before saying goodbye, my phone dropping to my lap as I sit in silence, letting the joy and the ache settle side by side.

When I get home, Damian's in the bedroom getting ready for his evening shift. He's standing in front of the mirror, buttoning his shirt with that quiet confidence I never get tired of watching.

"Hey," he says, catching my eye as I walk in. "How'd it go?"

"Good," I reply, leaning against the doorframe. "A lot to take in. I'm definitely going to need some time before I feel like I know what I'm doing."

"You'll find your rhythm," he says, crossing the room to pull me into his arms. "You always do."

He kisses my forehead, and just like that, the tightness in my chest softens. He doesn't have to say much—sometimes it's just the way he holds me that makes the world slow down.

I rest there for a second before pulling back slightly. "Oh—Karina and Oliver are eloping," I say, watching his face carefully. "They're doing something small in Austin, then having a reception in Australia."

His eyes light up. "No way! That's amazing. How cool would it be to go there?"

"It really would be," I say, my voice quieter now. "But I can't. I just started this job. There's no way I can afford it right now."

He nods, but he's already glancing at the clock, grabbing his keys. "I've got to run. I'll text you when I'm headed home, okay?"

"Okay," I say softly. "Be safe."

The door clicks shut behind him, and I stand there for a beat longer than necessary, the echo of his excitement still hanging in the air while mine fades into something else—something bittersweet.

After he leaves, I peel off my clothes like they're made of cement, throw my hair up, and grab a cold Dos Equis from the fridge. I step out onto the patio, barefoot, beer in hand, and watch the sky turn to gold.

With my new journal in my lap—the one with the soft watercolor ocean scene on the cover that I picked up from a little shop off the pier—I press my pen to the first page and write: *July 8th, 2009.*

There's something about a new journal that always feels like a fresh start. Clean pages. Untold stories. Space to become someone new.

And that's exactly what this is.

I exhale slowly and begin to write:

"Everything still feels a little surreal. The new job is intimidating—like I'm walking into a room where everyone already knows the dance steps but me. I keep waiting to feel like I belong. But then I come home to him... and somehow, I do.

With Damian by my side, it's like I can breathe deeper. Like maybe I really can figure all of this out, one piece at a time. He makes the scary parts feel less sharp, less lonely. I didn't know love could feel like that—like safety and freedom at the same time.

And then there's my sister, completely swept up in something real. She's glowing, and watching her fall in love makes me believe we're both finally stepping into the lives we used to dream about when we were little. Like our love stories are actually coming to life—side by side, just in different cities."

I close the journal gently, running my hand over the ocean waves on the cover. The pages are blank, and I'm so excited to see how they get filled—with this new life, this new love, and everything that comes next.

Around 10:30, my phone buzzes.

Damian: *I'm on my way home.*

I smile, heart flipping in that way it always does with him. No flights. No countdowns. He's coming home to *me*.

I slip into bed, pull the sheets to my chest, and wait.

The door opens quietly ten minutes later. I hear his shoes hit the floor, the soft rustle of clothes, the creak of the mattress.

He slides beneath the covers and reaches for me.

He pulls me close, his lips grazing my shoulder, then my neck—soft, slow, reverent. The day melts away in his touch. The world disappears in the way his fingers find mine, the way his body folds around mine like a prayer.

"I love coming home to you," he whispers, his voice a soft rumble that settles deep in my chest. "Knowing you're mine to come home to."

A smile tugs at my lips as I take in his words— words I've longed for, words that settle something in me.

I turn to face him, my hand sliding along his jaw. "I love being yours."

He shifts, guiding me gently onto my back, his body pressing over mine with a weight that makes me feel claimed in the most delicious way.

Our lips meet—slow at first, tender and full of knowing—then deeper, more urgent. His hips press into mine, the length of him teasing, then sliding just enough to make me gasp, to make my body chase more. I arch against him, needing the full length of him, needing *us*.

His hands pin mine above my head, fingers laced tight, holding me there as his hips roll into mine—deeper, claiming, driving us both mad with pleasure.

His mouth returns to mine, then trails lower—across my jaw, my neck, the hollow of my throat—each kiss a slow burn that leaves me aching.

I breathe him in, lose myself in him, feel everything fall back into place.

When we finally settle, his arms around me, his chest rising beneath my cheek, I whisper:

"I made it through day one."

"You did," he murmurs. "And you'll make it through all the rest."

And in the dark, in this unfamiliar life, I start to believe him.

That weekend, Damian actually had the weekend off from work. We plan to drive up to Santa Clarita to visit his mom and his best friend, Mike—and I'd be lying if I said I wasn't a little nervous. Meeting the best friend is a test. One I *really* want to pass.

After work on Friday, we start the three-hour drive. The LA traffic is insane—I've never seen anything like it, long blanket of red brake lights stretching ahead of us. By the time we make it up there, we're exhausted. We drop off our things at his mom's house and have a quick dinner before heading over to Mike's place.

Mike is hosting a party for a friend's birthday.

The house is buzzing with laughter, music, and the clink of glasses. Damian introduces me to Mike first—a tall guy with a big, easy grin and arms that swallow me in a warm bear hug.

"You must be Talia," he says. "We've heard a lot about you."

"Only the good stuff, I hope," I joke.

"Oh yeah," he grins. "And most of it's probably true."

His girlfriend, Veronica, hangs back a little. She offers a half-hearted hug and a lukewarm "Nice to meet you," her expression unreadable. Not rude, exactly. Just... reserved. I get the sense she's sizing me up—and not quite ready to make a call.

Still, I don't let it rattle me. I'm here to be *me*.

An hour later, we're in the middle of a spirited poker game. There's booze, music, and the kind of lighthearted chaos that makes strangers feel like teammates.

I've played plenty of poker before—tournaments with Edgar, late-night games with friends—so I hold my own. Maybe even too well.

When Mike flips over his hand and beats me on the river, I let out an exaggerated groan.

"You *called* with that?" I shout, pointing at his cards. "What a dumb call!"

Everyone laughs as I dramatically toss my cards and pretend to pout, punching Mike lightly on the shoulder. He howls with laughter, and someone across the table calls out, "I like her!"

Veronica watches, smiling faintly but staying just on the edge of the circle. I'm not sure what she's thinking, but I remind myself—this isn't about winning *her* over. It's about showing up for Damian.

The next morning, as we pack up our things, Damian wraps his arms around me from behind.

"You were great last night," he says into my neck. "Mike thought you were hilarious."

"Well, I *am*," I reply with a grin, nudging him with my elbow.

There's a pause before I say, "I don't think his girlfriend liked me very much, though."

Damian shrugs. "That's just Veronica. She's cautious around new people. She'll come around."

His quiet confidence calms me. I lean into him, feeling the warmth of something that feels like trust.

On the drive back to his mom's house, he reaches across the console and laces his fingers with mine. I exhale slowly. I passed the test—and not just the best friend one. The "Can I be part of this world?" test too.

We spend the rest of the day shopping.

I need more work attire, and Damian has a specific sneaker shop he wants to check out.

The moment we walk in, I blink. It's like stepping into a futuristic bodega—sneakers displayed inside vintage convenience store refrigerators, glowing under neon lights like prized artifacts.

"This place is insane," I say, peering through the doors at sneakers that look more like collector's items than something you'd actually wear.

Damian nods. "Yeah, it's a sneakerhead's dream."

Damian scans the shelves, his eyes lighting up when he spots a pair he likes. He waves over a store employee. "You got these in a 14?"

The guy disappears into the back, returning a moment later with a single box. "Man, I've got bad news—we only have a 13 left."

Damian exhales sharply, shaking his head. "Figures." He glances at the shoe, contemplating for a second before setting it back. "Nah, I can't do it. Too tight."

"Story of my life," Damian mutters as we head for the door.

We spend the next hour wandering through eclectic boutiques, each shop offering something different.

Eventually, we find our way to the designer section of the shopping district. As we pass Tiffany & Co., my steps slow, my gaze catching on the familiar blue storefront. Through the window display, a delicate silver necklace with a peace sign pendant sparkles under the soft lighting.

I tilt my head, admiring its simple elegance. "I've always loved their classic pieces," I murmur.

Damian follows my gaze. "Yeah?"

I nod, my voice wistful. "I've always wanted something in one of those little blue boxes."

He's quiet for a moment before saying, almost too casually, "Noted."

I turn to him, raising an eyebrow. "Noted?"

He shrugs, smirking. "Just making mental notes."

I roll my eyes, but the way he looks at me—like he's already planning something—makes my stomach flip in a way I don't entirely hate.

Our last stop is Nordstrom, where I browse through racks of workwear, eventually picking out a few blouses and pants to add to my wardrobe. As I pay, I think back to the only designer piece I own—a Burberry scarf my sister, Esme, bought me years ago when she worked at Nordstrom and got a discount during their Friends & Family sale. She always said every woman deserved one thing in her closet that made her feel expensive, even if her life wasn't.

Back in the car, shopping bags rustling in the back seat, Damian squeezes my knee.

"You okay?" he asks.

I nod. "Yeah. I think I am."

As we ease onto the highway, the sky turns molten gold. The kind of late afternoon glow that makes everything feel soft and safe. Damian taps through music on his phone, and I open mine, casually scrolling through notifications.

That's when I see it.

Nicole liked a photo you were tagged in.

I blink.

It's a picture from Mike's party—me and Damian mid-laugh during the poker game, arms draped casually around each other. One of Mike's friends must've posted it. I hadn't even realized I was tagged.

"She liked this?" I murmur aloud, more to myself than him.

Damian glances over. "What?"

"Nicole. She liked a photo from the party. I didn't realize Mike and Veronica were still friends with her on Facebook."

Damian lets out a short breath. "So what?"

I pause, watching his profile as he drives. "I don't know. I guess I just didn't expect her to still be in the same social circle."

"She's just on Facebook, Talia. Who cares?"

I hesitate. "Do you plan on staying friends with her on there?"

He shrugs, eyes on the road. "I don't know. Maybe. Why does it matter?"

"I don't know," I say quietly. "It doesn't. Maybe."

But in my mind, it *does*.

It matters because she wanted him back. Because she told me I was just a phase. Because I'm building a life here, one piece at a time, while she's still quietly watching from the sidelines—liking photos, holding on.

It matters because I left my past behind, and sometimes I wonder if his past is still riding in the backseat.

Damian changes the song, humming along to something low and familiar, completely unbothered.

I stare out the window, watching the coastline blur past. I don't want to be the jealous girl. I don't want to pick fights over Facebook likes. But I also don't want to pretend I don't feel it—that flicker of unease, that low hum of *what if.*

I tuck it away for now, folding the discomfort into a neat little box and placing it beside the rest of the unspoken things.

The sun dips below the horizon as we near Dana Point, and he reaches for my hand again, his thumb tracing soft circles against my skin.

And even though the doubt still lingers quietly in my chest, I hold on to him anyway.

Twenty-One

My first birthday in California should feel like a celebration. And in many ways, it does.

I've survived the first few weeks at Carver Reed— somehow. I'm still finding my footing, still battling the wave of nerves that hits every time I stare down a list of cold calls. But I'm learning. I'm growing. And on most days, I no longer feel like I'm holding my breath.

There are moments I even catch myself exhaling. Smiling. Settling in.

But this morning, with the sun rising over the coast and the sound of Damian breathing beside me, the familiar ache is there too. The one that reminds me I'm far from home. From the birthday desserts with my mom's cheesecake. From my sisters showing up in their pajamas with iced coffee and loud voices.

This year, it's different. It's beautiful. But it's also not *them*.

Still, I'm here. With the man I love. In a life I chose. And that has to mean something.

At exactly 9:00 AM, my phone vibrates against the nightstand, a steady stream of birthday messages flooding in. I groan, burying my face deeper into the pillow. Damian shifts beside me, his arm draped over my waist, his warmth lulling me back into a half-sleep.

But then—of course—my mom calls.

I sigh, reaching blindly for my phone. "Hi, Mom," I mumble, my voice thick with sleep.

"Oh, were you still sleeping? Sorry, honey! Happy birthday!" she says, her voice bubbling with affection.

"Happy birthday, Mija!" my dad chimes in from the background.

A sleepy smile tugs at my lips. "Thank you."

"Okay, go back to sleep. We just wanted to be the first to say it," she says sweetly, though we both know there's no going back now.

After we hang up, I peel myself from the sheets and head to the kitchen, craving caffeine. As the coffee brews, strong and rich, Damian sneaks up behind me, his arms circling my waist, pulling me flush against him.

"Good morning, birthday girl," he murmurs, his lips tracing a slow, deliberate path along my neck.

A shiver runs down my spine. "Good morning, my love," I whisper, turning to face him. My arms drape over his shoulders as I kiss him, slow and indulgent, tasting the heat of his lips.

He deepens it, his hands roaming over my hips, his touch possessive and intoxicating. "I can't wait for tonight," he murmurs against my mouth.

"Tonight?" I tease, smiling between kisses.

His dark eyes smolder. "Your birthday dinner. You didn't think I'd let the day pass without making it special, did you?"

Before I can respond, my phone vibrates again. With a reluctant sigh, I pull away and grab my coffee, stepping onto the patio to answer.

"Happy birthday!" Jess' voice bursts through the phone, loud and full of excitement.

I laugh. "Thanks, lady!"

"So, what's the plan? Tell me you're doing something fabulous."

"Well, Damian has a surprise dinner planned, but first, we're heading to the beach."

"Ugh. You're such a Cali girl now with your beach weekends. I swear, I need to book a flight ASAP."

"Yes! You definitely do. I miss you."

We chat a little longer, making promises to plan a trip soon before hanging up.

Back inside, Damian is packing a picnic basket, his focus on the selection of fruit, cheeses, and wine. I watch him for a moment, my heart swelling at the simple beauty of this—of him, of us.

The day couldn't be more perfect. The sky is a flawless stretch of blue, the sun warm on my skin as we step onto the sand. The beach is nearly empty, the sound of the waves rhythmic and soothing.

"Come on, birthday girl!" Damian calls, already waist-deep in the water, his broad shoulders glistening under the sun.

Laughing, I race toward him, the ocean lapping at my ankles. The moment I reach him, he lifts me effortlessly, spinning me as the waves crash around us.

I shriek, clutching at him. "Wait—my sunglasses!" I reach for them before they can slip into the water.

He grins, brushing wet hair from my face. "Forget the sunglasses," he says, his voice low, hypnotic. "Just be here. With me."

His gaze locks onto mine, and for a moment, the world falls away—the ocean, the sand, even the sun itself.

Just him. Just us.

And I know, without a doubt, this will be a birthday I'll never forget.

That evening, he surprises me with dinner reservations at a charming Italian restaurant in Newport. The ambiance is perfect—warm lighting, flickering candles, clinking glasses, the smell of garlic and fresh herbs in the air. The food is delicious, but the moment that steals the night comes after dessert.

Damian pulls out a large, sky-blue box.

At first, I laugh—he's written "Tiffany's" across the top in Sharpie, just like the joke we shared last week.

But when I open the box, my breath catches.

Inside is a real Tiffany's box.

"Damian!" I exclaim, wide-eyed. "You didn't!"

He just smiles, eyes twinkling.

With trembling hands, I lift the lid. Nestled inside is the delicate silver necklace with the peace sign charm—the one I'd admired behind the glass not long ago.

I'm glowing. Speechless.

He gently takes it from the box and moves behind me to fasten it around my neck. The cool silver rests perfectly against my skin, sending a wave of emotion through me.

"It's beautiful," I whisper, my voice thick.

He kisses my shoulder, his hands smoothing over my arms as if anchoring me in this moment.

It's not just a necklace. It's that he remembered. That he *listened*. That he turned something small into something unforgettable.

And in that moment—wrapped in candlelight, love, and the tiniest blue box—I know it with complete certainty:

This is the man I want to build a life with.

The birthday glow lingered for days. Every time I caught a glimpse of the necklace resting just above my collarbone, or thought about Damian's eyes over candlelight, I felt the same flutter in my chest. But life doesn't pause for perfect moments.

It's late. Damian's still at work, and I'm curled up on the couch in one of his old hoodies, the apartment dim except for the soft blue light of my phone screen.

A notification pops up: **Karina is calling you — FaceTime video**.

I swipe to answer, and there she is—radiant, windswept, glowing in a way I've never seen before. Her hair is pinned back with tiny flowers, and the golden Australian sun is setting behind her like something out of a postcard.

"Talia," she breathes, eyes shimmering. "We did it."

She turns the camera so I can see Oliver— grinning, tousled, his white shirt open at the collar as he pulls her into his side. He kisses her cheek, and she laughs, that familiar sound that always made me feel like home.

"Oh my god," I whisper. "You look... beautiful. Both of you."

Karina's eyes glisten. "I just needed to see you. Even if it's through a screen."

I nod, swallowing the lump rising in my throat. "I wish I was there."

"You are," she says firmly. "You're with me. Always."

For a moment, neither of us speaks. The camera shifts slightly, catching a glimpse of the ocean beyond the ceremony site—waves crashing gently, lanterns flickering in the breeze.

I memorize every detail. Burn it into my heart.

When the call ends, I sit in silence for a long time, phone still in my hand.

It's strange—how love can stretch across time zones, how joy and sadness can live in the same breath. Karina had found her calm in Oliver. Her *home*. And even though I'm a thousand miles away, watching her find it made me believe—maybe I could too.

The weeks that followed slipped into something quieter. Something real. A rhythm I hadn't quite expected—but one I found myself learning how to live in.

This is the new rhythm of our lives: me working Monday through Friday, eight to five, and Damian working evenings at the restaurant. His days off rotate—Sunday and either Monday or Tuesday depending on the schedule.

Sundays have officially become "Sunday Funday." It's our sacred time together, untouched by work or routine. Damian takes the lead, planning everything from beach days and shopping trips to comedy shows and brunch with friends. It's the one day a week where we can pretend the rest of the world doesn't exist. Where we can just be *us*.

Saturdays, however, are for sleeping in until Damian has to head to work. Then it's time for chores. I tackle laundry, clean the apartment, and stock up on groceries for the week. Damian usually handles his errands during the week before work, so by Saturday, we naturally fall into our own little routines.

I'm running on less sleep than usual these days— it's hard not to wake up when Damian gets home late at night, his presence instantly pulling me from sleep. We're still in that honeymoon phase, where the sound of his keys in the door is enough to make my heart beat faster. And somehow, the nights have become our time for long, unfiltered conversations. The kind you only have in the dark, when everything else is quiet.

Most evenings, I catch up with Jenni, my sisters, or my mom over the phone. I miss them terribly. I love my life here, but there's still an ache for home— one that creeps in during the quiet moments, soft but persistent.

One evening, I'm catching up with Jenni on the phone while folding laundry.

"So guess who I've been hanging out with lately?" she says, her voice dancing with mischief.

"Oh no," I laugh. "Who?"

"Bad Brad," she announces.

I blink. "Wait—Brad? This is the first I'm hearing of Brad."

Jenni groans. "I know. I didn't tell you because I thought it would be a one-week thing. But he's sticking around. He's still making questionable decisions, hence the nickname, but he's also been...surprisingly sweet. And funny. And he might be paying for my plane ticket, so I'm not asking too many questions right now."

I smirk. "Wow. Bad Brad with the grand gestures."

She laughs. "Okay, hear me out: Cabo. For my birthday. Come with me. You and Damian need a getaway."

My eyes light up. "Wait, really?"

"Yes! Let's go. Sun, beach, tequila. Just say yes."

By the time Damian gets home, I'm practically vibrating. "So… Jenni and I had an idea."

His eyes spark. "Yeah?"

"Cabo. For her birthday. In November. You in?"

Without missing a beat, he nods. "Absolutely. And my mom has a timeshare—Cabo's one of the locations. We'll just need to cover airfare."

My jaw drops. "You're kidding."

I can already see it: sand, sun, the way he looks at me when we're away from the world. Our first real escape. Just us.

Yes, we've fallen into a rhythm here— comfortable, steady—but something about the idea of getting away, of rediscovering each other outside of our routines, feels right. A romantic getaway could be exactly what we need.

October brings fall—or at least, that's what the calendar says. In California, it's just another stretch of golden sunshine, endless blue skies, and barely a whisper of seasonal change.

Still, change is in the air.

It also brings my niece's birthday. I call Maya to hear what she has planned for her birthday party. She fills me in on the party and life with her two little girls. Preschool drop-offs, bedtime stories, tiny voices asking for one more hug before lights out. Her home sounds chaotic, but warm—brimming with giggles and the kind of love that spills over without trying.

I smile and laugh in all the right places, but as she talks, something begins to stir. It's not just the nostalgia or the ache of missing them. It's deeper. A gentle but persistent longing that I've tucked away for years.

When we hang up, I don't move right away. I just sit there, holding my phone, staring at the screen like the answers I'm avoiding might suddenly appear.

Without really thinking, I open FaceTime and call Bella.

She answers from the living room, her hair a little longer, her smile just as bright. "Talia!" she squeals, holding the phone too close to her face.

"Hi, mama," I say, smiling through the lump in my throat.

"I miss you! Can I come visit you? And go to Disneyland?" she asks eagerly.

My heart twists. "I miss you so much too! I'll talk to your mom, okay? We'll figure it out."

Before I can tell her I will see her for Thanksgiving, Edgar appears behind her. He looks

274

surprised to see me on the screen. "Hey," he says, rubbing the back of his neck.

"Hey," I reply, careful to keep my tone neutral.

He leans against the wall, folding his arms. "So…how is California? You still like it out there?"

There's something in his tone—not quite judgmental, but laced with something else. Jealousy, maybe. Or doubt. Maybe even hope.

"Yeah," I say, keeping my voice even. "I do."

We hang up not long after, but something inside me doesn't settle. The question lingers. Not just Edgar's—mine. About this life. About what I want. About what Damian wants.

I step outside to the patio—the place I always go when I need to think.

I light a cigarette, the smoke curling into the warm night air like a secret. I've cut way back since the move—down to just one most nights, and always when he's not around. Damian hates it. He's made that clear in the way he winces every time he smells it on my clothes or kisses me after. But there's something about this ritual—being out here with the ocean breeze, a cigarette in one hand and my journal in the other—that I'm not ready to give up just yet.

I flip to a fresh page.

October 10th

I've always wanted to be a mom. That truth feels louder now than it has in a long time. Maya's chaos, Bella's tiny voice

asking to visit—they've stirred something I can't ignore anymore.
I want that. All of it.
I want to be a mom. Not years from now. Not in some abstract, distant future. Soon. And more than that—I want to be married. I want the stability. The promise. The partnership. Maybe it's because I've finally found someone I can picture building a life with. Or maybe it's because I've spent so long wanting to feel safe and chosen, and this—this version of life— feels like the beginning of that.
I haven't brought it up with Damian yet. Not seriously. We've touched the edges of these things, but never fully leaned in. Maybe I've been waiting to feel more settled. Or maybe I've just been scared of what I'll hear.
But I think it's time.
I need to know what kind of future we're building.
And if we're building the same one.

I take one last drag from the cigarette, stubbing it out carefully before flicking the ashes into the tray. The smoke lingers, faint and fading, like the last thread of something I've outgrown but still crave.

Inside, the apartment is dim, quiet. I clean up quickly, brush my teeth, and crawl into bed. The Tiffany necklace rests against my skin, cool and steady—a beautiful reminder that I'm loved. But not all reminders bring peace.

I'm not sure if I'll bring it up tonight. But the thought won't leave me alone.

Damian gets home just after midnight, the soft click of the lock coaxing my eyes open. I hear the rhythm of his steps, the low creak of the bedroom door. He moves through the space like he belongs here—which, of course, he does. But tonight, I'm hyper-aware of the weight of what I'm about to ask.

He slips off his shirt, leaving it slung across the chair, then slides into bed beside me. His body is warm from the night, his scent a familiar blend of cologne and kitchen and something purely him.

I curl into him as soon as he's close enough. This part is easy. This part always is.

His hand finds my hip, then my hair, threading through the strands slowly. "You awake?" he whispers.

"Mm-hmm," I murmur.

There's a moment of stillness. Our bodies, our breath, completely in sync.

I take a breath I hope he doesn't feel. "Do you want to have a family someday?"

His fingers hesitate—just for a beat—but I notice. Then they resume, slower this time. "Yeah. I want kids eventually."

Eventually.

The word hangs in the air like steam—warm, vague, impossible to hold.

I nod into his chest, willing my voice to stay casual. "I guess I always thought I'd be married and have kids by now."

He exhales, and I can almost feel him weighing his next words.

"I'd rather have kids now than get married," he says.

It's not defensive. Not dismissive. Just... honest. Like it's something he's said before in his head and this is the first time it's made it into the air between us.

I lift my head, just enough to look at him. "Really?"

He shrugs. "Marriage is... a lot. It didn't work out for my parents. I don't know if it's for me. But I definitely want kids."

His eyes don't waver. There's no uncertainty in them—only a kind of settled truth, like he's already made peace with this part of himself.

I smile. Not because I'm totally at ease, but because I *understand*. And that has to be enough—for now.

"Ok, so yes to kids then." I say, keeping the smile but my heart skips, just a little.

Because I want both. I want the chaotic mornings and the scribbled coloring pages on the fridge—but I also want the vow. The shared last name. The forever kind of love. Not just because it's tradition, but because it's commitment. Out loud. In front of the world.

And right now, I don't know if he'll ever want that.

Still, I press my cheek to his chest, letting his heartbeat settle against my ear.

Don't push, I tell myself. *This was good. Honest. Let it be enough.*

But even as I lie there, letting the silence wrap around us like a blanket, the words I didn't say curl up beside me too.

Maybe the order doesn't matter.

Maybe love is enough.

Maybe this is just the beginning.

But part of me wonders if I'll ever be able to fully let go of the things I still secretly want.

We drift toward sleep, and I hold onto the image of a future family—a blend of his dreams and mine.

Twenty-Two

The flight to Cabo from Orange County is quick and smooth, and excitement buzzes in the air as we step off the plane. Jenni is already in town, and we're set to meet her at the airport. But the moment we leave the terminal, chaos erupts. Salesmen shout over each other, offering rides, excursions, and discounts. Damian takes my hand and leads me towards the pick-up area. With no cell service to coordinate, we're left wandering through the bustling crowd, scanning every face for Jenni.

After what feels like an eternity—thirty frustrating minutes, to be exact—we finally spot her at an outdoor airport bar. She's perched on a stool, sunglasses on, beers already ordered, with a broad grin on her face. Standing beside her is a guy I've never met.

"Took you long enough!" Jenni teases, lifting her glass in greeting. "This is Brad, by the way."

Brad extends his hand, his smile easy and warm. "Heard a lot about you guys," he says.

"Likewise," I reply, exchanging a knowing glance with Damian.

"Cheers!" we say in unison, raising our glasses and taking big gulps.

"Our driver's over here," Jenni says, motioning for us to follow.

Jenni, who lived in Mexico City, during her childhood, switches effortlessly to Spanish as she chats with the driver. Brad watches her like she's magic.

I speak Spanish too—well enough to get by—but I've always been a little self-conscious about it. Edgar's family used to tease me whenever I messed up the grammar or used the wrong word. I'd laugh along like it didn't bother me, but it did.

Watching Jenni now, confident and effortless, I wish I could speak like that. I wish I *felt* like that—unapologetic and sure.

Soon, we're piling into a van, bags in tow, and heading to the resort. As we pull up, the sight takes our breath away. The property is stunning—tropical flowers in full bloom, cascading pools glinting in the sunlight, and a sprawling ocean view in the distance.

When we get to the room, it's even better than the photos promised. A two-bedroom unit with a full kitchen and a balcony overlooking the pool and ocean. Damian and I claim the bedroom with the luxurious jacuzzi tub and rain shower, while Jenni and Brad settle into the second room.

Without wasting a second, we throw on our swimsuits and head to the pool. The swim-up bar is calling our names, and before long, shots are flowing.

"It's like swimming in a fishbowl!" Damian marvels, diving under the water and resurfacing with a grin. "There's no chlorine—it's so clear and refreshing!"

Jenni and I laugh as we sip our cocktails, chatting about the resort's amenities and what we plan to do the next day. Out of nowhere, Damian appears at my side, dripping wet with a mischievous smile.

"Hey, you," he says, leaning close.

"Hey yourself," I reply, matching his grin.

Before I can react, Damian scoops me into his arms, grinning mischievously. "Damian! What are you doing?" I squeal, clinging to my drink. Laughter bubbles up as he carries me into the water, where his kiss melts away my protests, leaving me breathless.

He carries me into the water, and as soon as we're waist-deep, he presses his lips to mine in a kiss so passionate I momentarily forget where we are. The warmth of his arms, the cool water surrounding us, and the buzz of the tequila make it feel like we're the only two people in the world.

When he finally pulls back, his eyes are alight with mischief. "You looked too good sitting there not to do something about it," he says, brushing a strand of wet hair from my face.

Jenni and Brad cheer from the bar, and I roll my eyes, laughing. "You're crazy," I say, but my smile betrays the fact that I wouldn't have it any other way.

That night, we hit up a club, where the energy is intoxicating. Damian, ever the life of the party, ends up teaching a server how to do the Stanky Leg, much to everyone's amusement. At one point, Jenni leans in and whispers, "Brad's such a good dancer. I think I'm in trouble."

When my heels become unbearable, Jenni and I duck into a shop to buy $5 flip-flops. The flimsy sandals don't even last until we're back at the resort, leaving us doubled over in laughter as we hobble barefoot through the lobby.

The next day, we venture into town to grab groceries. Fish tacos are the unanimous decision for dinner. While wandering through the store, Jenni stumbles upon a rack of adult onesies.

"Look at these!" she says, holding up a bright red one emblazoned with chili peppers. "Should I try it on?"

"Absolutely," I say, egging her on.

She shimmies into the onesie right there in the middle of the store, striking a dramatic pose. Brad claps, grinning. "I think it's a keeper."

Damian, not one to be outdone, tries on a blue one with penguins but gives up when it won't go past his shoulders. "I think these are made for children," he complains, drawing laughter from everyone.

Dinner that night is a success—the fish tacos are perfectly seasoned, and we toast to a trip that already feels unforgettable.

The following morning, I wake up with a scratchy throat and a runny nose. Despite my better judgment, I down some cough syrup and join everyone at the pool, where bloody mary shots flow freely. It's a regrettable combination, and I spend a solid hour in the bathroom questioning my life choices.

After a nap, some water, and more medicine, I manage to rally just in time for our final night out. We stumble upon a cozy bar tucked between the bustling streets, its charm undeniable. The walls are covered with signatures and messages left behind by past visitors, each one a tiny story etched into its history. Damian heads to the bar and returns with beers for all of us, his easy smile making the dimly lit space feel even warmer.

"This has been an awesome trip!" Jenni exclaims, grabbing her beer from Damian's hand.

"It really has been," I agree, lifting my glass to hers with a smile.

Damian glances at the walls, his eyes lighting up as he points to a black marker resting in a mason jar on the table. "Should we leave our mark?"

Jenni is the first to snatch the marker, signing her name boldly on the wall. Damian and I follow, finding a spot just big enough for both of us. He carefully writes his name close to mine, then adds a simple "&" between them: "Damian & Talia." Seeing our names together like that feels almost poetic, as though we're carving our future into the stars.

As the night winds down, Damian takes my hand, and we return to the room for one last shared moment of this unforgettable trip. When I step into the bathroom, my breath catches. Damian has drawn a bath in the jacuzzi tub, the warm water dotted with delicate rose petals. Their intoxicating fragrance fills the air, a mix of romance and pure indulgence.

Damian climbs into the tub first, his hands resting on the edge as he looks at me. His eyes are soft but filled with longing as he motions for me to join him. It's impossible to resist. Slowly, I slip out of my dress and matching pink lace bra and underwear. His gaze follows my every move, his appreciation evident in the way his lips part slightly, the way his eyes darken with desire.

I step into the tub, the warm water caressing my skin as I settle into his arms. He wraps himself around me, his breath hot against my neck as he whispers, "I love you, Talia," before pressing soft kisses along my shoulder.

I close my eyes, letting his words and the weight of his affection wash over me. "I love you more," I whisper, my voice barely audible but heavy with truth.

The heat between us builds as he holds me closer, his body pressing against mine. I feel his rising need and instinctively move, bracing myself against the edge of the tub. He follows, his hands covering mine, his breath warm against my ear. His fingers trace the curve of my hips before he pulls me gently back toward him. With one smooth motion, he glides inside me, stealing my breath and igniting every nerve in my body.

Each thrust is slow at first, deliberate, as if he's savoring every second, but the intensity builds quickly. His movements grow more eager, each one sending waves of pleasure crashing through me. I match his rhythm, driving my hips back, meeting him with the same urgency. The water sloshes around us, but it's barely noticeable as our bodies move in perfect sync, reaching an uncontrollable crescendo. When release finally comes, it's shattering—leaving us trembling, breathless, and utterly consumed by each other.

Damian lifts me out of the tub, carrying me with ease to the bed. He lays me down gently, and we collapse together, still naked, still wrapped in each other. His arms encircle me, his lips pressing one last kiss to my temple as sleep claims us both.

On our last morning, Jenni and I sit on the balcony, sipping coffee as the sun rises over the ocean.

She lights a cigarette, offering one to me. I hesitate, then take it. Just this once.

"I'm so happy for you and Damian," she says, her voice soft but sincere. "You seem really happy together."

"We are," I reply, my smile softening as I look out at the horizon. The gentle crash of the waves below seems to echo the steady rhythm of my heart. "I feel like this is it. This is where I'm supposed to be—with him."

I hesitate, then add, "The other night, we talked about having kids..." My voice trails off as I gauge her reaction.

Jenni's eyes light up. "Are you serious? You two would have the cutest kids ever!"

"I know, right?" I say, laughing. "I've always wanted to be a mom."

Jenni leans back, exhaling a cloud of smoke. "I always knew you'd find your way," she says, her voice carrying a certainty that surprises me.

As we sit in companionable silence, I think about what lies ahead—our future in California, and maybe even kids. It feels like I'm on the edge of something big, something that could define everything.

November is a whirlwind of activity. After returning from the sun-soaked beaches of Cabo, Damian and I barely have time to catch our breath before packing our bags again—this time for Austin to spend Thanksgiving with my family.

The trip home is exactly what I need, a much-needed dose of familiarity and warmth. As we pull into my sisters' driveway, I'm hit with a wave of nostalgia. The house is adorned with fall decorations—pumpkins on the porch, a wreath of golden leaves on the door, and the faint scent of cinnamon wafting out as my mom swings the door open.

"There's my girl!" she exclaims, pulling me into a tight hug. Then, turning to Damian, she beams. "And Damian! Come here, you're family now, too."

Damian laughs as she envelops him in a hug, and I can see the way his shoulders relax. He's always been good with my family, but seeing him welcomed so warmly makes my heart swell.

The highlight of the trip is our annual visit to the Elgin Christmas Tree Farm. It's a tradition my family has cherished for years, and I'm excited to share it with Damian for the first time. Plus Jess and her family always go too so we will get to see her.

As we arrive, the familiar sights and sounds fill me with joy—the scent of pine in the crisp air, the laughter of children running through the fields, and the distant hum of a tractor.

"We're on a mission for the perfect tree," my dad declares as we pile onto the tractor that will take us out to the fields.

Damian sits beside me, his hand in mine. "So, what's the criteria for the perfect tree?" he asks, leaning in with a grin.

"It's got to be full, tall but not too tall, and have no bare spots," I explain. "And bonus points if it smells amazing."

"And don't forget it has to 'speak to you,'" my mom chimes in, winking at Damian.

288

When we reach the fields, we scatter in different directions, everyone scanning the rows of evergreens with the determination of hunters on a quest. Damian and I walk hand in hand, inspecting tree after tree.

"How about this one?" Damian asks, pointing to a tall, symmetrical pine.

"Hmm." I step back, scrutinizing it like an art critic. "It's nice, but I don't think it's *the one*."

"Oh, the tree has to speak to you," Damian teases, mimicking my mom's words. "Got it."

After what feels like forever—and a lot of playful banter—we finally find it. A beautiful, full-bodied tree with just the right height and the most intoxicating pine scent.

"This is it," I say, placing my hands on my hips triumphantly.

Damian grins. "Alright, let's make it official." He grabs the saw and, with my dad's help, cuts it down.

Dragging the tree back to the tractor, Damian pretends to struggle under its weight, exaggerating his effort. "I don't know how you do this every year, Talia. You're stronger than you look."

"Oh, please," I laugh, rolling my eyes. "I've been doing this since I was a kid."

Back at the main barn, the tree is shaken clean and wrapped in a net, ready to go. We wander into the cozy little shop filled with Christmas knick-knacks, twinkling lights, and the scent of freshly baked cookies.

"Alright, everyone," my mom says, clapping her hands. "It's ornament time! Pick something that speaks to you."

Damian picks up a tiny Santa surfing on a wave. "This feels appropriate," he says, holding it up.

"Perfect for California," I agree, grabbing a glittery star for myself.

Just as we're checking out, the door swings open and Jess steps in, her eyes immediately locking on mine like she'd been scanning the room just for me.

"Talia! I knew I'd find you all in here," she says, her voice full of that easy confidence, already moving in for a hug before I can answer. She holds on just a beat longer than casual—just long enough to say, *I've missed you* without the words.

"I was just about to call and see where you were," I say, though I can already feel that familiar comfort settling in just from having her near.

"This place is massive. We were out wandering through the trees like it was some enchanted forest," she says with a laugh, brushing a leaf from her shoulder and raising an eyebrow at me like she knows there's more I'm not saying—and she'll wait for it, on my time.

We walk arm in arm outside toward the corn maze, catching up like no time has passed at all.

The day ends with hot cocoa by the fire, everyone chatting and laughing. Damian fits seamlessly into the chaos, joking with my sisters and sharing stories with my dad.

As we head to the hotel, the car is filled with the scent of pine and the warm buzz of the day's memories. I glance over at Damian, his profile illuminated by the glow of passing streetlights, and my heart feels full.

"Thank you for coming home with me," I say softly, reaching for his hand.

"Are you kidding?" he replies, giving my hand a squeeze. "I wouldn't miss this for the world."

The next day, we have plans to meet up with Bella and Lindsay. It's been far too long, and I've missed them both so much. This will be Damian's first time meeting them, and I can't wait to see how it goes.

As soon as we step into the café, Bella rushes over, arms wide open. "Talia!" she shouts, pulling me into a tight hug. We cling to each other for a moment before she finally lets go, her excitement radiating. "It's been forever!"

Lindsay steps in next, and we exchange a warm hug. "I've missed you," she says softly.

"I've missed you too," I reply, grinning as I turn to Damian. "Ladies, this is Damian."

Bella gives him a quick once-over, her protective side evident, but Damian doesn't miss a beat. With his easy smile and natural charm, he dives into a conversation about the menu. "So, Bella, what's the move? Are we going for something adventurous, or sticking with the classics?" he asks with a playful tone.

She laughs, the hesitation melting away. "Well, I was thinking about the chicken and waffles, but now I'm second-guessing everything!"

Within minutes, Damian has won her over, and the atmosphere is light and relaxed.

As we settle into our table, Lindsay turns to me, her voice filled with sincerity. "It's so great to see you happy, Talia."

"You too," I reply, reaching for her hand. Lindsay's been seeing a new guy, Scott, and the difference in her is obvious. He's kind, sweet, and everything she deserves. We share a knowing smile, silently acknowledging the rocky roads we've both left behind.

Of course, I can't help myself. "So... I saw Edgar when I called Bella last month. Has Edgar been spending time with Bella?" I ask, treading carefully.

Lindsay sighs, her expression turning weary. "You know Edgar. He makes promises, and sometimes he keeps them... but mostly, he flakes." She looks down, disappointment falling across her face.

She leans in, lowering her voice. "Just a couple weeks ago he got arrested—for a DUI."

My eyes widen. "What? Seriously?"

She nods, her tone resigned. "Yeah, he's not even supposed to be driving right now. When he does see Bella, it's at his mom's place when we're in Houston. That's the best I can do."

My heart aches for her as she explains, the weight of co-parenting with someone so unreliable etched into her features. As I listen, a pang of guilt creeps in—an uncomfortable reminder of my own uncertainties about stepping into parenthood.

Lindsay has weathered so much, balancing love for Bella with the constant frustration of Edgar's failures. I wonder if I'd have her strength if I faced similar challenges. The thought lingers long after the conversation shifts to lighter topics.

We spend the rest of the afternoon laughing, reminiscing, and catching up. Sitting there, surrounded by the people I love, I'm reminded of how far we've all come—and how much stronger we've grown along the way.

The trip is everything I didn't know I needed. A warm, grounding reminder of the people and traditions that shaped me. Sharing it all with Damian only deepens my sense of gratitude. It feels like the perfect blend of old and new, past and future. I leave feeling whole, recharged, and more certain than ever of the life we're building together.

Back at the airport, I hug everyone goodbye a little longer than usual. There's a small tug in my chest as the plane takes off—a gentle ache for home, but also something else. A pull toward the life I'm creating.

I grab Damian's hand and smile at him, at our life together.

Damian almost instantly falls asleep. I swear he could sleep anywhere.

Somewhere over Arizona, I pull out my journal.

November 29, 2009
It's strange, how home can be two places at once.
This trip reminded me of who I am and where I come from...
but also of how much I've grown.
For the first time, I'm not afraid of what's next.
We talked about the future.
Really talked.
And for once, it didn't feel like a question mark.
It felt like hope.
Like something we could actually build together.
I never thought I'd get to feel this way again. Safe.
Loved.

I close the journal and exhale, looking out at the clouds stretched endlessly below. A sudden wave of nausea rolls through me—sharp and unexpected. My hand instinctively goes to my stomach.

I swallow hard. Shake my head.

No. It can't be. We just talked about the future... we weren't supposed to be there yet.

I lean back in my seat, heart fluttering in a rhythm I can't quite place.

The seatbelt light flickers on.

And somewhere deep inside me... a new kind of possibility begins to stir.

Bonus Chapter

From the upcoming sequel, Look At Us...

The following Monday, we're back in Dana Point, slipping into the rhythm of our life like we never left.

Damian meets me for lunch at a little restaurant near my office. The sun is warm, the breeze smells like salt and grilled fish, and for a minute, everything feels normal. Easy.

We order burgers, clink our beers together, and talk about the usual—work, the house, maybe taking a weekend trip soon. He makes me laugh, like he always does, and I feel... good. Settled.

Until I don't.

The nausea hits mid-sentence. Sharp and sudden, like being sideswiped. My fingers tighten around my glass, and for a second, I think I might actually pass out.

"Damian," I say, barely above a whisper.

He leans in, concern flickering across his face. "What's wrong?"

"I—I don't feel right." My hand drifts to my stomach, and the fear starts to bloom. Not just physical discomfort. A knowing...

Can't wait to see what happens next? Look At Us will be available October 2025 - sign-up at www.readlookseries.com to be the first to know when it's live!

Author's Note

Dear Reader,

This book is incredibly special to me because it's inspired by my own love story. While some parts have been fictionalized, the emotions, the journey, and the deep connection between Damian and Talia are very real.

Writing this novel allowed me to relive some of the most beautiful moments of my own love story. It was also incredibly helpful in processing the darker place I was in before finding that love. I hope it resonates with you as much as it did with me.

This story does touch on domestic violence, a painful reality for many. If you or someone you know is in an abusive situation, please know that help is available, and you are not alone. Organizations like the National Domestic Violence Hotline (1-800-799-7233 or thehotline.org) offer free, confidential support 24/7.

With Love and hope,

Tania Dilworth

Dedication & Acknowledgements

To my younger self - thank you for being brave and following your heart out of the darkness and into a love so radiant.

To Mi Vida, the reason I believe in love stories. Thank you for showing me what an incredible love story can truly be, for always believing in me and for continuing to look at me the way you did that night under the stars. Besos!

A heartfelt thank you to my friends and family for your endless love and support especially through the moments of doubt. I am forever grateful for your encouragement.

A special shoutout to my beta readers, early supporters and everyone who helped shape this novel. Your feedback, enthusiasm and love for romance mean the world to me.

This book wouldn't exist without you **all.**

And finally, to you—the reader. Whether you're here for the love story, the emotions, or just an escape, I'm grateful you've chosen to spend time here. Thank you for believing in love and in stories that make our hearts race.

With love and gratitude,

Tania Dilworth

www.ingramcontent.com/pod-product-compliance
Lightning Source LLC
Chambersburg PA
CBHW020357110726
47899CB00006B/1752